Like her central character, Barbara Murphy became Musical Director to a concert party and went into advertising. Later she switched to publishing, as a secretary to the editor of *Home Notes* and *Modern Woman* magazines, before moving to Hampshire with her husband and two children.

She is a keen member of a local music and drama group. Barbara's first novel was JANEY'S WAR.

A RESTLESS PEACE

Janey Harrison is only nineteen and, with the War behind her, she should be looking forward to happier times. But there is an emptiness inside her that Janey can't explain away. One thing she is sure of is her dislike of Sandy, the boy next door, now grown up and a successful doctor. She is convinced he is responsible for the tragic death of her lovely twin sister, Rose. Only as her career begins to take off does Janey come out of her dead sister's shadow. The men begin to flock around her as they did Rose — but to Janey's intense anger, it is Sandy who she cannot keep out of her thoughts . . .

Books by Barbara Murphy
Published by The House of Ulverscroft:

JANEY'S WAR
FIVEPENNY LANES

BARBARA MURPHY

◆

A RESTLESS PEACE

Complete and Unabridged

ULVERSCROFT
Leicester

First published in Great Britain in 1997 by
Judy Piatkus (Publishers) Limited
London

Large Print Edition
published 2002
by arrangement with
Judy Piatkus (Publishers) Limited
London

British Library CIP Data

Murphy, Barbara, *1928* –
A restless peace.—Large print ed.—
Ulverscroft large print series: general fiction
1. Domestic fiction
2. Large type books
I. Title
823.9'14 [F]

ISBN 0–7089–4710–7

Published by
F. A. Thorpe (Publishing) Ltd.
Anstey, Leicestershire

Set by Words & Graphics Ltd.
Anstey, Leicestershire
Printed and bound in Great Britain by
T. J. International Ltd., Padstow, Cornwall

This book is printed on acid-free paper

For Derrick —
because he adds fun to our marriage

A time to love and a time to hate:
a time for war and a time for peace.
                              Ecclesiastes 3:8

Acknowledgements

Again my thanks go to the staff of Hythe Library, who are always so helpful with my research, also the Museum of Army Flying at Middle Wallop, and the Medical Officer Recruitment, RAMC Training Group.

And I continue to be grateful to my agent, Judith Murdoch, who has patiently helped and advised me — and to Judy Piatkus, for saying, 'Yes'.

1

Jane pulled the scarf higher, trying to protect her face from a wind that blasted snowflakes into her mouth. If the newspapers were to be believed, 1947 would go down in history as the coldest English winter on record. How she hated dressing quickly under the bedclothes each morning, pulling on so many layers of clothes she could hardly walk, yet still feeling cold. Hated sludging through the streets around Piccadilly Circus to an unheated office with brown paper wrapped around her desk, and hated typing in old woollen gloves minus the fingers.

As she rammed the front gate hard against the packed snow and squeezed through the narrow gap, Jane wondered how the family would react to her news.

'I'm home.' Wrestling with her boots, she called her usual greeting from the hall, then paused, her numb fingers dropping the front door key as she recognised the voices from the living room. Mrs Randall and . . . oh, God, no! The last person she wanted to see now, or at any time, was Sandy. For the past two years she had managed to avoid him, but

now she was trapped — one boot on, one off
— the front room door opening and nowhere
to hide. Not even time to decide what to say
to him. Would she be able to control her
anger?

He stood in the doorway, taller than she
remembered, his hair still resembling thatch.
'Hullo, Jane,' he said. 'Long time, no see.' His
smile reminded her of the schoolboy who had
once been her best friend.

Hopping on one leg, Jane grabbed at the
banister.

'Let me help you.' Sandy crouched to take
the boot in both hands.

'No!' Her cry was so sharp, he looked up in
surprise.

Jane moderated her voice, 'No — thank
you. I can manage.' With an almighty tug, she
yanked off the boot and frantically unfastened
her coat, throwing it roughly over the
hallstand, hoping she could escape upstairs.

Her mother squeezed past Sandy and
handed a newspaper to Jane. 'You're home
early,' was her only greeting.

'We had no electricity, so Miss Reynolds
sent us home when it was too dark to work.'
Jane spread the newspaper on the floor to
catch the puddles from her boots.

'Didn't she have any candles?'

Jane shook her head. 'They've disappeared

from the shops. I used nightlights to make some phone calls, but most of our clients had packed up as well.'

'Well, you can make yourself useful when you've put your slippers on,' Mrs Harrison said briskly. 'We could do with another tray of tea. Come back into the living room, Sandy. It's freezing out here.'

It would have been nice if her mother had said 'please', Jane thought. She was always such a stickler for good manners, except when she spoke to her daughter.

As she put clean cups on to the tray, Jane was surprised to find Sandy at her side, staring at her ringless left hand.

'I thought you were engaged to a Norwegian,' he commented.

'I was.'

'What went wrong?'

'It didn't work out.'

'Too young?'

'Something like that. I really don't want to talk about it.'

'Sorry. It's just that I only get snippets of news from Ma, and I haven't seen you for ages — not since Rose's funeral.'

For a while they were silent, until Sandy said, 'I wrote to you, the next day.'

Jane busied herself with the teapot. She couldn't explain that she had burned his letter, unopened. Words — wrong words, right words, stuck in her throat. If she attempted to speak, she would either scream at him, or burst into tears.

Sandy soldiered on, 'I wanted you to know that I was there — if you needed help you only had to ask.'

Shocked at his arrogance, Jane almost snorted. My sister needed help, she thought. When she was carrying your child, she appealed to you, but you abandoned her. So much for your precious help.

Memories flooded back as Jane remembered the dreadful day when she'd overheard Rose tearfully quarrelling with Sandy, accusing him of not caring for her. They hadn't realised that Jane was nearby, too stunned to run after her sister. That night Rose had a back-street abortion before she staggered out into the path of a V-2 rocket. Much as she longed to confront Sandy, to let him know that she held him responsible for her sister's death, Jane couldn't allow her parents to discover the truth. They hadn't even known Rose was pregnant. As it was, her mother had never really recovered from losing her favourite daughter.

Angrily, Jane picked up the hissing kettle. If you had been an honourable man, she thought, my beautiful twin would still be alive. But your career had to come first. Marriage was not on the schedule for an ambitious medical student.

Engrossed in her thoughts, she dropped the teapot as boiling water splashed on to her skin. Sandy moved quickly forward and took the kettle from her shaking hand.

'Here,' he said, turning on the tap. 'Hold it under the running water for a while. You need to reduce the heat. Do you have a first-aid box?'

'Of course.' Her tone was abrupt. 'I don't have to be a doctor to know how to deal with a simple burn.'

As he bent to pick up the broken pieces of china, Jane snapped, 'Leave it. I'll clear it up in a minute.'

Looking uncomfortable, Sandy backed away, watching thoughtfully as Jane held her hand under the tap. Then he quietly said, 'I was sorry to hear about your grandmother. If the new M and B tablets had been available, it might have been a different story.'

'I doubt it, at her age. It wasn't the first time she'd had pneumonia.'

'Your grandfather seems to be coping quite well.'

Jane didn't answer. She wasn't in the mood for polite chit-chat, and it was too late for Sandy to show concern for her family.

But he was relentless.

'Actually, I called round to see Jack, but I understand he's just moved into one of the new prefabs.'

Jane nodded.

'How's Betty getting on with running her own home, after relying on your mother for so long?'

'Ha!' Jane couldn't prevent a curt little laugh. Since her brother had returned from a Japanese prisoner-of-war camp, her mother had nursed him back to physical health and taken care of his child, while her sister-in-law claimed she was too delicate to manage more than the simplest chores.

'That sounds as though nothing much has changed.'

Jane shrugged. 'Mum does all their washing and ironing, as well as the heavy cleaning. They might as well still be living here.'

'I'll try to see Jack before I go back to King's. Did you know I've applied for a House Officer post at the Queen Elizabeth Hospital — in Birmingham?'

'No.' At least he would be further away, Jane thought.

Sandy turned off the tap. 'Let's have a look at that burn,' he said.

'I'm all right. Just leave me alone!' As Jane pulled her hand away, her mother stormed

6

into the kitchenette.

'Why on earth is it taking you all night to make a pot of tea, Janey? Mrs Randall has to be on duty in . . . ' Her gaze rested on the broken china.

Quickly, Jane said, 'I'll buy another one tomorrow. Sorry, Mum.'

'That's not the point. If you weren't so clumsy — '

Sandy interrupted, 'Jane scalded her hand, Mrs Harrison. Is the first-aid box in the bathroom?'

'I told you I can manage perfectly well.' Jane couldn't keep the irritation from her voice. 'I don't need your help.'

'Janey!' Mrs Harrison flashed an apologetic smile at Sandy. 'If you wouldn't mind bringing the box down, I'll get the other teapot.' As soon as he had left the room, she turned on Jane. 'You ought to be grateful Sandy's taking so much trouble over you. He's a proper doctor now, not a student.' As she brushed broken china into the dustpan, Mrs Harrison added, 'Mrs Randall says he plans to be a surgeon.'

'I bet he does,' Jane muttered under her breath.

'So you just treat him with a bit more respect.'

Respect? Jane found it difficult enough to

be civil to the wretch. But there was no point in provoking a family row, not if she couldn't justify her mood. So Sandy was politely thanked after he had dressed the burn and carried the tea tray into the living room, and Grandad and Mrs Randall greeted with genuine warmth.

As Sandy's mother fastened her scarlet-lined cloak over her nursing sister's uniform, she smiled at Jane.

'Come with your mother next time she visits. I'd like to hear more about your work. Advertising sounds much more interesting than enemas and bedpans.'

Jane made a non-committal reply, knowing she wouldn't take up the offer, even though she had always liked Mrs Randall. The slightest connection with Sandy must be severed.

As she closed the front door behind the visitors, Jane asked her mother when Kathleen was expected home.

'About the same time as your father. She's joined a debating society or something at school.'

Jane nodded. Kathleen O'Connor had lived with the Harrisons since her own family had been killed during the war, and Jane regarded the younger girl more as a sister than a friend. She couldn't wait to tell

8

Kathleen what had happened today in the office. For a moment she was almost tempted to tell her mother, as she desperately needed to put all thoughts of Sandy from her mind — but she decided to wait until the family were all together for the evening meal. Nell Harrison had shown little interest when Jane announced that she had won best student of the commercial course award, but her father was different. He cared. And his opinions were worth listening to.

* * *

'Did you have any idea this was going to happen?' Fred Harrison leaned his elbows on the table, listening intently to his daughter.

'Not until Miss Reynolds called me into her office this morning. We were all — I suppose shocked is the best way to describe how we felt.'

Grandad slurped a little soup into his mouth, then said, 'I can't make out why your boss wants to sell up and go to Canada in the first place, Janey. Thought she had a nice little business already.'

'The advertising world is in the doldrums, I'm afraid, Grandad,' Jane sighed. 'After two years of peace, we still have rationing, and there's no chance of picking up any new motoring accounts until the petrol restrictions are lifted.'

'What about the clients you've already got? That whisky firm, and the travel company. You brought a lot of work home before Christmas, so they must be keeping you busy.'

'We were desperately trying to hang on to those accounts — that's why I was reworking their budgets.' Jane smiled sadly at her grandfather. 'But the simple truth is — people haven't got the money to spend on luxuries, so the clients are reducing the amount they spend on advertising.'

Mr Harrison cut another slice of bread. 'I can understand her going to Canada,' he said. 'They've got plenty of money for luxury goods out there. But I can't understand anyone wanting to buy an advertising firm over here. Surely they'll be inheriting the same problems?'

'Grafton and Hughes are a huge outfit, Dad,' Jane explained. 'They've got agencies up and down the country, and a much wider range of client. So they can absorb some of the losses into other branches until the economy is better.'

'And what about you?' Mr Harrison wiped his soup dish with a piece of bread. 'You say

10

they want you to run the firm until they bring in their own manager. Are they giving you a rise?'

'Ten shillings a week, from the first of next month, when Miss Reynolds leaves.' Jane turned to her mother. 'I'll be able to give you another five shillings housekeeping, Mum,' she said.

'I can do with it, the way everything keeps going up.' Mrs Harrison collected the soup plates.

Kathleen had followed the conversation with great interest. 'How safe will your job be with a new manager?' she asked.

'I don't know. There's always a chance they might prefer to choose their own secretary.'

Grandad scoffed at the idea. 'They'd be daft if they did, girl. That firm couldn't manage without you, I reckon.'

'Thanks for the vote of confidence, Grandad.' Jane laughed. 'I just hope I can live up to their expectations meantime. Managing an advertising agency is a different kettle of fish to being a secretary, and they're a bit bothered about my age.'

'They don't know our Janey, though, do they?' Grandad said. 'You've always had an old head on young shoulders, and you'll be nineteen in April.'

Mr Harrison patted Jane's hand. 'You'll do

fine, dear,' he said. 'And we're proud of you, aren't we, Nell?' He smiled up at his wife. 'First she's best student, now she's in charge of her firm.'

'Only for the time being.' Nell Harrison handed her husband a plate of faggots and mashed potatoes. 'That's all I could get, I'm afraid. The fishman didn't call, and I've had to save the last of the meat ration for the Sunday joint. There's rice pudding for afters, with evaporated milk.' Not once did she look at Jane.

★ ★ ★

'I'm so pleased for you, Jane,' Kathleen said, pouring water from the kettle on to the soda crystals in the bowl. 'But do I detect just a wee bit of — reservation?'

For a fifteen-year-old, Kathleen was more than a little perceptive, Jane thought, as she struggled to put her doubts into words. 'It's just that I feel I have reached a very important crossroads in my life,' she said slowly. 'Do I keep going on the same road and take my chances with the new boss? Or do I turn off onto an unknown path that may be even more risky?'

'And why would you be wanting to do that?'

'Well, like I said, advertising is not growing too healthily just at the moment, and there's no sign of any let up in the near future. Perhaps I should look around for a job in another industry.' Jane polished the soup spoons on a clean cloth. 'Or I could go to Canada.'

Mouth open, Kathleen stopped scrubbing at a saucepan. 'You wouldn't really be leaving home, would you?'

'I'm in a rut.' Jane shrugged. 'And I feel the time has come for me to move on. Miss Reynolds said she would vouch for me — but perhaps Canada is too big a step.'

'I saw a marvellous documentary film about Canada not so long ago,' Kathleen mused. 'It looks a grand place to live.'

'Well, you might like to consider emigration yourself later on. You're bound to get good grades when you go to university, and it's the right country for young people.'

'I wouldn't want to go too far away from you, Janey — ever.' Kathleen renewed her attack upon the saucepan. 'But if you do leave home, later on, when I'm working — I wouldn't mind being your flatmate.'

'Now that is a good idea.' Jane smiled. 'To be honest, I'd start looking tomorrow if I could afford it.'

'Just wait for a few years, and we'll look

together.' Changing the subject, Kathleen said, 'I'm glad you were in for once when Sandy called. I was beginning to think you'd gone off him.'

Startled, Jane looked at her friend. 'What do you mean?' she asked.

'Well, whenever your mam mentions that he's coming round, you say you have to go out somewhere. And if you are at home, you're usually just running a bath.'

Jane shrugged. 'That's the way it is sometimes.'

'Oh, I know. But you used to be such good mates. And the fact is . . . ' Kathleen paused, a mischievous little smile on her face. 'I used to hope that you and Sandy might — you know . . . '

'No, Kathleen, I don't know.' Jane had a pretty good idea what the little Irish girl meant but she couldn't think what else to say.

'Well, before you met Olaf, you were especially close to Sandy. More so than Rose, although he took her out a few times. Sure and I wouldn't have been too surprised if you'd been a wee bit jealous.'

'Of course not! We were just part of the crowd from school, that's all.'

'And now he's a tall, handsome doctor.' Kathleen dried her hands. 'Do you think they'll be calling him up once his studies are over?'

'I expect so. Even doctors have to do their national service.' Fumbling with the ties of her pinafore, Jane went quickly on, 'Are you doing any homework out here tonight?'

'Oh, yes. It's warmer than the dining room.'

'Then I'll leave the oven on low.'

When Kathleen had run upstairs to fetch her books, Jane recalled her words. Jealous? No, she didn't hate Sandy because he'd once loved Rose. She hated him because he hadn't loved Rose enough.

★   ★   ★

The following morning Jane was cleaning the stairs when two further visitors arrived. There was something vaguely familiar about the tall man with the charming smile and pencil moustache, but Jane was sure she had not seen the woman before.

'We're looking for Miss Harrison,' the man said. 'Jane Harrison. Would that be you?'

Puzzled, Jane nodded.

'I'm Bernard Berwick, and this is my sister, Eunice.'

At first, the name meant nothing to Jane, until prompted by the man.

15

'Delia Berwick's husband. We've not met, but she told me a lot about you.'

'Of course! I've seen your photograph. Please come in.' Jane led the way into the dining room and switched on a bar of the electric fire. 'May I offer you a cup of tea?'

As she prepared the tray, Jane glanced at her visitors through the open hatch. Rose had been the lead dancer of Madame Delia's Dancettes, and Jane had been the accompanist for most of the war. She knew Delia had fallen in love with an American sergeant while her husband was in a German prisoner-of-war camp, and was now living in New Jersey, but she hadn't a clue as to why Bernard Berwick and his sister should call.

'I hope your mother doesn't mind us coming round without telephoning or writing first,' he said, warming his hands around the cup of tea.

'Actually, she's out at the moment — and we're not on the telephone.' Jane switched on the second bar of the fire. 'I'm sorry it's so cold in here, but we don't use it much in the winter, and my grandfather is in the living room.'

'Please don't apologise.' Mr Berwick smiled. 'I should be used to the cold. Several of us had frostbite in the camp. However, I expect you're wondering why we are here.'

16

He produced a packet of cigarettes. 'Do you mind?'

Jane shook her head, and again when he offered her one.

When he'd lit his sister's cigarette, he went on, 'The reason we are here, Jane, is because we're planning to form our own amateur concert party, and we need a good pianist.'

For the first time, his sister spoke. 'Delia told us you were one of the best,' she said. 'I may not have much time for my two-timing sister-in-law, but she was a good judge of talent, just like Bernard. And I was one of Miss Bluebell's dancers, so can handle the choreography.'

Jane studied Eunice Berwick. Tall and slender, with her bleached hair swept up and make-up expertly applied, she looked every inch the professional dancer. Although there was a resemblance between brother and sister, it was the expression in their hazel eyes that marked the difference in their personalities. Bernard's eyes were warm, with a smile not far below the surface, whereas Eunice looked as though all animation had been suspended. This woman would make a formidable enemy.

Jane turned to Bernard. 'How do you propose to put your plan into action, Mr Berwick?'

'Bernard — please. An ad in the local paper should do the trick.'

'What sort of talent are you looking for?'

'Singers, dancers, comedians, musicians. Anything and everything.'

Eunice pointed her cigarette holder towards Jane. 'But most of all, we need a first-class pianist and musical director, and you've got the experience.'

'I'm not sure that a concert party would take off around here. Isn't it the sort of thing people expect to find at the seaside? End of the pier and all that? And there's a lot of good entertainment in London.'

'That's the point,' Bernard said. 'It's all in London, and expensive. Not much on their doorsteps, apart from cinemas, pubs, and one or two variety theatres. Just think how successful Delia's concerts were.'

'It was wartime then. People didn't want to go far in the blackout, and children are always popular.'

'Good entertainment can be just as popular in peacetime.' Bernard reached for an ashtray. 'There must be a wealth of untapped talent around. We had some splendid chaps in the stalag and I produced some jolly good shows.'

Eunice took up the story. 'If I have the right material to work with I can form a good chorus line. You must know some of Delia's

18

older dancers who would jump at the chance, Jane?'

Jane glanced at a photograph on the sideboard. Rose would have jumped at the chance. 'I can think of three or four girls who might be good enough,' she said.

'In that case . . . ' Bernard rubbed his hands together gleefully. 'There's nothing to stop us going ahead. You are interested, I hope?'

'Oh, yes. I'm interested, and it's very good of you to think of me, but I'm not sure that I can . . . ' Jane faltered at the disappointed expression on Bernard's face.

'Is there a problem?' he asked.

She explained about her job. 'So you see,' she concluded, 'for the next few weeks I shall be too busy to give the commitment that you would need.'

'We're not expecting to have a show ready until next winter,' he said. 'So we won't be auditioning just yet, will we, Eunice?'

'Do you think you'd be ready to join us in about a month?' Eunice asked.

'Probably — but are you sure I'm the right person?'

'I've heard how well you performed under extremely difficult conditions during the war — bombs falling around and so on . . . ' That lovely warm smile lit up Bernard's face. 'And

19

I'm sure you are the right person.' Reaching inside his jacket, he produced a business card, turned it over, and wrote a telephone number on the back. 'As soon as you feel ready, please contact me, either at my business or at home.'

Jane read the card. 'Bernard Berwick: Theatrical Ticket Agency.'

'I've rented a little office near Barking Station,' he explained. 'It's coming along slowly, but one thing being a prisoner teaches you is patience.'

Turning the card over, Jane recognised the telephone number he had written on the back. 'You're still at the same address, then?' she said.

'Yes. Delia made her share of the house and studio over to me, and Eunice has moved in.'

His sister sniffed. 'That was the least she could do after the disgraceful way she deserted you.'

Bernard frowned slightly, then stood up. 'Thank you for the tea, Jane. I look forward to hearing from you.' His handshake was as warm as his smile. Eunice barely touched Jane's fingertips.

Upstairs, from the window in Kathleen's room, Jane watched Bernard and his sister walk away.

At her side, Kathleen commented, 'It's a

strange little lopsided walk he has, or perhaps it's the snow?'

'He lost two toes through frostbite. Tough for a champion ballroom dancer.'

'Oh, the poor soul!'

'But there's not a scrap of self-pity in Bernard Berwick. Or bitterness.' Jane turned back and straightened the curtain. 'Can't say the same about his sister.'

Kathleen polished her dressing table with vigour. 'How old do you think they are?' she asked.

'Not sure. Thirty-something, I suppose.'

'You'll have your work cut out, being the boss lady at work, and a musical director.' Kathleen met Jane's eyes in the mirror. 'Do you feel a little nervous, as well as excited?'

Not for the first time, Jane marvelled at the beauty of her friend, who had inherited a mane of lustrous black curls and deepest blue eyes from her Celtic ancestors. Rose's blonde prettiness had turned heads from a very early age, but she had never had Kathleen's absolute innocence — even as a child there had been a look of guile in Rose's eyes as she twisted every adult around her little finger. Jane was accustomed to having the plainer reflection, with dark hair which refused to remain permed for more than a month, problem skin, and brown eyes which she felt were too large for her thin face. Sometimes it bothered her, but not often, although she missed the fun of Rose's encouragement to try different hairstyles and cosmetics.

Softly, Kathleen said, 'Are you thinking about Rose?'

Surprised, Jane said, 'How did you know?'

'There's a sad little look comes over your face. What were you thinking?'

'Oh, just how different Rose was to you — and me — and how much I miss her.' Jane smiled in the mirror and answered Kathleen's earlier question. 'And yes, I am a little nervous about being a musical director. It will certainly be the most challenging thing I've done. I just hope I'm good enough.'

'Of course you're good enough. Those shows you did with Madame Delia were grand. But this time you'll be able to choose the music, and help create the shows.'

'Gosh! So I will. I must admit, I've missed the rehearsals, the buzz on opening nights.'

'Well, then . . . ' Kathleen turned and hugged her friend. 'And I wouldn't be in the least bit surprised if you don't run that agency so well they'll end up offering you the job for keeps.'

Jane laughed. 'Isn't life crazy? Yesterday I was bored rigid. And now . . . '

Kathleen clipped the lid back onto the tin

of Mansion Polish and grinned at her. 'And now do you know which path to take at the crossroads?'

Lifting her chin, Jane said, 'I can't wait to take the first step.'

2

'If I have to play 'Your tiny hand is frozen' one more time, I shall scream,' Jane muttered under her breath as yet another tenor with more vibrato than voice left the studio. 'It wouldn't be so bad if the temperature wasn't way up in the eighties!'

With a wry smile, Bernard consulted his list. 'Only two more to go,' he commented. 'What do you think of the chaps we've heard so far?'

'Not much, I'm afraid. The second one was passable, but he doesn't read music and he tried to race me.'

'So I noticed.' Bernard sighed. 'Ah well, let's hope the next one is better.'

Jane's heart sank as the man produced the familiar copy of the solo from *La Boheme*, misjudged the introduction, and ploughed on with complete lack of pitch, making three unsuccessful attempts to hit the final top note. She dare not look him in the face as she thanked him and returned the music, desperately hoping he wouldn't notice her shaking shoulders. As soon as the door closed behind him she exploded, stuffing her handkerchief into her mouth so the poor man wouldn't hear. She wasn't the only one having difficulty controlling her mirth.

'Oh, my God!' Bernard gasped. 'I'm not sure I can listen to any more tonight and remain sane.' He leaned against the piano, trying to regain his composure. 'Would you like a drink before we hear the last one?'

Shaking her head, Jane wiped her eyes and took a deep breath. 'Let's get it over and done with,' she said. 'Then I'll have a drink.'

The well-built man who introduced himself as David Roberts looked more like a baritone or bass singer. In fact, Jane thought, he looked as though he would be more at home on a building site than a concert platform, but at least he showed originality with his choice of music — and as soon as he began to softly sing the opening bars of 'All through the night', in the Welsh language, Jane knew they had found their tenor.

'That was beautiful,' she said, as the final glorious note died away. 'By far the best we've heard, wasn't it, Bernard?'

Strangely, Bernard was frowning. 'There may be a problem,' he said.

Too surprised to speak, Jane stared at him. David Roberts was perfect. There couldn't possibly be a problem.

'It's your size.' Bernard was tall, but he had to look up at the Welshman towering over him. 'I'm not sure we'll be able to hire a dress suit for you.'

'I have a very nice dress suit of my own.' David's speaking voice was as lyrical as his singing. 'Sung with the Briggs Male Voice Choir for years, I have.'

'Really?' Jane wondered why he had answered their advertisement. 'They are a superb choir.'

'The best — well, apart from the one we had back in the valley.' David smiled at her. 'And — in case you are wondering — I haven't fallen out with them.' He hesitated, then went on, 'We all work together, rehearse together, and perform at concerts together, see. There are times when a change is good for you, don't you agree?'

★ ★ ★

'I've kept the bottles in the bread crock, but nothing stays cool for long in this heat.' Bernard handed Jane a tall glass of shandy and heaved his front-room window up another inch.

'Mmm. Just what the doctor ordered.' Jane downed half the glass in one gulp and moved closer to the window, trying to gain a breath

26

of air. 'Now we have our tenor, plus a baritone and contralto. And when you were answering the telephone, David told me his wife plays a piano accordion. I've arranged to hear her next week, when we audition the drummers — is that OK?'

'Wonderful! If she's half as good as him, we'll be in luck. Pity he couldn't stay for a drink.'

Jane nodded, then continued with her mental list. 'If we can find a reasonable soprano, I can work on some duets with David.'

'Anything particular in mind?'

'Something by Ivor Novello, I think. Possibly, 'We'll gather lilacs.' '

'Fine by me.' Bernard finished his drink. 'Eunice needs another couple of dancers, and I'd like some unusual acts — a juggler or magician; maybe a mind-reader if there's one out there. But most of all I need a good comedian before we can put the show on the road. I'm OK at being Master of Ceremonies, but I'm useless at telling jokes.'

Jane laughed. 'Like the time at Eunice's birthday party, when you forgot the punch line?'

'Don't remind me.' Bernard became serious again. 'We need a guy who is lively, perhaps slightly risque, but not too blue. I'll put another ad in the paper.' He picked up her empty glass. 'A refill?'

'Please. I've been thirsty all day. It was like an oven in the office.'

'How's it all going?'

'Fine. Managed to get another account — a building society.'

'Good for you. It's a growing market. Do you think they'll keep you on as manager?'

'I don't know.' Jane pulled a face. 'They're still dubious about my age, even though I've brought in two new accounts since I started. I'm surprised they haven't found someone by now, with so many officer types being demobbed.'

'Ah, well it's one thing leading chaps into battle, but a different matter persuading industries that they need you to market their goods. You've obviously got the knack.'

Jane smiled. 'Maybe if they haven't found someone by my next birthday . . . '

For a few minutes they sat silently sipping their drinks, then Bernard asked, 'Have you eaten?'

'No. I came straight from work.'

'There's a new little cafe up the road that I have been meaning to try. Would you care to join me?'

'Thanks just the same, but Mum asked me to collect the laundry from Betty.'

'Let me run you over there and take you home afterwards.'

'That's very kind of you, Bernard, but I couldn't put you to all that bother.'

'It's no bother — Eunice won't be back till late and there's not much on the wireless.'

It was too hot to argue, and the thought of hoisting a heavy bag on and off buses was not particularly appealing to Jane. As Bernard parked the car outside the neat row of prefabs, where once an ugly bomb site had scarred the street, he commented, 'I wonder whether these will be as temporary as the old wooden huts in Woolwich were supposed to be?'

'Goodness! I remember Gran telling me about those. They even wrote a song about them.' Jane softly sang, ' 'I wouldn't leave my little wooden hut for you' . . . ' Then chuckled, 'I wouldn't leave my prefabricated house, doesn't have quite the same ring, does it?'

Laughing, Bernard shook his head. 'And some of the little wooden huts are still standing, I believe.' He walked around the car and opened the passenger door. 'Still, at least the prefabs have helped solve the problem of rehousing.'

'They're rather nice inside,' Jane said. 'Come and see for yourself. You've not met my brother, have you?'

'No, and I'd like to — if his wife doesn't mind my calling unexpectedly.'

'I don't think Betty will mind, although I should warn you that my sister-in-law is not as houseproud as Mum.'

That was an understatement, Jane thought, as she picked her way through the clutter of toys and piles of magazines littering the floor.

Jack had answered the door, apologising for the mess after he'd been introduced to Bernard. 'I've been putting Johnny to bed. He takes a while to get settled.'

'I expect it's the heat,' Bernard said, as Jack cleared a space for him on the settee.

'Not really. He's always difficult. I expect Jane told you he's handicapped.'

'Yes. Something to do with a tricky birth during the Blitz, I believe.'

'Afraid so. My wife has never fully recovered her strength.'

Jane stacked the magazines into a pile. 'Where is Betty?' she asked.

'Sitting out in the garden. She said it's been too hot for her to do anything today. That's why . . . ' He waved an apologetic hand around the room.

If it's not too hot, it's too cold, Jane thought. Or too wet, or windy. She gazed with affection at her brother. Once a fine athlete, and a glider pilot during the war, he was only a shadow of his former self and, even now, after months of hospital treatment, none of the family knew the true story of his experiences in the prisoner-of-war camp.

'What's it like, being back at work, Jack?' she asked. 'Have things changed much in the drawing office?'

'A couple of the lads didn't make it back, and the supervisor stayed on in the navy, but the rest of the old gang are still there — seven years older of course, but aren't we all?'

'Is the work more difficult?'

'It seems so, but I think that's mainly because I find it hard to concentrate for long.' Jack threw some toys into a cardboard box in the corner. 'The boss said I could go part-time if I want, which was jolly decent of him — but we really need the money, Sis, for furnishing this place.'

Bernard glanced around the room. 'It's much more spacious inside than I imagined.'

'We were lucky to get it, with so many on the waiting list. Mum's been a brick, but it's nice to have our own home. Now, Bernard, can I offer you a cup of tea, or would you prefer . . . ?' He was interrupted by a knock at the front door. 'Excuse me.' Jack took a football coupon from the sideboard drawer and foraged in his pocket for a shilling. 'I won't be a minute.'

But it wasn't the pools collector. It was Sandy. And he wasn't at all surprised to see Jane. 'Your mother said you'd probably be here, so I can kill two birds with one stone.' He grinned at Jack. 'Just called round to say goodbye — I'm off to Birmingham next week.'

What has Birmingham done to deserve you? Jane thought. And what have I done to deserve this? Yet again I have to fix a polite expression on my face, and suppress the urge to wipe the smile off yours.

'Phew! What a summer.' Sandy loosened his tie. 'Last time I saw you two, it was cold enough to freeze the . . . ' He stopped himself just in time. 'Sorry, Jane, but you know what I mean. In fact, I thought that was why you were such a grizzly guts. You never liked the cold. Perhaps that's why you didn't want to live in Norway?'

Unable to think of a smart reply, Jane looked away, but Sandy put his hand under her chin and turned her face back towards him, his head on one side. 'So, why the sour expression today? Don't you like the heat, either?'

To her intense embarrassment, Jane felt the colour rising from her throat. Jack made matters worse by joining in the laughter with

Sandy. In front of Bernard, too!

'Actually,' Jack said, still grinning, 'I was about to offer Jane's friend a cold beer. By the colour of Jane's face, we'd better tip hers over her head — it might cool her down a bit.'

As Jack went through to the kitchen, Sandy noticed Bernard, who looked at Jane, as though waiting for an introduction.

'Bernard Berwick — Sandy Randall,' she murmured, unwilling to prolong the moment with explanations.

The two men shook hands. 'Is that your jalopy outside?' Sandy asked. 'My dad used to have a Morris just like that. Sold it when petrol rationing started.'

Bernard peered through the window. 'Nice little sporty job you've got. I've always fancied an open top myself.'

'It's OK in this weather, but a bit draughty in the winter, even with the hood up. Still, you've got to put on a bit of a show if you expect to stand a chance with the nurses.'

The man's incorrigible, Jane thought, wondering how much more she had to endure.

'Oh.' Bernard's eyebrows were raised. 'I didn't realise you were a doctor. Jane never mentioned you.'

Why should I? she thought. I'd buried him

in my past — or thought I had!

To Jane's horror, Sandy slipped his arm around her shoulders. 'We're old mates, Jane and I. Went to the same school. Met when we were evacuated.'

Mortified, Jane realised he was about to reminisce, and there wasn't a thing she could do about it. She managed to side-step from his arm by picking up a stray toy engine. Sandy was in full flow.

'Silly goose fell off a haystack and was badly winded — everyone was flapping around. She was only a first former and I thought, as a more mature fourth former, I ought to show off some of my feeble medical knowledge. Mother's a theatre sister and Dad works in pharmaceuticals.'

'Ah, so you're following in the family tradition.'

'Of course. Anyway, Rose — Jane's sister — and I managed to get Jane back to her billet in one piece, and we've been good friends ever since.'

Not quite true, Jane thought, as Sandy took a cigarette case from his pocket and offered it to Bernard.

'Thanks.' Bernard bent his head to Sandy's lighter. 'Delia told me about Rose. Great tragedy, especially for someone so young — and talented.'

'I think Rose could have been a professional dancer if she'd really set her mind to
it.'

And if she hadn't been carrying your child,
Jane silently accused.

'She certainly had the looks . . . ' Sandy
paused, as though a thought had just
occurred to him. 'Delia? Madame Delia, the
dancing teacher? Are you her husband?'

'Ex-husband.'

'Oh, yes. I'd forgotten about the Yank.
Hard luck.'

'I wasn't the only one.' Bernard smiled
briefly. 'And it's becoming easier now I'm
starting up the concert party — with Jane's
help.'

'Jane?'

How dare they discuss her as if she wasn't
in the room? Jane thought.

Now it was Bernard's turn. 'She's my
musical director and pianist. Didn't you
know?'

'No, but I'm not surprised. Rose wasn't the
only talented twin. I used to listen to Jane
playing the piano for hours.'

This was too much. Jane knew she had to
get out of the room. At that moment, her
brother reappeared with three foaming
glasses. 'Excuse me, I need to have a word
with Betty,' she muttered.

'Here, take your shandy with you.' Jack handed the other two glasses to his guests. 'While you're doing that, we can have a look at the cars, can't we, fellas?'

Her sister-in-law sat outside the back door, reading a sixpenny romantic novel, her feet in a zinc bath of water. 'Just what I need,' she said, taking the glass from Jane's hand.

'Actually, that was my drink!'

'Was it? Oh, well, you can get yourself another one when you go back in.' Betty finished the glass without stopping, then asked, 'Who was the bloke talking to Sandy?'

'Bernard Berwick. Aren't you coming in to say 'Hullo'?'

'I've only just got comfortable.' Betty slapped at an insect. 'If it wasn't for the creepy crawlies, I'd sleep out here tonight,' she said. 'Then I wouldn't have to put up with Jack's nightmares. They've been worse since the heatwave.'

'It probably reminds him of the jungle. Have you told the doctor about them?'

Betty shrugged. 'He hasn't asked, so there doesn't seem much point.' She handed the empty glass back to Jane and turned the page of her book. 'Tell Jack to put more beer and less lemonade in it next time — and to run the cold tap on the bottle a bit longer. It was lukewarm.'

Jane felt like emptying the footbath over her sister-in-law's head. Instead, she said, 'Betty, I really don't think it's fair that you expect Jack to do everything. He's finding it very tiring now he's back at work.'

A belligerent expression on her face, Betty looked up from her book. 'Then he shouldn't have moved away from his mum's, should he? I never wanted to come here in the first place.'

'It's only natural that he should want a home of his own. When you married him you didn't expect to live with us for ever, did you?'

'If I'd known what was going to happen, I'd never have married him in the first place. It was rotten, being left on my own all those years, especially with Johnny.'

'The war wasn't easy for anyone, Betty, but most people are trying to get over it and build new lives for themselves.' Jane tried a different tack. 'Now that Johnny's at the Special School, you could get a little part-time job, buy some nice things for the house. Wouldn't you like that?'

'Don't you start! They asked me if I wanted to go back to the baker's, three mornings a week. I told them to get stuffed.'

'But why? It's not far.'

'Because I can't be on my feet all the time,

that's why. It's all right for you, sitting in your posh office just answering the phone and getting paid well.' Betty glared at Jane. 'Anyway, it's none of your bloody business.'

There wasn't much point in trying to explain that her job wasn't that easy, Jane thought, and Betty was right. It was none of her business. 'Have you got the laundry for Mum?' she asked.

'It's in the bathroom. The bag's around somewhere.' Betty swatted another insect. 'And tell Mum the oven could do with a clean, next time she's over.'

On the way home, Jane wondered why on earth Jack had married Betty in the first place. His other girlfriend, Sheila, had a much livelier personality. Perhaps it was the helplessness of Betty that had attracted him. She had always relied upon him to do everything, but couldn't cope once their roles were reversed.

'A penny for them?' Bernard's voice interrupted Jane's reverie.

'Oh, I was just thinking how the war has changed people.'

Bernard negotiated a road junction without speaking, then quietly said, 'I'm not sure whether it's really change, or circumstances revealing our true natures.'

'How do you mean?'

'Well, in the camp, most of the chaps were supportive to each other. But there were one or two who would hog the best things from the Red Cross parcels, or even steal from their mates. And then there were the 'Dear John' letters. Some coped, others went to pieces. At least Delia spared me that.'

'But it must have been quite a blow. Surely it changed your outlook on life?'

'I suppose it did, in some ways. But I still loved her, and wanted her to be happy, whether it was with me, or someone else. That's not being noble, Jane. It's being honest. It wasn't really her fault that she fell in love with Chuck.'

'She fought it for a long time.'

'I know. And what sort of man would I be if I refused her the chance of a happier marriage than the one she had? It would be like making her a prisoner, and I know only too well what that is like. I couldn't do that to anyone, especially someone I love.'

'Eunice doesn't see it in quite the same way, does she?'

'No. But Eunice is a different sort of prisoner. She has things locked inside her, just like your brother. Maybe one day she'll tell you about them.'

As the car slowed down outside her house, Jane thought, not for the first time, what a genuinely fine man Bernard was. Then he spoiled it.

'It's the first time I've met a doctor outside surgery hours,' he mused. 'Sandy seems like a decent chap. We've arranged to have a drink next time he's home — he thinks his dad might know someone who can retune the car.'

Oh, God! Jane thought. How can I forget Sandy if he and Bernard are going to become buddies? Next thing, they'll be suggesting threesomes. I had enough of that when Rose was alive.

3

'Happy New Year! Happy New Year!'

Jane's cheek was kissed by Eunice, her lips by Bernard — quite warmly. She backed away a little, then noticed that he also kissed the lips of Audrey and Monica, the two sopranos.

While she played 'Auld Lang Syne', Jane wondered what the coming year held in store for her. Less than a year ago she had been very much in the doldrums, trying to recover from a broken engagement, afraid she might lose her job, and frustrated beyond belief by the attempts of Sandy to resume their old relationship — something she would never do — ever! But 1947 had worked out quite well. She was still Acting Manager for the advertising agency, and had heard on the grapevine that she would probably be offered a permanent post on her twentieth birthday in April. If she managed to clinch the deal tomorrow with a new cosmetic company, that would go in her favour.

Then there was Bernard. She admired his professional approach and the way he was picking up the pieces of his life again, although she was still wary of his sister. Jane felt he had more understanding than most men and he was obviously lonely, so she'd been a willing listener when he needed to talk to someone more sympathetic than Eunice. But although Jane enjoyed their conversations, there were times when she wondered if he was reading more into their relationship than she intended.

For the next hour, she didn't have a moment to reflect on Bernard's feelings towards her, or her own towards him. The hall had an extended licence and Jane took her little group of musicians into a non-stop medley of dance tunes. In addition to a drummer, they had acquired a double bass player just in time for Berwick Productions' opening show in December, which was so successful they had been asked to perform at the Masonic New Year Dinner-Dance. The audience had really entered into the spirit of the evening, and Jane knew that every member of the company had given of their best. David had been over the moon when she asked him to sing a Frank Sinatra song.

'I've always fancied myself as a bit of a crooner, see, and 'Time after Time' became a bit special for Ruth and me after we saw *It Happened in Brooklyn*.'

David's wife had also passed her audition with flying colours, becoming Jane's fourth musician as well as soloist, her fingers flying nimbly over the keys of her glittering piano accordian.

One last chorus of 'Auld Lang Syne', and the National Anthem, then Bernard took the microphone and wished the audience goodnight and a safe journey home.

'Thanks, everyone.' Jane shook hands with Harry and Gordon, kissed Ruth's cheek. 'I've never heard you play so well.'

Harry smiled back at Jane as he began to release his kettle drum from the stand. 'Haven't enjoyed myself so much in years,' he said. 'Reckon we might get a few more engagements out of tonight, don't you?'

'Could be. And Bernard has booked the Winter Baths for another full show on the thirty-first. Are you OK for a rehearsal on Friday week?'

All nodded agreement.

'That got nineteen-forty-eight off to a flying start, didn't it?' Bernard was back, still wearing his paper hat.

'I thought everyone performed beautifully.'

'That's what I've just been telling them. And you were wonderful, Jane. No wonder Delia spoke so highly of you.' He helped pack away her music. 'Your arrangement of 'Sweet Georgia Brown' was really something.'

'Thank you.' Jane had been surprised and

43

delighted at the response from the audience,.

'And I'm not the only one to appreciate your talent.' Bernard nodded towards a man still seated at a table, scribbling on the back of a menu. 'That's Charlie Davenport.'

Both name and man were unfamiliar to Jane.

Bernard slid the music rest back inside the piano. 'He's a talent scout for Sol Jacobs.'

That name did have a familiar ring. 'The man who's trying to outrival Caroll Leviss and his Discoveries?' she asked.

'The very same — and he told me he was quite impressed with our show.'

'Really?' Jane waited for Bernard to go on, but he was infuriatingly hesitant. 'Oh, come on, Bernard,' she cried. 'I know there's more to come. You look just like the cat that ate the cream.'

He continued to play the waiting game just a little longer, then swung Jane around in a half circle. 'Sol Jacobs is planning a series of talent contests around here, and he wants some of our acts to enter the opening show.'

'That's wonderful!' Now it was Jane's turn to grin like the proverbial Cheshire cat. 'Who is he interested in?'

'Maureen — he thinks her impressions compare with Florence Desmond.'

'I agree. She's terrific. Who else?'

'David and Ruth; Audrey and Monica . . . '

'Oh, yes. Monica sang 'Musetta's Waltz Song' with such feeling.' Jane jotted down an idea then popped her notebook into the music case. 'I'd like to try them in a duet. We're lucky to have two trained sopranos, and I think their voices would blend.'

'Anything particular in mind?'

Jane nodded. 'Do you know 'The Flower Duet' from *Lachme*?'

'No, but if you think it's right for our audiences, go ahead.'

'It's by Delibes, and so beautiful it makes the hairs stand up on the back of my neck. They'll love it.'

Bernard nodded. 'Fine. Now come and meet Mr Davenport. He has a proposition to put to you.'

Charlie Davenport stared shrewdly at Jane and came quickly to the point. He needed a good accompanist and Jane obviously had a flair for bringing out the best of the various artistes, without stealing the limelight herself. She would have to adapt to the needs of untrained and inexperienced performers — would sight-reading present a problem? Good. The contests would be monthly, at a local cinema, and she would be paid three pounds for each performance. Oh — and she must be prepared to enter the contest herself if there was a shortfall.

Jane sank onto the chair vacated by the talent scout and watched him disappear through the entrance, coat collar turned up against the chill dawning of the first day of the year. As usual, when she didn't quite know what to say, she reverted to her schoolgirl expression.

'Gosh!'

Bernard's eyes crinkled as he gazed down at her. 'Pity the bar is closed,' he said. 'You look as though you could do with a drink — I know I could.'

'I feel intoxicated enough as it is, and I've only had lemonade. What an evening! We're going to need some extra rehearsals before the first contest.'

Bernard nodded agreement. 'And I've an idea for your solo for my next show.'

'Oh?'

'Gershwin's *Rhapsody in Blue*. I've asked Eunice to dye the rest of that parachute stuff a deep blue and make you another evening gown.' Bernard touched a fold of her skirt. 'This colour isn't really you.'

Jane agreed. When Eunice had been offered a length of shop-soiled brocade, it had seemed perfect, especially as Jane had no clothing coupons to spare. But the dull gold made her skin appear sallow.

Thoughtfully, Bernard went on, 'Something off the shoulders and glamorous. I'll put a blue spotlight on you. What do you think?'

'The music is wonderful.' Jane was embarrassed. 'But I'm not so sure about the glamour — I'm not really the type.'

'You might surprise everyone, including yourself. Why don't you ask Eunice to try something different with your hair?'

'My sister used to spend hours coaxing it into various styles, but it never lasted.' Jane changed the subject. 'I thought young Patrick did very well as Merlin the Magician, didn't you? He's got an amusing line of patter.'

'If he hadn't mucked up the last trick, I think Charlie Davenport would have been interested. Actually, the lad told me he might build a new act around making mistakes.' Bernard thought for a moment. 'With his Irish accent and charm, it might work, and he certainly got a few laughs tonight. But it's not the same as a stand-up comedian.'

'No luck with your last ad?'

'I've got a chappie coming to see me on Sunday morning. Says his act is funnier than Sid Field's.'

Jane laughed. 'They all say that.'

'Don't they just?' Bernard waved to the chattering chorus dancers as they left, gipsy costumes draped over their arms. Then he turned back to Jane. 'Any chance of you coming over and sitting in with me on the audition?' he asked. 'I'd value your opinion.'

Surprised, Jane said, 'I don't know much about comedy acts. Eunice would be a better judge.'

'She's off down Petticoat Lane to see if she can find some bargains for costumes. But this fellow plays trumpet, and you know about music.' He cleared his throat. 'We could have a spot of lunch afterwards, if you like? I know quite a nice little place in Gidea Park.'

'Sorry, Bernard. I'm going to Westcliff for the day. Family lunch with a friend of Mum's — Mrs Marshall. I introduced her to you at the Christmas show. Do you remember?'

'As if anyone could forget meeting the beautiful widow. It's incredible that a good-looking woman like Laura Marshall hasn't remarried.' He paused for a moment, then went on, 'I'm surprised that you haven't been snapped up by now, either. You're intelligent, talented, and a very nice person to have around.' He smiled at Jane. 'Perhaps you haven't met Mr Right yet, eh?'

'Perhaps.' Jane picked up her music case. 'Ready?' She was glad that Eunice was eager to talk about the next show on the drive home. The last thing Jane wanted just now was to discuss her personal life — and certainly not with Bernard.

★　★　★

The rough drawings for posters on the London Underground were quite promising, Jane thought, and certainly should catch the eye if strategically placed alongside the escalators. The new range of cosmetics were aimed at working girls who wanted quality but couldn't afford Helena Rubinstein or Elizabeth Arden prices. But Jane needed more information on the advertising rates before she could show the cosmetic company her proposals, and the file was in Miss Dawson's office.

Her ideas for the new campaign were put to one side by the sight of Miss Dawson standing over her desk, blackened hands clutching a tangled mess of typewriter ribbon, her expression defying description. For a moment, Jane watched the book-keeper with amused affection.

Augustine Dawson had once lived in Edwardian grandeur, cosseted by Nanny and Cook. Any prospects of marriage were slim — the Great War had claimed too many young men — and when the stock market crash wiped out the family fortunes, she was forced to seek employment for the first time in her life, and enrolled at the Phyllida Lawson Secretarial Academy for Young Ladies. Three years later, still totally unqualified for the commercial marketplace, she replied to an advertisement for a clerical assistant. Miss Reynolds soon realised that her new clerk had no aptitude for office machinery, but the books were painstakingly and neatly kept. Normally, she would not need to use a typewriter, but she had been helping out by typing the costings for Jane.

'Would you like me to put the new ribbon on for you, Miss Dawson?' Jane asked.

Startled, her colleague looked up. 'How very kind of you, my dear.' Relief was apparent in her voice. 'It is incomprehensible to me why I cannot master such a simple task.'

Jane smiled as she deftly fastened the end of the new ribbon to the spool. 'You only have to ask, you know.'

'Yes, I do know — but you are so busy today preparing for your meeting . . . Were you looking for the 'Lovely Lady' file? It is safely locked away in my drawer.'

'Good.' Jane despatched the tangled mess into the waste paper basket. 'If I can get that account I'm hoping the directors might agree I'm capable of doing the job permanently. At

50

the last count it was three in favour, one against.'

'Of course you are capable!' Miss Dawson was quite vehement. 'You are every bit as efficient as Miss Reynolds, more so in some respects.' Her lips twitched. 'You do not leave the petty cash tin unlocked. As for your age — after all your achievements during the past year, I should think that was quite irrelevant.'

'If only the powers that be agreed with you,' Jane muttered. 'But until I am twenty-one I shall be regarded as a minor, unable to even carry my own library ticket without my parents' permission. As for managing a business — tut-tut for even considering it!'

Miss Dawson gingerly held the door open with one elbow. 'When those laws were made, life was somewhat different. Young girls were quite content to remain sheltered by their parents until they came of age.' She followed Jane into the cloakroom. 'I remember that I had no wish to be independent, and it was quite a shock when circumstances forced me to go out into a wider world.'

'And tackle monsters like typewriters and Gestetner copying machines,' Jane teased.

'Indeed.' Miss Dawson began to scrub her hands. 'But two world wars have changed so many things, and more young ladies than ever

51

have been introduced to new responsibilities. Surely it is time for some reassessment?'

'Nice in theory, but men make the rules, and they won't give up their superiority so easily,' Jane sighed. 'I really would like to stay with this post. The work is so satisfying.'

'Then we will keep our inky fingers firmly crossed.' Miss Dawson carefully examined her hands. 'Before I forget, Jane, there is a recital of music by Schubert and Brahms at the Albert Hall next Thursday. Shall I try to book two tickets?'

'Please do. We haven't been to a concert together for ages.'

When Jane joined the agency, she had been drawn to the gentle spinster who still plaited and coiled her grey hair over her ears, as she had for twenty years, and they had often attended lunch-time recitals by Myra Hess at the National Gallery. In Miss Dawson's tiny flat in Kensington, Jane heard about a genteel world so very different to her own, and admired the treasured painting by Turner, rescued after the family home was bombed. In fact, despite the difference in their ages, Miss Dawson was Jane's closest friend, apart from Kathleen. The other girls in the office were more interested in films and dancing and fashion, just like her sister. And yet she and Rose had been so close, sharing innermost thoughts in a way that was almost telepathic. No one could ever take the place of Rose in her life.

This won't do at all, she thought, shaking herself out of her melancholy. I must look to the future. On the way back to her own office she asked Stella to hold her calls for an hour so that she could work on 'Lovely Lady' uninterrupted.

A little later, her head buried deep in figures, Jane was vaguely aware that her office door had opened. It would be Rachel with a cup of coffee.

'Thank you, Rachel,' she murmured. 'Would you put it . . . ' But it wasn't the nervous little junior who stood in the doorway. It was a man. Annoyed that Stella had allowed such an unsavoury character to slip through the net, she stared at the stranger. 'I didn't hear you knock,' she said.

Undaunted by her cool tone, the man closed the door behind him. Wearing a camel overcoat with a velvet half-collar, over a pair of checked trousers, he looked as if he would be quite at home selling black market goods from the pavements of Oxford Street. To her amazement, he took off his jauntily tilted pork pie trilby and placed it firmly on her hat and coat stand.

'Sorry, me darling. Rather remiss of me.

You might have been changing your stockings,' he said. His accent was Irish, but not the gentle brogue spoken by Kathleen. It was a northern voice, harsh from the back of the throat.

Her voice still icy, Jane said, 'Miss Downey handles all the purchasing of stationery supplies, but she will not see anyone without an appointment, and she is rather busy just now. Perhaps you would like to telephone her in a week or so. Good morning.' Pointedly, she looked at the hat stand.

His smarmy smile revealed a glint of gold from a front tooth filling as he closed in and leaned across the desk. Jane felt the full blast of his breath, strongly laced with halitosis and beer fumes, and as for his nose — Grandad would have called it 'a right boozer's hooter'.

'I'll not be needing an appointment, Jane.' He held out his hand. 'Me name's Seamus O'Rourke and, as from the first of January, 1948 — that'll be today according to the calendar — I'm your new manager.'

★ ★ ★

Laura Marshall's house at Westcliff was detached, on a rise above the road, with a pleasant view overlooking the Thames Estuary. The sort of house that local estate

54

agents described as a 'desirable property'. Jane loved visiting the Marshalls. She loved the house, and the garden, and the warmth of the atmosphere. But most of all, she loved the Marshalls.

They were all there for lunch on the first Sunday in January. Bea Marshall, Laura's mother-in-law, valued her independence too much to give up her little bungalow nearby, but she usually joined the family for Sunday lunch. Her eldest grandson, Lawrence, was about to go to the Royal Naval College at Dartmouth, so the luncheon party was partly in his honour. His younger brother, Desmond, was the same age as Kathleen but, whereas Kathleen had learned to accept the loss of her family, Desmond still grieved deeply for his father, and Jane suspected that was the real reason his mother had not remarried. Then there was Laura's brother, Robert. He was about to have his final skin graft at East Grinstead for the burns he'd suffered when his ship was torpedoed.

The large lounge was a hubbub of chatter as the ladies sipped sherry and the gentlemen quaffed light ales. Kathleen talked to Desmond; Grandad and Fred Harrison questioned Lawrence about his plans for a naval career, and Robert reminisced with his old shipmate, Nell Harrison's brother, Len, who was now in charge of the Seamen's Hostel at London Docks.

Sitting on the window seat in the curved bay, Jane's attention was taken by the little group of women by the fireside — her mother, Mrs Marshall, and Auntie Bea, as she had been asked to call the older lady. All three had one thing in common — they had been young widows. Bea Marshall's husband had gone down with the Titanic, Laura Marshall's husband had died trying to rescue soldiers from the beaches of Dunkirk, and Nell Harrison had lost her first husband when Jack was just a toddler. Jane's mother was the only one who had remarried, but Jane had never heard her mother's friends complain about loneliness, or the problems of bringing up sons single-handed.

Jane admired Mrs Marshall tremendously and wished she had her sense of style. Today, she looked far younger than her forty-two years, absolutely stunning in a glowing red woollen dress, her dark hair dressed in sweeps, with a page boy roll. Jane glanced at her uncle and knew, from the expression on his face, that he still loved Laura Marshall with an intensity that only a confirmed bachelor of many years can feel when he has met the woman of his dreams.

Suddenly, Jane realised that her name had

been mentioned. Mrs Marshall was talking about the Christmas show.

'We thought Jane was superb, didn't we, Bea?'

'Oh, yes. You must be so proud of her, Nell.'

Jane was curious to know how her mother would answer.

After a pause, Mrs Harrison said, 'I suppose she did quite well but, to be honest, I was rather upset.'

'Oh, dear. Why was that?' Bea Marshall asked.

'Well, I didn't want to go in the first place, but Fred made me. I knew what it would be like, and I was right. As soon as the dancers came on, I expected to see my Rose, and I couldn't enjoy anything after that. It wasn't fair to expect me to.'

'Nell, dear.' Mrs Marshall put a comforting hand on her friend's arm. 'It's true you have lost one daughter, but remember that you have another, equally talented.'

'It's not the same. Never will be.'

Laura Marshall glanced across the room at Jane, and a sympathetic expression crossed her face as she stood up. 'I'd better see to the roast, or we'll be having burnt offerings.'

Without looking up, Mrs Harrison said, 'Jane will help you.'

Jane was already on her feet. As she helped Mrs Marshall spoon the vegetables into tureens, she said, 'I'm afraid this is a bad time of year for my mother. It's almost the third anniversary of Rose's death.'

'I know, dear, and I'm sure she doesn't mean to hurt you.'

'That's what I keep telling myself.' Jane blinked back the tears. 'But it doesn't help.'

'Would you like me to speak to her when we are alone?'

Jane shook her head. 'Thank you, but I really don't think it would do any good. I've tried, but Mum has no time for me, and that's that.'

After a pause, Mrs Marshall said, 'Can't your father do anything about the situation?'

'Not really. He's sympathetic and I think he knows how I feel, but Mum still blames him for having a row with Rose before she went out that night, so it's just as difficult for him.'

'Surely your mother realises that Rose would have gone to the theatre whether she quarrelled with your father or not?'

Jane had told everyone that Rose had been killed outside the Ilford Hippodrome. Nobody knew the truth, only Jane.

'So far as Rose is concerned, my mother is totally blinkered. She thinks only what she wants to think.' Jane put a lid on the dish of Brussels sprouts. 'If things are no better when I come of age, I might consider leaving home. But for now, I have a bigger problem.'

Before she could tell Mrs Marshall about Seamus O'Rourke, Kathleen came into the kitchen, offering to help. It wasn't a good time, Jane really wanted to ask Mrs Marshall's advice while they were alone.

Throughout lunch, the conversation was general and light-hearted, which helped lift the atmosphere. Afterwards, a walk along the beach was suggested, and warm scarves and gloves were donned to protect against the east wind blowing into the estuary from the North Sea.

Eventually, Mrs Marshall and Jane dropped behind the others. 'Do you want to talk about your other problem?' the older woman asked.

'Oh, yes, please.' Jane described the new manager, and how she feared he was not the right person for the job. 'It's not jealousy, I can assure you. He just doesn't have any business sense at all. I don't think he's managed anything in his life.'

'Then how on earth did he get the post?'

'Ah, that's what really annoys me. I telephoned the managing director's secretary, because nobody had informed me he was coming. She'd heard some gossip that Mr O'Rourke had met Mr Grafton at a race meeting before the war and given him a good tip which won enough money to start up his first agency.'

'I see. And Mr Grafton told him that if he ever needed the favour returned . . . ?'

'Exactly. At the time, Mr O'Rourke was going abroad. In fact, he spent the war in Casablanca, but he's very cagey about his time there.'

'Shady dealings, no doubt.'

'More than likely. Anyway, now he is broke, and he has come back to call in the debt. I dread to think what will happen to the agency. The market place is difficult enough as it is.'

'Surely they could have found him a less responsible post elsewhere?'

'There's a much more suitable vacancy at the head office in Liverpool. But the managing director has killed two birds with one stone by putting him in our office.'

'In what way?'

'Mr Grafton is the only director who still considers I'm too young for the job.'

'Ah. And the other bird?'

'Our managing director lives in Lancashire.'

'And this keeps O'Rourke off his back.'

Mrs Marshall was thoughtful for a moment, then asked, 'How have the rest of the staff taken the news?'

'As you can imagine, he is too uncouth for Miss Dawson to even contemplate, and Stella complained that he stood with his sweaty hand on her shoulder while she was working the switchboard. Also, he managed to leave a portfolio of artwork in a taxi.'

'Not a very good start.'

'The artist is furious.' Jane held onto the brim of her hat. 'The only thing in our new manager's favour is that he wants me to continue working with the three new accounts.'

'So you were successful with the cosmetic firm? Well done.'

'Thanks. After the meeting they gave me a huge box of samples. Rose would have loved trying them all out.'

'That's true — but what do you think of the range?'

'I haven't got a clue about make-up, so I just kept a mascara and pinky lipstick for the shows and gave the rest to the girls.' Jane laughed. 'They had a lovely time sorting through the box. It helped to make up for having Mr O'Rourke sitting in Miss Reynolds' office, reading the racing papers.'

'It sounds as though he's the sort of

person who might well leave you to carry on much the same, Jane. Would that be very difficult?'

'Probably not, but then I'd just be an overworked secretary without any real authority. I'm not sure if that's what I want.' Her eyes fixed on the mile-long Southend Pier jutting into the river ahead of them, Jane murmured, 'Maybe I should leave now, and look for another job.'

'Is that what you really want?'

'Yes . . . no.' Jane sighed. 'To tell the truth, I just don't know what to do for the best. What do you think I should do, Mrs Marshall?'

'For a start, you can stop calling me Mrs Marshall.' Jane's companion smiled. 'It makes me feel like an elderly aunt, and I'd like you to think of me as a friend.' She tucked her hand into Jane's arm. 'And my advice, for what it's worth, is to do nothing hastily. Why not give it six months, see how things work out?'

Jane nodded. It sounded like a reasonable idea. As they walked a little faster to catch up with the others, Robert turned round and waved. From that distance, his scars were barely visible, just a slight puckering around one eye.

'You must be relieved that Robert's

operations are almost over,' Jane commented. 'Will he go back into the merchant navy afterwards?'

'I don't think so, although he would still like to work at something connected with the sea.'

'Could Uncle Len help him? There might be a vacancy at the hostel.'

Laura Marshall pursed her lips. 'I don't think that's quite what he has in mind. He's talking about convalescing at your aunt's place in Torquay, and looking around while he's there.' She stopped walking and turned to Jane. 'I've had an idea. If I go with him, I can visit Lawrence in Dartmouth.'

'Aunt Grace would love to see you again.'

'Why don't you come with us?'

It was tempting. Jane hadn't seen her mother's sister for some time. She had lived with the Harrisons until she had joined forces with Uncle Len's best friend, Nobby Clarke, and bought a guest house in Babbacombe, adapting it into a holiday home with a difference. All the guests had some kind of disability and found it difficult to use other hotels, sometimes because they were in wheelchairs, sometimes to avoid the curious glances of other guests.

'When are you thinking of going?' Jane asked.

'Oh, not before Easter at least. Could you get away?'

'I don't see why not. I didn't take my full two weeks last year. And the first phase of talent contests should be over by then.' Suddenly, Jane felt happier. 'Yes, it will be something to look forward to. Thank you — Laura.'

4

Jane's favourite aunt settled herself more comfortably into her armchair and smiled at her niece over the rim of her Devon Pottery teacup. 'Now we can have a nice, cosy chat while Laura and Robert stretch their legs.'

It had been a long drive and Jane had been tempted to join them, but she could enjoy the views from Babbacombe Downs later. For now, she was happy to have Aunt Grace to herself for a while.

Aunt Grace had been one of the many young women who had lost their beloved at Ypres in 1915, and she had settled for a career in a solicitor's office. Unlike Miss Dawson, she learned to cope with the vagaries of cylinder recording machines and became supervisor of the typing pool. It was taken for granted that this was her mission in life, and expected that Jane would follow in her footsteps as the spinster of the family, and the shocked reactions to Grace's decision to leave a secure job and go into partnership with Nobby Clarke had not quite subsided, even after two years.

As if reading Jane's mind, her aunt

chuckled. 'Nell still thinks I'm mad,' she said, offering a plate of assorted biscuits. 'But I'm happier than I've ever been — it was worth running the gauntlet of all the gossip.'

'Poor Gran was convinced that you and Uncle Nobby were living in sin, right to her dying day.'

Colouring slightly, Aunt Grace smiled. 'Nobby did ask me to marry him, you know,' she said. 'Before we moved in.'

'Did he?' Jane stared in surprise.

'I gave his proposal serious consideration but — when I looked deep into my heart — I realised that a loving friendship is one thing, marriage is another. It should not be chosen out of propriety.'

'Couldn't agree more.' Jane was thoughtful for a moment, then she asked, 'Was Uncle Nobby very disappointed?'

'On the contrary.' Aunt Grace chuckled again. 'He was relieved. We're both too set in our ways, really, but he felt he should protect me from gossip. And for the first time in my life I have my own little flat. From up here in the attic I have the finest view in the house, and can entertain my friends whenever I wish. Now — ' she poured a second cup of tea for Jane. 'Tell me about your new boss. I can't get any information out of Nell, and when I telephoned you at the office the line was appalling. Is Mr O'Rourke making life very difficult for you?'

'Let's just say, he could make it easier, if only he would listen. He forgets appointments, even when I've reminded him. I waste so much time making excuses for him and Stella is threatening to leave unless he stops hovering around the switchboard.'

'Some people do become nervous when they are watched, I am afraid.'

'Angry would be a better word for Stella. He has a nasty habit of peering down her neckline. I've tried having a discreet word with him, but he just laughs and says she shouldn't wear such pretty blouses if she doesn't want to be looked at.'

'Why don't you leave, dear? You could get a job anywhere, with your experience.'

'There's not much available that's really interesting and pays as well. I couldn't bear to be in an office where I took shorthand all morning and typed all afternoon.'

'Mm. That's what it was like when I first started work. I agree, it is quite horrid.'

'Anyway.' Jane helped herself to another biscuit. 'I'm stuck now until the end of the summer at least.'

Aunt Grace raised her eyebrows enquiringly.

'Remember how excited Jack became when

he heard the 1948 Olympics were being held in London?'

Aunt Grace nodded, but still looked puzzled.

'Well,' Jane continued, 'Bernard was let down over his tickets and Mr O'Rourke said he knew someone who might be able to get some, and he was prepared to pay the tout's price so that Jack could go.'

'He can't be all bad then.'

'There's a catch.' Jane grimaced. 'He insists that I go along, as his guest, and for dinner afterwards.'

'Oh. I can see that would be very awkward. What are you going to do, dear?'

'I've accepted.' Jane shrugged her shoulders. 'It means so much to Jack, and there are times when I can't bear to watch the expression on his face, when he thinks no-one is looking and I know he is remembering a war that was more dreadful than anything we experienced.'

Tears moistened Aunt Grace's eyes as she patted her niece's hand. 'You have such a good heart, Jane. I just wish . . . ' She hesitated.

For a moment, Jane thought her aunt wasn't going to say any more, then she slowly went on, 'I just wish my sister appreciated you more.'

'Ah. That's another story altogether.'

Silently, Aunt Grace studied Jane's face. Then she quietly said, 'If it ever becomes too much for you, there's always a home for you here, you know.'

Surprised, Jane said, 'That's terribly kind of you — but there would be an almighty row if I left home to live with you.'

'Tosh and fiddlesticks! If I can survive the scandal of coming down here, I can survive your mother's tantrums. So can you, Jane. Remember, you don't have to be the doormat of the family, any more than you have to remain a secretary, just because everyone thinks that is your chosen lot. You are worth better.'

Jane smiled at her aunt. It was good to know that someone was fighting in her corner.

While they washed the teacups in the tiny kitchenette, they talked about the talent contests.

'Is that the ultimate prize, a recording contract?'

'And a chance to tour with the production. If David wins, we'll lose our star attraction.' Jane was pensive for a moment. 'His wife might not be too keen on him travelling all over the country without her — she only got as far as the semi-finals.'

'And I suppose he would have to give up his job?'

'I hadn't thought of that — another bridge to cross if it comes to it.'

'Will you be accompanying them for the finals?'

'No.' Jane laughed. 'Full blown orchestra for the finals, a la Stanley Black.'

'What about you, dear? Wouldn't you have liked to enter for yourself, and have a shot at a career in show business?'

'Funnily enough, I was asked to be a contestant one night, when someone didn't turn up. I actually got through to the next round — but I asked Mr Davenport to let the runner-up go in my place.'

'For goodness sake, why? You might have gone on to the finals!'

'That's what Mr Davenport said, but he understood my reasons and agreed I had made a wise decision.'

'It seems foolish to me to turn down an opportunity like that.'

'I did give it careful consideration, like your proposal . . . ' Jane smiled mischievously at her aunt. 'But you have to be a particular type of person to have a career in show business. You need personality and glamour as well as talent. Rose had all those things.'

'But she didn't have your ability to work

hard to get what she wanted, or she would have been a professional long before she was sixteen.'

'Poor Rose was convinced she would be discovered by a talent scout, and I'm the one who has turned it down. Ironic, isn't it?' Jane hung up the tea towel. 'Anyway, I've decided that I would rather keep my music as a hobby and enjoy it than have to worry about earning my living from it.'

'You have a point there, which reminds me. Would you play for us this evening? I know our guests would appreciate it.'

'I'd be delighted to.'

'Thank you, dear.' Aunt Grace untied her apron. 'Now, let's go down and see Peg. She should be back from the shops by now.'

'Probably in the kitchen, up to her elbows in flour, as usual.'

Some of Jane's happiest childhood memories were of annual holidays at the guest house, especially the mouth-watering smells that greeted them after a day on the beach. Uncle Joe was the older brother of Nell Harrison's first husband, 'Big Jack' Taylor, and in 1918 he brought home a bride, the nurse with the warm heart and delightful accent who had tended him in France. For years, they happily ran the guest house as a family 'home from home', until Uncle Joe

71

was badly injured in a hit-and-run raid across Babbacombe Downs in 1943. Now, the old couple were quite happy to let Aunt Grace and Nobby Clarke take over the place, as long as Aunt Peggy could make her feather-light Devonshire splits and dumplings, and Uncle Joe could help tend the garden from his wheelchair.

Wiping floury hands on her apron, Aunt Peggy held out her arms. 'You're still too thin, my pretty,' she commented, 'but us'll put flesh on they bones soon enough.'

Jane loved her aunt's soft west country burr, and her insistence that good food was the answer to all the world's problems. If only life was that simple!

As she helped lay up the afternoon tea-trays with warm scones and dishes of home-made strawberry jam and thick golden cream, Jane said, 'I thought I'd go over to the farm tomorrow, Aunt Peggy — unless you have anything else arranged.'

'Oh, my dear! The farm was sold last Michaelmas Day. Didn't you know?'

Every time they stayed in Babbacombe, Jane had visited Aunt Peggy's sister. The farm was part of her childhood, where she had learned to milk the cow and bottle feed orphaned lambs. Even during the war, she had helped the Land Army girls gather potatoes and clean the pigsties. Rose hadn't been so keen on the farm chores, but she was popular with the farm hands and village boys. Jane couldn't imagine a visit to Torquay without the farm.

'I always thought their sons would take it over,' she said.

'So, did I, my dear. And so did Amos and Jess.' Aunt Peggy's chins wobbled as she shook her head. 'But the boys emigrated to Australia as soon as they came back from the war, and it was too big for Amos on his own.'

'What about the Italian prisoners? Rose told me that one of them was talking about staying on.'

'He did, but he's gone into catering in one of they big hotels down Paignton way, and the local lads wanted better paid jobs. I suppose us can't blame them.' Aunt Peggy sighed. 'Jess and Amos have one of they new little bungalows over by Teignmouth, but he'd rather be ploughing a field than planting a few beans in his back garden.'

The farm had belonged to Amos's family for generations, handed down from father to son. For a while Jane pondered on the aftereffects of the war. Families struggling to pick up the pieces of their shattered lives, trying to recapture a lost era. Like her own family. Ten years ago her mother had been a contented woman, proud of the spick and span home she created, prouder still of her pretty, blonde daughter. She happily washed Jack's cricket whites or muddy rugby gear and stitched sequins to Rose's dancing costumes. Jane had not minded that Rose was the favourite, as long as Rose was there. When Rose was alive, the house was alive — their parents laughed. But now . . .

'Why the big sigh?' Aunt Grace asked.

'Oh, I was just thinking about the old days, before the war.'

'Ah, those days are gone for ever, I'm afraid, dear.'

'I know, but I always believed that the war would cleanse away the evil, and we would return to normal family life again once it ended — loving each other, staying together.'

Laura appeared in the doorway. 'A time to love and a time to hate; a time for war and a time for peace,' she murmured.

'Yes! I've heard that saying before, and it sums it up so well.'

'You can't beat the Bible for getting at the truth.'

Jane was thoughtful for a moment, then said, 'But when will we have our time for peace? We still have legacies of war, like national service and rationing and shortages — yet everything else is changing. I'm very

74

confused about the future.'

Aunt Peggy took another batch of scones from the oven. 'I remember saying that after the first war,' she said. 'Nursing those poor boys in France was quite an experience for a young country girl, and I yearned for the peaceful life we'd once had. But everything was changing so fast around me I was quite dizzy. The Suffragettes were chaining themselves to railings, and as for our clothes!' She chuckled. 'After years of covering up our ankles with skirts trailing in the dirt, they flappers were showing their knees — and more!'

Aunt Grace nodded. 'I remember arguing with Mum over the length of my skirt. I had good legs in those days, but if you worked in an office you had to dress very properly in navy or brown with little white collars.'

'So what you are all saying is — there will always be change, and we have to adapt.'

'Unless we're dinosaurs.' Laura pulled a funny face. 'And look what happened to them.'

'True.' Jane picked up a tray. 'Where's Robert?' she asked.

'In the garden, talking to Joe and Nobby. Shall I call them in for tea, Grace?'

'Yes, please. Will you bring that tray through to the lounge, please, Jane? I'll introduce you to the guests.'

The guests included a lady who had been deafened by bomb blast, and Jane was astonished to see her aunt deftly conversing in sign language. There was also a rear gunner who had been blinded — he was revisiting some of his old haunts from when he was stationed near Torquay, and he was talking to Jane about his favourite Chopin nocturnes when an attractive young woman wearing a District Nurse's uniform wheeled her bicycle into the garden.

'Just in time for tea, as usual.' Smiling, Aunt Grace poured another cup and introduced the nurse to Laura and Jane. 'Yvonne usually calls in about now to see if we have any guests who might need her assistance — at least that is her excuse.'

'I will make any excuse possible for one of these scones. Oh, hullo . . . ' The nurse smiled at Robert as he wheeled Uncle Joe up the ramp from the garden. 'Miss Davies told me you were coming. One of Archibald McIndoe's guinea pigs, aren't you?'

Looking slightly nonplussed at her directness, Robert half-smiled, then nodded.

Yvonne tilted her head to one side and studied his face. 'I'd heard he was good, but didn't realise he was this good. Were you in fighters, or bombers?'

'Merchant navy.'

'Oh.' She grinned. 'I just assumed.'

'Most were flyers, but he took the occasional patient from other services.'

'I'd like to hear more about his methods if you can bear to talk about it?'

'It doesn't bother me now.'

'Good.' Yvonne gulped down her tea. 'Tell you what. I'm off tomorrow and I told Dad I'd pop in on him. He's got a sailing school in Brixham. Would you like to come with me?'

'Rather!' Robert looked questioningly at his sister.

'Fine by me,' Laura said. 'I'm going over to see Lawrence, anyway.'

'Good.' Yvonne looked at her watch. 'Must dash. I've a crotchety old man to bath in ten minutes. Pick you up after breakfast, Robert. Bye all.' Then she was gone.

There was a moment's silence, then a burst of laughter. 'Is she always so full of beans?' Laura asked.

'Oh, yes.' Aunt Grace smiled. 'Yvonne is like a breath of fresh air, the way she breezes in and out of here. But she's also a very good nurse. You'll enjoy her company, Robert.'

'I'm looking forward to tomorrow,' he answered slowly.

★ ★ ★

Later that evening, Jane sat at her bedroom window, thinking how good it was to see light shining along the road, after years of blackout, when Laura knocked at the door.

'Peg asked me to bring you this.'

Jane giggled as she saw the mug of Ovaltine and plate of biscuits. 'She's determined to fatten me up, bless her,' she commented.

'And me.' There were two mugs on the tray. 'Do you fancy some company for a while?'

'Yes, please.' Jane sighed. 'I don't know why I'm so — disgruntled? No, fidgety is a better word, like Tibs used to be when he was choosing the best lap.'

'I expect you still miss him.'

'We'd had him for eighteen years, Laura. I grew up with him. And I lost him and Gran in the same month.' She sipped her drink. 'I wish I could do something useful, like Aunt Grace, or Yvonne. It might put back some purpose in my life.'

'You wouldn't say that, my dear, if you had seen the expression on that young airman's face when you were playing the piano tonight. I would love to be able to play like that.'

'Really?'

'Yes, really. And you give such pleasure to people at your concerts. You must not put yourself down so much, you know.'

'I suppose it's habit, really.'

'Then for goodness' sake, break the habit — before it breaks you.' Laura paused, then went on, 'Have you thought any more about leaving home?'

Slowly, Jane nodded. 'Aunt Grace offered me a home here, but it would cause such a rift in the family.'

'That's one of the reasons why I didn't suggest you move in with me, although I would have liked that.'

'Would you? That's a nice thought — but it wouldn't be fair.'

'Exactly. I value my friendship with your mother and, to be honest, I feel I am of more use to you both from the sidelines. However . . . ' Laura Marshall covered Jane's hand with her own. 'If ever it becomes unbearable, don't be afraid to ask.'

'Thank you. I'll remember that. In the meantime, I'm saving every penny I can just in case I'm lucky enough to find an unfurnished place. It's quite frightening how much it is costing Jack to buy just the necessities for their home, and Mum has given him a lot of things, so I can't expect much help.'

'You will need to stick with your job for a while longer, then?'

'Afraid so.' Jane grimaced, then laughed.

'I'll give Mr O'Rourke until the Olympics to mend his wicked ways.'

Smiling, Laura replaced the empty mugs on the tray. 'Who knows, you might even enjoy the Olympics.'

'Oh, I'm sure I shall enjoy the Games. My only problem is the company I'll be keeping.'

★ ★ ★

The languages and accents were richly colourful. French, Scandinavian, Dutch, American, Australian — even Czechoslovakian supporters of the great distance runner, Emil Zatopek — and regional accents from the length and breadth of Great Britain. It reminded Jane of the Mall on VE Day, when their destination was Buckingham Palace, whereas now the solid mass of humanity pushed her along the Olympic Way towards the white domes of Wembley Stadium — the flag with five linked circles proclaiming that London was host to the first Games since 1936.

From the moment they met at Wembley Station, Jane tried to keep Jack in between herself and Seamus O'Rourke, but the Irishman would have none of it. Wherever she turned, his hand was at her elbow, and the density of the crowd made escape impossible.

'Where are we meeting Bernard and Eunice?' Jack asked.

'Near the turnstile at Block A, in an hour's time. He had to go into his office first, otherwise he would have driven us up.'

Mr O'Rourke manoeuvred Jane through a noisy group of Americans. 'I thought he wasn't able to get any tickets,' he said.

'They came through at the last minute. That's why he will be late, he is contacting people who tried to order tickets.'

'Ah, well. We'll say hullo and leave them to it. I doubt they'll be wanting to tag along with us.'

'Actually, they do want to join us — if that's all right with you two?' Jane looked hopefully at her brother, who came to her rescue.

'Of course. Bernard's a good bloke. And he knows the track records of most of the athletes. He'll be useful.'

Mr O'Rourke conceded. 'So your friend is a bit of a sporting lad, like meself,' he said to Jane.

Jane repressed a smile. Seamus O'Rourke hadn't been a lad for twenty-five years and his only claim to sporting knowledge was the form of certain horses in racing stables. 'He was a PE instructor in the army,' she said, 'and he has always been interested in athletics — like Jack.'

When they reached the turnstile, Mr O'Rourke had to go through first as he had the tickets, and Jane took the opportunity to whisper to her brother, 'Thanks for backing me over Bernard. I feel more comfortable if we're all together.'

They watched as Mr O'Rourke flashed a wallet full of notes in front of the attendant. 'He'd better watch out for pick-pockets,' Jack murmured. 'There must be at least a hundred pounds in there.'

'Most of it belongs in the petty cash tin,' Jane quietly observed, 'although the three-thirty at Goodwood yesterday may have had something to do with it.'

Once inside, Jane became too absorbed to worry about her manager, or his wallet. There was a buzz of excited anticipation, rather like waiting for the curtain to go up on a show — the main difference was that performers they had come to applaud were visible as they warmed up in preparation for their events. People jostled to find their seats, friends, programmes, toilets, and refreshments, while they watched field contestants flex their muscles as they tested grips on javelins and discus, or aborted trial run-ups to the high and long jumps.

Jane was so fascinated, she hadn't noticed

an hour had passed, until her brother stood up. 'Time to meet Bernard and Eunice, Sis,' he said.

The gold filling glinted as Seamus O'Rourke leaned across and grasped Jane's arm. 'No need for you to go as well, me darling,' he said. 'They probably won't be sitting in this block, anyway — but there's no reason why your brother shouldn't sit with his friends, if there's room.'

Jane was on her feet in an instant. 'Bernard told me they will only be a few rows behind us,' she said, 'and I want to find the Ladies.' Taking Jack's arm, she moved swiftly along the row before her manager could argue further.

As they pushed through the crowds, Jack glanced sideways at Jane. 'Perhaps I shouldn't say this — he did me a great favour, and he is your boss, but . . . '

'But what?'

'I wish O'Rourke wouldn't keep — touching you.'

'So do I!'

'Do you want me to have a word?'

Jane shook her head. 'It will be easier once Bernard and Eunice are here.'

'Sit with them if you can. I'll try and keep O'Rourke out of your way.' He frowned thoughtfully. 'Is he like this at work?'

She shook her head. 'I'm usually too busy, and I try to keep on the move when he's around. He pesters Stella more than anyone, because she can't get away from the switchboard.'

'Doesn't anyone say anything?'

'Oh, yes. But he's so thick-skinned, he really thinks he's the cat's whiskers, and we're all begging for his attention. He's a bit of a joke really.'

'He wouldn't last five minutes in our place. The shop stewards would soon sort him out.' Jack pointed to his right. 'There's rather a long queue for the Ladies. You get on it while I find the others.'

When Jane came out, Jack had found the others — all three of them.

'Surprise, surprise!' Sandy grinned down at her.

'I didn't know you were coming.' She had no choice but to shake his hand.

'Neither did I until this morning. I came off night duty, phoned Bernard to see if he had any tickets, jumped into the old flivver, and here I am!' Still holding her hand, Sandy smiled warmly. 'You're looking very smart,' he said. 'That colour suits you.'

She hadn't known what to wear that was suitable for the day at Wembley, and dinner afterwards, so had chosen a navy dirndl skirt with pink cotton blouse.

Sandy was still talking. 'And it's not too cold and not too hot, so I expect you to be in the very best of humour all day.'

My day is well and truly ruined, she thought, as she smiled a tight little smile. Mr O'Rourke I can just about stomach, but Mr O'Rourke *and* Sandy — not to mention Eunice . . .

'Have you been working all night?' Jack asked Sandy.

'On call, actually. I was lucky. Just one tiny baby that popped out after a couple of hours, and I was able to get my head down again.' He glanced across at the track. 'Hey look! There's Fanny Blankers-Koen warming up. How many golds has she won already?'

'Two, I think,' Jack answered.

'Well, we don't want to miss her next one. Where are our seats?'

For a short while, Jane was able to forget her problems as she admired the thirty-year-old Dutch housewife speeding along the track. Then the people sitting next to them moved away. Next moment, she found herself sitting next to Sandy.

'We decided we might as well have our sandwiches down here with you,' he said, moving closer to Jane to make room for Bernard and Eunice.

As Jane introduced them to Seamus O'Rourke, she noticed a flicker of surprise on Sandy's face and, later, a trace of annoyance on her manager's when he stood up to offer his hip flask around and found himself unable to slip in next to Jane. With a muttered apology, he took himself off in search of the Gents.

'While he's gone, I'll get some ice creams,' Jack said quietly to Jane. 'If he gets back before me, stick close to Sandy and Bernard.'

Sandy had overheard. 'Has that Irish guy been pestering you?' he asked.

'Not really. Jack's just a bit over-protective.' She didn't want to discuss her boss with Sandy — certainly she didn't want his sympathy.

'How can a spiv like that be a company manager?' Sandy exclaimed. 'I can't understand how you can bear to work with such an obnoxious man, Jane.'

Suddenly, Jane's emotions changed from embarrassment to anger. How dare Sandy criticise her companion, and her judgement? Who was he to judge others, with his heart of stone concealed beneath his charming exterior? For all he knew, Seamus O'Rourke might be the kindest of men despite his rather coarse exterior. After all, he had paid a lot of money for their tickets so that Jack could have a treat. Quickly she dismissed the reminder that an ulterior motive was behind the benevolence, by telling herself that her choice of work and colleagues had nothing whatsoever to do with Sandy, and he could jolly well keep his opinions to himself.

Coolly, she said, 'I do not have a problem being with Mr O'Rourke and, if you do, I can only suggest that you return to your own seat.'

Sandy stared at her in amazement, but before he could answer, the people returned to claim their place on the bench, and he was forced to leave her side.

When Seamus O'Rourke returned to sit next to Jane, it was obvious that he had revived his spirits with the flask.

'If you're so inclined, we could slip away and take a little drive before we dine?' he suggested.

Oh, Lord, Jane thought. I'd forgotten this evening. If only I could get out of it. But I'm blowed if I am going to be on my own with him one minute longer than necessary.

'Thank you for the suggestion, Mr O'Rourke, but I was really looking forward to these races this afternoon. Look . . . '

As she turned towards him with her programme, she noticed Sandy staring at her. His expression so annoyed her, she smiled sweetly at her companion and put her hand on his arm. 'You don't mind, do you?'

'Of course not, me darling. But why all this Mr O'Rourke nonsense? Isn't it time you called me Seamus?'

'Oh, no!' This was too much, she thought. 'I couldn't do that. It wouldn't be right in the office — a bad example to the other girls.'

'But we're not in the office now — who's to know?'

'I would know, and I would not be comfortable calling my superior by his Christian name. I'm sorry, Mr O'Rourke, but it really is out of the question.'

Now it was his face that was like thunder. Jane tried to engross herself in the events, but her heart wasn't in it. As she glanced over her shoulder again, she was only too aware of Sandy's tight-lipped scrutiny. Eunice was also stony-faced, and Bernard looked puzzled. Oh, dear.

She also realised that Jack had been gone rather a long time. Then she saw the reason why.

'It's Sheila Green!' Jane cried delightedly, pointing to the young woman walking beside Jack, both carrying rapidly melting ice cream cones.

Seamus O'Rourke whistled softly as he followed her pointing finger. 'Now there's a cracker of a girl, and no mistake,' he said. 'I've always had a bit of a fondness for redheads.'

Jack beamed as he handed round the ice creams and introduced Sheila. 'She was sitting in the stand just behind the ice cream kiosk,' he said. 'Haven't seen her since the old house was bombed in forty-one, but she hasn't changed a bit.'

He was right, Jane thought, Sheila had the same lovely smile that had captivated everyone when she lived next door to the Harrisons. They had all grown up together, and Jack had taken Sheila dancing a few times.

Jane and Sheila sat in the aisle, licking their ice creams and catching up on news. Sheila had been engaged to a Spitfire pilot who didn't survive the Battle of Britain, and she was still unmarried. Now she was the manageress of a photographic studio in Harrow, and had her own little flat above the shop.

'You'll have to come over one day,' she said. 'I mean it. Do you drive?'

'No, but it's easy enough on the train.'

'I could drive over and pick you up, if you like?'

'Gosh! Fancy you having a car of your own.'

'It's Dad's little Austin, actually. Did you know he had a stroke last year?'

'No! I don't think Mum has seen your mother for ages.'

'She doesn't get out much, with Dad being an invalid.' Sheila took a diary from her handbag. 'Why don't I bring her over to see your mother next Thursday afternoon? It's early closing day and I'm free.'

'Mum would like that. They can have a good old gossip.'

Sheila scribbled in her diary. 'And we must fix up an evening at my place.' As more people tried to step around the girls, Sheila stood up. 'There's an empty seat next to mine,' she said. 'Do you want to move over there?'

There was nothing Jane would have liked better than to be far away from O'Rourke and Sandy. But she had an obligation.

'Sorry, Sheila, but I'm with my boss, so I feel I ought to . . . '

Sheila nodded and glanced across at Mr O'Rourke, who didn't so much smile at her as leer at her. Quickly, she turned back to Jane and lowered her voice. 'Is he really your manager?' she asked.

Jane was not angry that Sheila expressed doubts, only when Sandy asked virtually the same question. 'Afraid so.' She shrugged. 'I'll tell you about it next time we meet — but why don't you ask Jack? I'm sure he'd love to chat to you a bit longer.'

'Good idea. He was asking about my photographic work.'

As Jane watched her brother escort his old girlfriend back to her seat, she couldn't help comparing the vivacious, intelligent Sheila with his wife. If only . . .

More and more medal winners were honoured on the rostrums, and the sun began to dip behind the stands. The moment Jane dreaded loomed nearer. Could she plead a sudden headache? Probably not. He was her boss, after all, and she'd offended him quite enough.

A few people near them were already leaving their seats as Jack and Sheila returned, and Bernard and Eunice came down to chat. Sandy remained in his seat. Bernard had a suggestion to make to Mr O'Rourke.

'I understand you and Jane are eating out?' he said.

'That's right. A perfect end to a perfect day.'

'Well, I was wondering — perhaps we could all have dinner together?' Bernard's arm embraced the whole party.

'What a lovely idea!' Jane was enthusiastic,

but Mr O'Rourke would have none of it.

'Sorry, folks, but I've booked a table for two at a rather exclusive little restaurant in town. They'll be fully booked by now. Some other time, perhaps?' He took Jane's arm, then turned to Jack. 'You don't mind me whisking your darling sister off, do you? I'll just give you your ticket in case . . . '

Her heart in her boots, Jane had turned away, but became aware of a sharp intake of breath, then silence.

His face drained of colour, Mr O'Rourke was frantically searching his pockets. 'Christ Almighty — I've been robbed!' he muttered. 'Me wallet's gone. It must have been that lad in the Gents . . . ' He turned to Jane. 'What shall I do?' he asked.

'You'll have to tell the police. Look — I can see one over the other side of the track. He'll know what to do.'

Without another word, Mr O'Rourke rushed off, and they watched him talking to the policeman, who nodded and led him towards the offices. They waited for a while, then Bernard said, 'Should we go and see if we can help?'

'No.' Suddenly, Jane knew she had to get away, put an end to this disastrous day. This was her only chance. 'They'll keep him hanging around for ages, searching for known pickpockets, filling in forms and so on. He hasn't got any other money, anyway, so he'll have to cancel the table booking.' She looked appealingly at Bernard. 'Can Jack and I come with you?' she asked.

'Of course.' Bernard looked back at Sandy, still sitting on the bench. 'We're going to find somewhere to eat,' he said. 'Want to join us?'

'Not this time — thanks. I think I'll get back to Birmingham. Thanks for getting me the ticket.' Sandy waved an airy hand towards them and hurried to the exit. He didn't look at Jane.

Bernard smiled at Sheila. 'I hope you can join us as well?' he said.

'I'd love to.' She looked up at Jack. 'Shall we go in my car and meet them at the restaurant?'

As they made their way towards the car park, discussing various eating places, Jane realised that she had not seen her brother looking so relaxed and contented since he had returned from the war, and she knew it was because of his companion's lively personality. For a moment, she felt a pang of envy when she thought of Sheila's lifestyle. A managerial job, flat of her own, car — and independence. But then she was older than Jane — twenty-six or twenty-seven at least. Perhaps next year would see the beginning of change for Jane — after her own coming of age.

For now, she was relieved that she didn't have to endure the company of Seamus O'Rourke for the rest of the evening. But she was sorry that Bernard had seen her pretending to enjoy the company of such a dreadful man, and hoped he didn't think too badly of her.

Sandy's opinion was of no importance. He was out of her life once again — hopefully for ever.

So why did she feel such a sadness in the pit of her stomach?

5

They had all signed the huge silver key 'With Love'. All except one, who had written, 'Best wishes, Mum'.

Jane supposed it was silly to expect anything else, and opened her presents. Boxes of handkerchiefs and soaps, two scarves, perfume — and an enamelled brooch from Kathleen: 'It's a shamrock, to bring you luck and remind you of me.' Then came a Conway Stewart pen and pencil set from Grandad; Basildon Bond writing case from Uncle Len; book token from Jack and Betty; selection of music from Eunice and a gold locket and chain from Bernard, with her name engraved on the locket. Thank you seemed inadequate for such a beautiful gift — her feelings had to be expressed with a warm hug.

She really missed Aunt Grace and Uncle Nobby. The hotel was full and they couldn't get away. 'You would have your twenty-first at Easter!' Aunt Grace had laughed on the telephone. 'So you'll have to come and get your present the week after. Peg has been saving her rations to make you a cake, bless her, and we'll have another party.' Jane's extension began crackling again and she barely heard Aunt Grace say, 'Will you tell Laura I'm very grateful . . . ' before they were cut off.

But Jane knew what her aunt had intended to say. When her father tentatively asked what plans were being made to celebrate Jane's coming of age, her mother had retorted that the rations wouldn't run to a party. Poor Grandad then had his head snapped off for suggesting that it would be nice to have a little bunfight for Janey, and he was sure everyone would pitch in if they were asked.

Cheeks flushed, Nell Harrison had replied that nobody had offered and she was not going to beg rations or help from anyone. 'And you know I still grieve for Rose,' she had said, 'so how on earth do you think I could possibly have a bunfight, as you call it, on her birthday. It would be like dancing on her grave!'

Jane had felt like screaming, 'It's my birthday, too — or don't I count?' But she hadn't, and Aunt Grace wasn't the only one to feel grateful when Laura Marshall stepped into the breach, tactfully suggesting that her house was bigger and more convenient for a coming of age celebration. Reluctantly, Jane's mother had given way to family persuasion and everyone had donated rations.

Even the sunshine had come out to wish Jane a happy birthday. With sparkling eyes, she looked around at her family and friends from the office and the concert party as they sat in the garden. 'It's lovely to see you all here, and thank you so much for the wonderful presents,' she said.

Two more parcels to open. A single strand of perfectly matched pearls from Bea Marshall and a small box, labelled, 'To our dear daughter Jane, with fond love from Mum and Dad', in her father's handwriting.

'Oh — Mum! Dad! It's beautiful!' Jane held up the gold watch to be admired, then hugged and kissed her father, before crossing the garden to bend over her mother's deck chair. 'Thanks, Mum. I'll always treasure it.'

As she leaned forward, her mother turned her face away, so Jane's kiss landed just below her ear. 'It was your father's idea,' she said, then stood up. 'Think I'll go inside. It's getting chilly.'

It was as painful as a slap in the face, and emphasised by a cloud which suddenly covered the sun, causing some of the guests to follow her mother, with murmurs of 'April showers'.

A quiet voice at her side. 'One more present, Jane, dear.' Laura handed her a large envelope.

'But you've already given me so much,' Jane protested. 'This party . . . '

'The party is from everybody. I wanted to give you something personal, just from me.'

Jane pulled the gold-edged card from the envelope. 'The Penelope Symonds Beauty Salon,' she read aloud. 'I don't quite understand . . . ' She looked enquiringly at her friend.

'Penny Symonds was a model before the war — we worked in Paris together,' Laura explained. 'Hadn't heard from her in years, then out of the blue came an invitation to the opening of her salon in Knightsbridge.' She walked with Jane a little further away from the house. 'I'd been wondering what to give you, and Penny came up with this wonderful idea.'

'A beauty treatment?'

'Better than that.' Laura paused by a raised bed of gaily coloured tulips swaying in the breeze. 'As well as the salon, Penny runs courses for beauticians. We went through her brochure and I selected a six-session evening course for you.'

'A beautician? Me?' Jane could not suppress a giggle.

'It's not so absurd.' Laura smiled. 'You know a great deal about many things, but hardly anything about skin care, cosmetics or manicures. It's something they used to teach young ladies in certain finishing schools, alongside elocution and deportment, so they knew how to make the best of their appearance.'

'You're right. I don't know anything about make-up. Rose was the expert.' For a moment Jane was solemn. 'Do you know, I still expect her to come dancing through the door, singing 'Happy Birthday to us', the way she always did.' She read the card again. 'This is a lovely thought. Thank you.'

'My pleasure.' Laura linked arms with Jane and lowered her voice. 'I hope the agency rewarded your coming of age with a decent raise in salary?'

'Actually, yes. Another pound a week, which will certainly help my savings campaign — that's if the firm survives, of course.'

'Oh? Is it very much at risk?'

'Well, we desperately need some new accounts.'

'And what is the infamous Mr O'Rourke doing about it?'

'Very little. He comes in late, gives most of the post to me to deal with, then studies the racing papers. After that, he borrows from the petty cash and drives down to Newmarket or Epsom.'

99

Laura pursed her lips. 'Does he lose much?'

'Let's just say the IOU's are rarely refunded — in fact, he still hasn't paid back the money that was stolen last year at the Olympics.' Her smile was rueful. 'Mind you, when he does win, he's generous to a fault. Boxes of chocolates for the staff, flowers for me, and a tenner in the petty cash — which usually disappears the next day!'

Laura looked concerned. 'The future doesn't look too promising, does it?'

Jane shook her head. 'We have several dissatisfied clients whose contracts are due for renewal fairly soon. If we lose them, Grafton and Hughes will have to invest more money into the agency, and they won't do that for ever.'

'Perhaps they'll sack him,' Laura said, hopefully.

'That would solve the problem, but I don't think Mr Grafton will welch on a gentlemen's agreement.'

'So what do you think he will do?'

'If we continue to run at a loss, he can't sell it as a going concern, so he'll probably cut his losses and close it down.'

As they turned back towards the house, they paused to watch Johnny attempting to chalk noughts and crosses on the back-door step, with Desmond's guidance.

'Johnny is such a handsome child,' Laura observed. 'He'll break hearts with those huge blue eyes and golden curls.'

Jane nodded, then murmured, 'Jack must have looked just like that when he was nine years old.'

'Probably. But such a tragedy — Desmond thinks more could be done about his speech, but it would take a lot of patience.'

'That's what they say at the Special School. Betty can't be bothered, but Jack and Kathleen have persevered and he does say a few words now, instead of just grunting.'

At that moment, Jack joined them, smiling as he followed their gaze. 'Your Desmond seems to have the knack of dealing with Johnny,' he said to Laura. 'It's usually almost impossible to persuade him to sit still for long.'

Laura nodded. 'He's seriously thinking of training to be a Special School teacher,' she said. 'I think he could be rather good at it.'

'If Johnny is anything to go by, Desmond will make a first-rate teacher.' Jack slipped an arm around Jane's shoulders. 'You know, I can't believe my kid sister is actually a fully paid up member of the Grown-up Society,' he teased.

'And you'll soon be drawing your pension, you poor old boy.'

'Not so much of the old, if you don't mind. I'm only . . . ' He stopped.

'What's the matter?' Jane asked.

'When I was Johnny's age, I told Uncle Len that thirty was really old — and I shall be thirty-two this year. What does that make me?'

'Ancient.' Playfully, Jane cuffed his chin. 'But you're in good company. Bernard is older than you, and I don't think of him as being old at all.'

'No, you don't, do you?' Jack's expression was thoughtful. 'I've not seen anyone get on so well as you two, despite the age gap.'

Laura smiled. 'When you get to my grand age you'll both realise that age is totally irrelevant. I still have the same feelings that I had as a teenager — the only difference is that I am a little more cautious. I don't rush headlong into things any more. And I do value friendships more, whatever the age gap.' She squeezed Jane's arm.

'Me too,' Jack quietly agreed. 'I lost too many friends during the war to ever risk losing any more. Which reminds me, Sis — you've got a surprise friend coming later on.' He turned to Laura. 'I hope you don't mind me inviting someone without your permission, but I didn't have your telephone number.'

'Not at all. It's Jane's party. Who is the surprise friend?'

'It's — oh, Lord . . . ' He stopped abruptly as his wife, empty glass in hand, attempted to push her way between Johnny's stiffly callipered leg and Desmond, smudging the chalkmarks in the process, and provoking howls of protest from her son.

'I'm sorry, Laura,' Jack said, 'but it looks as though my wife has helped herself to too many glasses from your punch bowl. I'd better rescue Johnny before . . . ' He sprinted across the lawn, but was too late.

Screaming, 'Shut up, you noisy little brat!' Betty slapped the child viciously across the face just before Jack grabbed her arm.

Jack didn't shout. He didn't need to. The anger was apparent in his voice, as he loomed over his startled wife. 'Don't you ever hit him again like that!' he warned, dragging her into the kitchen and dumping her unceremoniously onto a chair just inside the door. 'You will stay there until you have sobered up, and then you will apologise to Laura for your disgusting behaviour — and to Jane for spoiling her party. Do you understand?'

Betty whimpered something about wanting

another drink, but wisely noted the expression on her husband's face.

Horrified at the vivid red weal on his cheek, Jane tried to comfort her nephew, but he screamed for 'Nan' and she was relieved when her mother appeared and carried the child indoors.

'I'm sorry, Laura,' Jane said. 'That was embarrassing.'

'It's not your fault.' Laura looked concerned as she glanced through the door at the subdued Betty slouched in the chair. 'Is she often like this?' she asked.

'She started drinking when they moved into the prefab. It didn't seem too serious at first, but lately . . . ' Jane shrugged her shoulders. 'I think she's pawning things to buy drink.'

'Oh, dear. That's a slippery downward path, if you like.'

'I know, but I've not seen her hit Johnny like that before, and I know Jack won't stand for it. He's already angry with her that she doesn't keep the hospital appointments or help Johnny with his leg exercises.'

'I'll make her some strong black coffee.'

'Good idea — by the way, do you have any idea who my surprise guest might be?'

Foot poised on the step, Laura turned back. 'Could it be your cousin Peter? He must have finished his army training by now.'

'It won't be him.' Jane shook her head. 'He wrote from Scarborough to say he can't get leave until next month.'

'That's a pity. You were always close — I don't suppose his parents are coming, either?'

'No chance.' Jane snorted. 'Only Christmas Day is allowed to interfere with customers coming into the corner shop! They gave Mum a pound note for me when she went over there. Said it saved buying a postal order and would she get me a birthday card as they'd forgotten.' Jane followed Laura into the kitchen. 'The only person I can think of is Sheila Green. I had invited her but her father wasn't too well, and it is possible that Jack saw her. Mr and Mrs Green live quite near to the prefabs.'

After Betty had sobered up a little and everyone had enjoyed the splendid tea, it was time for Jane to blow out twenty-one candles and cut the superb iced cake. For a moment, she closed her eyes and wished — there were so many things to wish — that Betty would come to her senses and try harder to be a better wife and mother; that little Johnny would be able to run around and chatter like other children; that Kathleen's exam results would be good enough for the university entrance . . . then Jane remembered that it was *her* birthday, *her* wish, and she squeezed her eyes even more tightly shut and wished fervently that her mother could realise that she still had a daughter to love.

Now it was time for dancing. Furniture was pushed back, Desmond switched on the radiogram, and Bernard claimed the first dance with Jane. He was remarkably good, with only a slight roll to indicate he had lost two toes. Jane was not a natural dancer, but she found it easy to follow him as they moved slowly to the velvety tones of Frank Sinatra singing 'Nancy with the Laughing Face'. It was the first time she had been in his arms, and she felt comfortable as he swirled her into a reverse turn. After some applause, she signalled her guests to join them, and David swept his wife onto the floor. Like many large men, he was light on his feet, and Jane smiled as the music changed to 'Time after Time' and Ruth gazed adoringly up at her husband.

'It's still their special song,' Jane murmured.

Following her gaze, Bernard nodded, 'And they're so much in love, after ten years of marriage.'

Feeling his arm tighten, Jane steered the conversation away from the romantic. 'Although I'm sorry David didn't win the finals, I'm glad we still have him in the group, aren't you?'

Bernard's grip relaxed slightly. 'Of course. That reminds me, I'd like to discuss some ideas for next season's shows with you. If you're not doing anything next Saturday, perhaps we could drive out to Cambridge — you'd love the bookshops — and we could have dinner later?'

'Sorry, Bernard. I'm going to Torquay next weekend. But I'll be happy to call in one evening after work and talk to you and Eunice.'

He looked disappointed, but before he could say any more, Harry tapped him on the shoulder. 'Is this an 'Excuse Me' dance?' he asked with a cheeky grin, and whisked Jane out of Bernard's arms before he could answer. Harry was a better drummer than dancer, Jane decided, but he had a good sense of humour and kept up a light-hearted conversation throughout the dance.

Her brother was her next partner. He still looked tense, and glanced from time to time at his son, now sitting quietly on his grandmother's lap. Betty lit a cigarette, and glowered at the dancers. 'Has she apologised to you?' Jack asked.

Jane shook her head.

'I'm really sorry, Sis,' he began, but Jane

stopped him with a finger to his lips.

'Not another word,' she said. 'Relax and enjoy the party.'

He smiled affectionately down at her. 'You're right. And it is a good party, isn't it? Laura's been a brick.'

'The best friend anyone could have.' Jane was explaining about Laura's special gift when the doorbell rang. 'Could that be my mystery guest?' she asked, grinning at her brother.

'Probably. Let's see, shall we?'

They followed Laura into the hall. As Jane had anticipated, Sheila Green stood on the front doorstep, clutching two parcels.

'Sorry I'm so late.' She kissed Jane on the cheek. 'I wasn't sure about leaving Mum, but she insisted I come.' Sheila handed the parcels to Jane. 'Happy Birthday, love.' One contained a beautifully embroidered dressing-table set from Mrs Green, and Sheila had bought a cut-glass powder bowl.

'They're beautiful!' Jane gasped.

Laura took Sheila's coat. 'Come and have a drink, Sheila, then Jane can introduce you to the others.'

'Thanks — oh, Laura, don't close the front door. I'm not the only late arrival.'

Jack beamed at Mrs Randall as she came into the hall. 'Oh, good, I hoped you could make it.' He turned to Jane. 'I bumped into her at the hospital yesterday when I went for my check-up, and I knew you wouldn't want to leave out your old friend.'

'Of course not.' Jane hugged Mrs Randall and took her gift. 'I've been wondering about my surprise guest all evening.' As she unwrapped the pink-enamelled hairbrush and mirror set, she suddenly became aware of another figure standing hesitantly in the doorway, almost hidden by a huge bouquet of daffodils, tulips and mimosa.

'I told Jack that Sandy was coming home for Easter,' Mrs Randall said, 'and he insisted we both come to your party, dear. It is all right, isn't it?' She looked questioningly at Jane and then at Laura, who smiled and nodded.

Jane gulped, then forced herself to say, 'Of course.' What else could she say, without being churlish? 'Do come in.'

Looking a little anxious, Sandy thrust the flowers into her hand. 'Didn't have a chance to get a present,' he said quietly, 'so I hope you're not allergic or anything . . . ' His voice trailed.

Mrs Randall laughed. 'Trust a doctor to say something like that.'

Laura bent her head to smell the fragrance of the mimosa. 'How delightful,' she said.

'Would you like me to put them in water for you while you take your guests into the lounge?'

Betty had taken an instant dislike to Sheila on the one occasion they had met, so she soon took herself upstairs to sleep off her excesses on Laura's bed. Although Jane was annoyed at the lack of manners, she knew it was better than having her sister-in-law continue to sulk and glare daggers at Sheila, and certainly better than trying to steer her away from the punch bowl. Mrs Randall sat quietly chatting to Mrs Harrison, Sheila, dragged Jack onto the floor, and Sandy sat next to Bernard. Jane knew he was watching her as she danced with her father, and she prayed he wouldn't ask her to dance or, if he did, that she would be able to come up with a plausible excuse. But it didn't quite work out like that. Just as she was discarding one or two excuses that she knew wouldn't work, her father paused in front of Sandy's chair.

'Seems like only yesterday that you were all kids at school together,' he said. 'And now look at you, all grown up — you're a qualified doctor and our Janey a young woman. Doesn't seem possible.' He blew his nose on a spotless white handkerchief.

Oh, dear, Jane thought. Dad really shouldn't have had those two whiskies. Now he's going to be all emotional. I don't mind — it doesn't happen very often, but Mum won't be very happy.

Fred Harrison put the handkerchief back into his pocket and tapped Sandy on the shoulder. 'Now, young feller-me-lad, it's your turn to dance with the birthday girl,' he said.

'But, Dad, I was enjoying . . . ' Jane tried to protest, but her father would have none of it.

'Nonsense! You should have a partner of your own age, not an old fogey like me, isn't that right, Bernard?'

Bernard stammered something incomprehensible, Sandy looked equally embarrassed, and Sheila added to the confusion by calling out, 'Come on, Sandy. You haven't danced with the guest of honour yet.' Once Bernard had taken the glass of beer from his hand, Sandy didn't have much choice — and neither did Jane. Desmond put on the latest long-playing record and as Jane went stiffly into Sandy's arms there was a ripple of applause.

For a while, they danced in silence, then Sandy cleared his throat. 'I don't recognise this music,' he said.

'It's a selection from a new American musical, *South Pacific*.' Her answer was equally stilted as her mind went back to their last meeting, at the Olympic Games, when

111

she had been so rude to him. She resisted the temptation to apologise. After all, he had been rude first.

As if reading her mind, Sandy murmured, 'I think I ought — I feel I owe you an apology.'

Surprised, she looked up into his face, but said nothing.

'You were right,' he went on, 'I shouldn't have criticised your companion. It was extremely impolite, and I'm sorry.'

Stunned, Jane didn't know how to answer, so just nodded.

'I didn't know if I would be welcome here, but I wanted to make my peace. I hope I'm forgiven?'

If only she hadn't overheard that quarrel, Jane thought. Then Sandy would still have been her best friend. But she had heard it, and now she was trapped, unable to tell him the real reason for her hostility, and duty-bound to be a pleasant hostess. What a complex situation! She had no alternative but to smile faintly and nod.

'What's the name of this one?' Sandy asked, his voice a little more normal. He had obviously taken her silence as an acceptance of his apology.

' 'Some enchanted evening'.'

'Pretty tune.'

'Yes.' Jane glanced across the room at Kathleen, dancing with Desmond, her head thrown back as she laughed up at him. 'I shall miss Kathleen when she goes away,' she commented, making an attempt at conversation for the sake of the guests who were watching them.

Thoughtfully, Sandy watched the petite Irish girl. 'Is she still set on studying law?' he asked.

'Yes. If her results are as good as we expect, she'll go to Exeter University in the autumn.'

'And when she qualifies she'll be the most beautiful solicitor in London. I knew she was going to be a stunner when you first brought her home from school.'

For a moment, Jane stiffened. Was Sandy going to get up to his tricks again with Kathleen?

'And Desmond thinks so, too,' he went on.

'Desmond?' Surprised, Jane looked at Laura's son. 'They're like brother and sister.'

Sandy shook his head. 'Not any more, they're not. Just look at his expression.'

It was true. There was no mistaking that look. Jane had seen it too often on her uncle's face when he was with Laura.

'You smell nice. What's that scent?'

Jane was so surprised at the comment, she stumbled, and Sandy paused and held her more firmly until she regained her balance. 'Sorry,' she apologised, then answered his question. 'It's Coty's *L'aiment* — Sheila bought it for me.'

'Ah, that's a pity.'

'Why?'

'Only men should buy perfume for ladies.' He glanced at Bernard and Eunice as they gracefully executed an intricate step, their expertise apparent even on the small amount of floor space available. 'I thought it might have been a gift from Bernard,' Sandy went on, with a lift of his eyebrows.

Jane touched her throat. 'This is my gift from Bernard,' she said. 'He's even had my name engraved on it.'

For a moment, Sandy studied the locket, then he said, 'That is a very handsome present. Puts my flowers in the shade.'

Without stopping to think, Jane slipped her hand back into his. 'Your flowers are lovely,' she said.

'I'm glad you think so.' He grinned. 'To be honest, I thought you might throw them at me.'

'Oh, no! That would be . . . ' She stopped, not knowing what to say next, then curiosity got the better of her. 'Am I really such an ogre?'

'Only sometimes.' He smiled. 'But when

the weather is not too hot, or too cold, or she isn't being loyal to her employer, Miss Jane Harrison is one of the very nicest people I know.'

This is crazy, she thought. Here I am, dancing with the man I vowed to hate for the rest of my life, making small-talk, practically flirting with him and — God help me — I'm almost enjoying it. My family will never be the same again because of this man. Why should I care what he thinks of me? When will this record end, so that I can get away before I . . . ?

At that moment, someone dimmed the lights and the music changed to one of Jane's favourite ballads. As David waltzed with Ruth, he began to softly sing the poignant love song, 'This nearly was mine'. Jack was still dancing with Sheila, Uncle Len with Laura and Gordon with Monica. Now there was little room for dancing, so the couples swayed together, almost at a standstill, listening to the beautiful lyrics.

Suddenly, the atmosphere in the room became electric, and Jane was deeply conscious of Sandy's arms around her, his breath close to her cheek. She had danced with him before at school dances — but never like this. Her whole body tingled with a sensation she had not felt since Olaf . . . Was this how Rose had felt? No wonder she had succumbed. Jane tried to focus her thoughts on Rose, but the words of the song intruded — 'One partner in paradise, this promise of paradise' — and she felt herself melting into the warmth of Sandy's arms. He held her more closely, and she felt his body tremble. Just this one dance. Just this one moment of paradise.

As David sang, the true meaning of the final words, 'Now, now I'm alone, still dreaming of paradise', brought a tear onto her cheek, and she knew she had to break the spell, or she would be lost, as Rose had been lost.

Her moment came when the tempo quickened to 'Happy Talk'.

'Sorry, I'm no good at a quickstep,' she said, breaking free from Sandy's arms.

The expression on his face told her that he, too, had felt — something, and his voice was just a little breathless as he said, 'Shall we sit this one out, in the other room? Would you like a drink?'

'Not just now.' She looked around the room, searching for a straw to clutch. Johnny had fallen asleep on his grand-mother's lap, his golden head sprawled heavily across her arm. 'I must take Johnny upstairs before Mum's arm falls off. Why

116

don't you dance with Sheila?'

After she had laid the sleeping child on Desmond's bed, Jane sank onto a chair, trying to regain her composure. Her heart pounded and her knees felt so weak she really didn't know how she had carried Johnny upstairs. Then her gaze went to the bedside cabinet, where the lamplight illuminated a framed snapshot. It had been taken during the autumn of 1943 — before the invasion, before the flying bombs, before . . . oh, how vividly she remembered that lovely Sunday afternoon in Laura's garden. They had been harvesting the plums, and Rose had complained that she couldn't reach the branches because she wasn't as tall as Jane, so Lawrence had hoisted her onto his shoulders. Laura had taken the photograph just after Rose had bitten into the ripest plum and the juice had overflowed onto Lawrence's face as he looked up to see why she was laughing. Desmond and Jane were also in hysterics and Laura had captured the moment perfectly — four young friends, as full of fun and innocence as puppies. Even in that frozen moment as the shutter clicked, Rose's vitality was apparent, her tousled hair enhancing her beauty.

'Oh, Rose,' Jane whispered, tears streaming down her cheeks. 'He let you down so badly

— and now I've let you down as well. Forgive me.'

After a few moments, she pulled herself together, knowing what she had to do. Like Nellie Forbush in the musical, she had to 'wash that man right out of her hair'. For the rest of the evening she would avoid any physical contact with Sandy. Then he would go back to Birmingham and she wouldn't see him again for a very long time, if at all.

Closing the door quietly on her sleeping nephew, Jane slipped into the bathroom and splashed cold water on her face.

As she came down the stairs, Sandy was waiting in the doorway of the lounge. 'Desmond has found Lawrence's collection of Glen Miller records,' he said, holding out his arms. 'Shall we?'

'I'm sorry.' Her voice was calmer than she felt, and she managed a smile. 'I really ought to circulate. I haven't spoken to Miss Dawson all evening. Excuse me.' His expression was confused, rather like that of a child who has just had a toy taken away. But Jane steeled her heart, and slipped into an empty chair alongside her colleague. The quiet strains of 'Moonlight Serenade' allowed them to chat.

'I really do love the painting,' Jane said. 'It was very good of you.'

'I saw it when I visited your aunt, my dear,

and thought the artist had captured the rich colours of Babbacombe so well.'

Miss Dawson considered the party to be a splendid affair, but she was also troubled. 'I really do not think I can continue to work at the agency for very much longer,' she confessed.

'To be honest, I am surprised you have stayed on for so long.'

'As you know, Jane, I have only a small income from my investments, so it is an opportunity to add to my little nest egg. Also,' she patted Jane's hand, 'I do so enjoy your company. But if you should leave, I would tender my resignation immediately.'

Jane nodded thoughtfully. 'I have been trying to make up my mind what to do for the best,' she said. 'I keep hoping things will improve, but — ' She shrugged. 'I don't think I can bear to hang on and watch it all go down the drain because of that wretched man, so I will have to study the Situations Vacant columns again. Perhaps now I am twenty-one I can be considered for a more senior post.'

Across the room, Grandad was trying to catch her eye. He needed a refill of his favourite tipple — brown ale.

Jane was opening the bottle in the kitchen when she became aware of voices from the garden. Low voices, but clearly heard through the open window.

'But he'll be eighteen next year and away doing his national service.' It was Uncle Len. 'He'll hardly ever be here.'

'It's only for two years.' Laura's voice was just a murmur. 'After that he wants to become a teacher.'

'And if he meets a girl, he'll be off without another thought.' Uncle Len's voice was becoming angry. 'I know he's a sensitive lad, but I can't really believe you're prepared to sacrifice your life for him.'

'He needs to have me here, at least for a while longer. Please, Len, try to understand.'

'That's what you said the last time I proposed. But things are different now. There's nothing to stop us — not if you really want to . . . ' The silence was ominous, until it was broken by Uncle Len. 'I love you, Laura — have done from the moment I saw you — but I'm not prepared to hang around till I draw my old age pension, just on the off-chance.'

'Len . . . please . . . '

'You've made it quite clear where I stand.' The anger had gone from his voice, replaced by a terrible sadness. 'Better leave it at that.'

Standing in the far corner of the shadowy

kitchen, Jane was sure her uncle wasn't aware of her presence as he opened the back door and went through to the hall. But Laura paused to lean against the door as she closed it, her head turned towards Jane. When she opened her eyes, tears glistened on her cheeks, but she didn't speak, just stared for a moment then hurried through the hall and up the stairs.

Oh, dear, Jane thought, what's that saying about the path of true love not running smoothly? Even her own non-existent love life had hiccups, with a divorced admirer, an ex-fiancé sending birthday greetings with the message that he was marrying a girl from Ulvik on Midsummer's Day, and he hoped she wished them happiness. She did, but with a bittersweet poignancy, leaving her wondering why she had only felt goose-bumps again at the touch of a man she despised.

'Jane?' Bernard stood in the doorway. 'I've been looking for you.'

'I'm just getting drink for Grandad.'

'Don't you want the light on?'

'No — I can see fine, thanks.' She wasn't sure that her rapid repairs in the bathroom would stand up to the bright light in the kitchen. As she poured the ale into Grandad's glass, Jane was aware that Bernard was watching her closely, fidgeting from one foot to another, clearing his throat. When she turned to leave the room, he moved into her path.

'Jane . . . '

'Yes?'

'We've been friends for more than two years now.'

She thought for a moment, then agreed, 'Yes, I suppose we have.'

'And it has worked very well, hasn't it?'

'What has?'

'The concert party — us.'

'Oh, I see. Yes, we seem to have worked out quite a good routine between the three of us.' She felt rather foolish, standing holding a pint of ale and wondering what point Bernard was trying to make.

'And you have no complaints?'

'No. None at all. Why should I?'

'Well — it takes up a lot of your time, with rehearsals and so on — and I wonder sometimes whether you feel you should have more time for friends of your own age. Boyfriends. Like Sandy, for instance.'

'Sandy? I can assure you that Sandy is not my boyfriend!'

'Really?' Bernard's voice brightened. 'Only your Dad said — and I thought — well you are old friends and he's much nearer to your age than me, and — '

'Bernard,' she said firmly, 'Sandy Randall and I were at school together. That's all. I didn't even invite him to my party.'

'You didn't?'

'No. Jack invited him. Sandy is working in Birmingham, and it is highly unlikely that I will see much of him in the future.'

'Oh, I see. Only I didn't want to get in the way if you were — promised to him or anything.'

'Promised to Sandy!' Jane stared indignantly at Bernard. 'He is the last person on earth I would be promised to.'

'I'm sorry. I misunderstood.'

'Yes, you did.' Her anger abated. It wasn't Bernard's fault, and he didn't know the reason for her indignation. Her smile was kindly. 'And it couldn't happen to a nicer person. But can I come by, please? Grandad is waiting for his drink.'

Bernard didn't move out of the way. For a moment he gazed down at Jane, then he took the glass from her hand and put it on the table, held her face between his hands, and kissed her full on the lips. It wasn't a brotherly kind of kiss, or that of a friend, but it was a nice kiss, surprisingly pleasant — and definitely more skilful than Olaf's kisses had been. Then he lifted his head and smiled, as though he had quite enjoyed the kiss too. Jane was speechless, but Bernard wasn't.

'Will you marry me, Jane?' he asked.

Oh, gosh, she thought. What a birthday!

6

'Upward strokes. A little firmer. That's perfect. How does it feel, Hilary?' Penelope Symonds watched Jane as she massaged an exorbitantly priced cream into the other student's face.

'Gorgeous! Jane has such a gentle touch. Must be all that piano playing.' With a contented sigh, Hilary relaxed on the couch. 'Don't get carried away, though, and start playing a concerto.'

The beautician smiled. 'You have wonderful hands, Jane. I think I'll use you as my model in the manicure session. There's a new nail varnish and lipstick I want to try called Black Cherry. It's rather dark, but it should suit you with your colouring.'

'I've never used nail varnish.'

'You haven't lived — not as far as beauty is concerned, anyway.'

'It always seemed a waste of time for me. My sister was the twin with the looks — and the hair that didn't need a home perm.'

'Ah, yes. Laura told me about Rose.' Penelope looked at Jane's reflection in the mirror. 'She also said you shouldn't put yourself down so much, and I agree. You have good bone structure, and your skin is looking better already for the deep cleansing and masks.'

Jane laughed. 'When it erupted afterwards I thought I'd never put my face outside the front door again. But I agree, it has made quite a difference.'

'Are you enjoying the course?'

'Actually, yes. Much more than I expected. I just wish hair care was included. Mine is such a mess, it needs a miracle.'

Penelope fingered the ends of Jane's hair. 'Could it be too many cheap perms?'

'I know I have more than I should, but they don't last, and I don't know what to do with it otherwise.'

Speculatively, Penelope turned Jane's head sideways. 'You have a good profile,' she said. 'I think you could wear it drawn back and up into a bun — like Helena Rubinstein's style, but not quite so severe.'

Still massaging, Jane studied her own reflection. A crepe band held her hair back from her face, now clear-skinned. It might be worth considering something more sophisticated. 'Trouble is, I don't know how to pin it,' she mused.

'Make an appointment to see Mr Gerard at

Antoine's. He'll cut it properly, and give you good advice.'

'I don't know . . . what do you think, Hilary?'

Jane and Penelope's eyes met in the mirror, and they smiled. Hilary was asleep.

It took a while for Jane to master the art of restyling her own hair, but with the aid of Gerry Bernstein from Golders Green, professionally known as Mr Gerard from Paris, she was able to coil and fix her long hair with combs and pins into a sophisticated topknot that stayed in place all day. Stella looked up from her switchboard and gaped, Miss Dawson thought it was elegant, and Seamus O'Rourke used it as an excuse to run his fingers down Jane's neck and back while she was taking dictation. Even when she jumped up from the chair on the pretence of needing a file, he wasn't deterred.

'I'm glad you've not gone in for that New Look,' he drooled. 'To my ways of thinking, legs should be displayed, not covered up to the ankles. And why wouldn't you be wearing higher heels, showing off those shapely ankles?'

Jane turned round from the filing cabinet. 'Because I'm too tall, Mr O'Rourke.' Her voice was sharp. 'And you really should be talking to me about these budget figures, not my legs.'

'And who'd be wanting to do that when there's a more tempting figure right under his nose?' He continued to ogle. 'Talking of which, would you be coming with me to Wimbledon this afternoon? Gorgeous Gussie's through to the next round. Now there's a fine pair of legs in those frilly knickers and no mistake.'

The man was incorrigible. Jane said as much to Laura when they met for lunch. 'It's not that I can't handle him, he's too obvious to be a real danger. But I do find all that groping up my skirt or down my blouse a bit tiresome.'

'Oh, Jane! Is it really as bad as that?'

'To be honest, sometimes he's so drunk, he doesn't know what he's doing, only what he's thinking. There are times I wish I could ask Rose how she would handle him, although she'd probably tell me to put my knee in his crutch.'

'More than likely,' Laura agreed. 'So how do you handle him?'

'I just order a taxi and send him home.'

'Probably the best solution. And you really have to start looking for another job.'

'I go through the ads every day and I've registered with that new Brook Street agency.

128

Believe me, Laura, as soon as I can find something that pays well and is remotely interesting, I'm off!'

'Good.' Laura appraised her young friend. 'What are you doing on Saturday?'

'Apart from cleaning my room, nothing in particular. Why?'

'I'll meet you in Galeries Lafayette at ten. You need a new wardrobe, something more stylish.'

'But, Laura — '

'They have an early summer sale, and now there's no rationing you can buy whatever you can afford. It will be fun.'

It was fun. Jane chose two full-skirted dresses, nipped in at the waist and almost ankle length. White gloves and a rustling circular petticoat almost completed the picture, but Laura and the assistant per-suaded her to try on a pair of high-heeled court shoes.

'If madam would hold back her shoulders a little more and her head higher . . . '

'But it makes me look so much taller,' Jane protested.

Laura turned her towards the full length mirror. 'Try making the most of your height instead of hiding it,' she said. 'All the top models are tall, but they have good deportment so it doesn't matter.'

It was true, Jane thought — Laura's height never seemed to be a problem. But she was beautiful.

Jane was still turning this way and that, undecided about the shoes, when the assistant reappeared, holding an expensive-looking woollen coat in a rich burgundy colour. 'Having seen how well the longer styles suit madam, I am certain this would be exactly madam's style.'

'It's gorgeous,' Jane breathed, 'but it's a winter coat.' She stroked the soft grey fur lapels.

'That is why there is such a generous reduction on the price, and it has a matching fur muff. Let me help you slip it on.'

Once the coat was on her back, Jane knew she had to have it. She also fell in love with the silver-grey half-moon hat that curled round towards her cheeks, the tiny veil just covering her eyes. 'Well, that's blown my last bonus — and some!' She laughed. 'I suppose I should feel guilty.'

'Guilty?' Laura raised an elegant eyebrow. 'When did you last have a shopping spree — just for yourself?'

Jane thought for a moment, then said, 'I don't think I ever have. Certainly I've never spent so much money at one go.'

'If you feel guilty, the money will be

wasted, but if you are enjoying the experience . . . '

'Oh, Laura, I haven't had so much fun in ages. Anyway — ' Jane pirouetted in front of the mirror and liked what she saw, 'it's my money, and I don't feel at all guilty — well, not very much.'

* * *

Autumn golds had only just begun to tint the trees, but the brick-red Devonshire soil warmed the heart, whatever the season. Thinking aloud, Jane murmured, 'If I don't get a decent job by the end of the year, I might change my mind about coming to live down here. Perhaps the start of a new decade would be the right time to take a fresh path.'

'I suppose it was inevitable that the agency would close down eventually, but at least it has made the decision for you.' Laura glanced sideways at her companion, then concentrated on steering around the twisting bend. 'Did you have a leaving party?'

'Oh, no. When Miss Reynolds left, she gave us a slap-up do in the office and gifts all round, but this time . . . ' Jane sighed. 'Our hearts weren't in it and we knew Mr O'Rourke would get hopelessly drunk. So a few of us went out to lunch together. Not so much a celebration, more of a wake.' She made an angry gesture. 'I could cheerfully kill him.'

'Do you know what has happened to the odious man?'

'Mr Grafton couldn't find another job for him within the group.'

'Surprise, surprise! I wonder what he'll do?'

'I believe he has gone to America.'

'God help the Yanks!' Laura laughed, then said, 'I'm surprised that Grafton and Hughes haven't found a vacancy for you somewhere.'

'Actually, they offered me a post as secretary to one of their area managers.'

'Then why . . . ?'

'It's in Birmingham.'

'Oh.'

Jane sighed. 'I think I'd prefer Torquay.'

'But what about the temporary job you have now? Is there any chance that it could be permanent?'

'No. The agency told me the girl I'm covering for will be out of hospital in a few weeks.' Jane paused to admire the scenery, then went on, 'They did offer me a permanent job typing accounts, but can you imagine doing that all day?'

'Sounds pretty ghastly.'

Jane thought deeply, then said, 'With

Kathleen away at university, it will be even more miserable at home, but I haven't replaced all the money I spent on clothes yet, so there's no hope of my setting up on my own, and I can't find the right man to carry me away on a handsome white charger.' She smiled wryly. 'Although Bernard would like to.'

'Does he still propose at regular intervals?'

'Faithfully. He's a nice man, Laura. I hate hurting him.'

'So why go out with him?'

'Sometimes I can't think of another excuse, and sometimes . . . '

Laura prompted, 'And sometimes?'

Jane shrugged. 'I just get fed up with going to the pictures on my own, if Kathleen isn't available. Bernard was so thrilled when I agreed to see *The Glass Mountain* with him — bought me the theme music and a huge box of chocolates.' She pondered for a moment, then went on, 'That's one thing in favour of an older man. He knows how to make a girl feel special.'

Laura nodded, then asked, 'Does Eunice approve?'

Slowly, Jane replied, 'I'm not sure. We work well together, but she didn't seem very happy when Bernard said I looked just as he'd imagined in the blue gown she made.'

'Is that the crinoline you wore when you played *Rhapsody in Blue*?'

'Mm. Bernard designed it.'

'And you looked quite lovely in it.' Laura glanced at her young friend. 'It's no use your shaking your head like that. You played beautifully and looked perfect.'

'Thank you.' Jane didn't know what else to say.

'The blue spotlight was a nice touch,' Laura commented.

'There's no doubt that Bernard is very professional, and I do love the shows.'

'But not the man.'

'No-o . . . although I have to admit I find him quite attractive. But that's not love, is it?'

'If you have to ask the question, my dear Jane, then no — it isn't love.'

Jane lowered the window a little, still thinking out loud. 'I thought I loved Olaf, and his family were sweet, and the mountains beautiful, but . . . ' She sighed. 'If I had really loved him I wouldn't have minded the remoteness of the farm, or being cut off by snow for half the year.'

'Or not being able to get your piano up the mountain.'

'That was probably the final nail in the coffin of my first romance.' Jane's laugh was short. 'So I'm afraid I haven't a lot of confidence in my judgement as far as love is concerned.'

'There will be no doubts when it happens, believe me. And this couple of days in Torquay will do you good. Your Aunt Peg is guaranteed to chase the blues away — not to mention Yvonne.'

'Ah, yes. I'd forgotten Yvonne. How is Robert getting on at the sailing school?'

'Absolutely loves it. It was just the sort of thing he was looking for, and Yvonne's father is delighted to have a younger man working with him — his arthritis is becoming troublesome.'

'Do you think Robert and Yvonne will get engaged?'

'Wouldn't be at all surprised. They're coming to lunch tomorrow. Who knows? There might be an announcement!'

'That would be lovely.' Jane smiled, then her thoughts changed direction. 'It was good of you to suggest bringing Kathleen. She was dreading the train journey on her own, with all that luggage.'

'Well, I wanted to see Robert, so it made sense to drop her off at Exeter on the way through and have some company at the same time.'

'It's the first time I've been inside a university. Pity she's not in the main campus.'

'They seem to have an excellent law faculty in that funny little back street.'

'I know, but it's a bit isolated — I just hope she's not too lonely.'

'She'll meet the other students socially and, knowing Kathleen, I'm sure she will soon make friends.'

For a while they drove in silence. Then Laura said, 'My baby brother has turned up again.'

'I thought he'd settled in America.'

Laura laughed. 'Paul won't settle anywhere. He's a gipsy, just like Father. Just now he's trying his hand at freelancing in London before he returns to the States.'

'Is he successful?'

'Oh, yes. He's a very good photographer. Already has a commission for film stills and some fashion work for a couple of magazines and an advertising agency. I asked him to keep an eye out for any vacancies suitable for you.'

'That's very good of you, Laura. Do you think there's a chance?'

'Don't build your hopes up too much. My brother only thinks about his work, and beautiful women. His latest is one of the Rank starlets.'

'Gosh! What's her name?'

'Afraid I can't remember, and I doubt

136

whether Paul will this time next year. She's blonde, busty and brainless, just the way he likes them.' Smiling, Laura shook her head. 'You've not met Paul, have you?'

'No. I was in Norway when he came out of the navy, and by the time I came back he was off on his travels.'

'It's time Paul settled down. But he's a thirty-year-old Peter Pan, always chasing his shadow, and never growing up.'

'At least he's doing things, going somewhere,' Jane said, then wondered why she had never been able to pluck up enough courage to go somewhere, get out of her rut.

Suddenly, Laura asked, 'Have you ever thought about learning to drive and buying a car?'

'Buying a car?' Jane's laugh was incredulous. 'When we had the tyre stand at the Motor Show last year I liked the look of the new Morris Minor — but at three hundred and fifty-eight pounds . . . ! I can't even afford driving lessons!'

'I could teach you, if you wish — and some second-hand cars are quite affordable.'

'Really? Gosh!' Jane lapsed into her favourite schoolgirl expression. Uncle Nobby was the only member of her family to drive a car.

'We could start this weekend if you like.'

Laura lowered the window and rotated her hand to indicate she was turning left. 'Petrol's still two shillings a gallon at this garage. Might as well use up my coupons.'

★ ★ ★

The following July, Jane was behind the wheel of the car as she pulled into the same little garage on the road to Torquay, but this time it was her own car. Laura had sold her faithful little Morris to Jane for a ridiculously low price. It had taken the last of Jane's savings, but was too good a snip to miss. Although of 1938 vintage, the car had been kept in wraps for most of the war, and was still in pristine condition. So far she had only taken her parents and Grandad for trips to Epping Forest on a Sunday afternoon, so she was glad of the chance to give 'Little Mo' a good run.

'I see petrol has gone up to three shillings a gallon,' she commented to her passenger.

Uncle Len nodded. 'I guessed that would happen as soon as they ended the rationing.' He opened the passenger door. 'Might as well stretch my legs for a minute.' Stiffly he walked up and down, then said, 'Whatever made Laura buy a Consul? Surely it's much too big for her needs?'

'She was quite smitten by it at the launch, and once she had taken it for a trial run, the temptation was too great.' Jane handed a pound note to the petrol pump attendant.

'Shouldn't have thought Laura was the sort of woman to succumb to impulse.'

'Oh, she's quite surprising at times.'

'Hmm.' Uncle Len frowned as he scuffed at the ground, and Jane wondered how he would react when he met Laura again today.

Putting the change back in her purse, Jane went on, 'Actually, Laura was looking for something bigger so she can take her old dears out.'

'What's she doing now, then — running an old people's home?'

'She helps at a little club for the elderly, something to do with her WVS work.'

As they drove on, Jane knew her uncle's thoughts were with his lost love. He broke the long silence. 'Are there going to be many people at this do?' he asked.

'Just family and a few close friends. Yvonne's mother was killed in an air-raid at Exeter, so Aunt Grace offered to do the wedding breakfast.'

Laura's shiny blue car was already parked outside the Babbacombe Bay Holiday Home when they arrived. Looking as gorgeous as ever, in black trousers and white shirt, a multicoloured scarf knotted loosely at her throat, she ran down the front steps to greet Jane.

'Saw you from the window. Did 'Little Mo' perform well?'

'Wonderful! Our first really long run. What about yours?'

'It's certainly a faster car, and Bea and Desmond had much more leg room — but it drinks up the petrol! Hullo, Len. How are you?'

'Very well, thank you.' He took her outstretched hand with the barest glimmer of a smile.

'And what do you think of my pupil?'

'Jane? She drives very well. Excuse me, I'll just take the cases in.'

Laura watched him thoughtfully for a moment, then turned to Jane. 'Is the new job still going well?' she asked.

'Fine! Really fine.'

Aunt Peggy bustled out of the front door. 'Us'll have a nice cup of tea while you tell us all about it.' She beamed at Jane. 'And don't you look the part, my dear? Why, in that pretty dress, you've stepped right off the cover of your posh magazine!'

As she clasped Jane to her bosom, Aunt Peggy smelled of home-baked bread. Then she held Jane at arm's length, her expression slightly concerned. 'Just don't you ever stop being our nice Janey underneath, though, will you?' Still chattering, she led them back into the hall. 'There's no other guests this weekend, so us'll have plenty of time for catching up on all the news. How's the poor little toad? It's time they took that brace off his leg.' Not waiting for an answer, she ploughed straight on. 'By the way, dear, if your wedding outfit is creased, give it to me and I'll run the iron over it. I do so hope the weather is fine tomorrow.'

★ ★ ★

Granting Aunt Peggy's wishes, the sun shone brilliantly as they donned their finery. Jane was pleased with her choice of a full-skirted turquoise dress with broad-brimmed matching hat and white accessories, and Laura looked every inch the ex-model in a figure-hugging, navy-blue silk dress topped with a loose coat in the same material. Lawrence had managed to get a weekend pass, wore his naval cadet's uniform, and shared the duty of usher with his brother. After he had pushed Uncle Joe's wheelchair along the side of the picturesque little church, Nobby Clarke took his place at the side of the groom.

Laura and Jane had volunteered to wait at the door of the church to assist Yvonne. In white lace, she was as radiant as every bride should be, and her father looked proud as he patiently watched the women arranging the long train and frothy veil. Predictably, Aunt Grace made a delightful, if slightly tearful, matron of honour.

'There!' Laura stood back and nodded. 'You look wonderful! Robert will think he's died and gone to heaven!' She smiled at Desmond, anxiously tapping his watch. 'Just let us slip into our seats, then you can give the organist the signal . . . '

She was interrupted by the sound of a roaring engine as a racy sports car screeched to a halt. Turning, Laura sighed with exasperation. 'About time, too,' she reproved, as a tall young man leaped out of the car. There was no mistaking the family likeness — the dark eyes inherited from their Italian mother — but there the familiarity ended. With his windblown dark hair, formal morning suit, and grey topper clutched to his chest, it was easy to imagine him in a world of dashing young bucks and pistols at dawn.

'Hullo, bossy boots,' Paul said, planting a kiss on his sister's cheek before turning to Yvonne and her father. 'Sorry to hold up your entrance,' he said, with an apologetic smile.

'The plane was dreadfully late, but thanks to a complete disregard of speed limits — ' He glanced at his watch. 'I'm only two minutes late. They say the devil looks after his own.' He grinned cheekily at Jane. 'Hi, Jane. Recognised you from your photo. Doesn't do you justice — I would have done the lighting much better.'

Dryly, Laura said, 'Jane, this is my brother Paul, as if you didn't know.'

'Of course she knows. I'm the one who got her that wonderful job on *Lady Fair*.' His handshake was warm, his smile devastating. 'And so, Miss Jane Harrison, you are beholden to me — for ever. Shall we go in?'

Too breathless to speak, Jane felt the thrill of goose bumps as Laura's brother tucked her hand into the crook of his elbow and led her into the church.

7

The carpet tickled her ankles, sheer curtains filtered the September sunlight so that no glare bounced from the snowy tablecloths, and immaculate waitresses appeared to float between the tables, quietly placing a silver tea-tray on each one, complete with short-bread fans that literally melted in the mouth. As she dabbed at her mouth with the damask napkin and poured a refill into the delicate porcelain cup, Jane felt she should pinch herself just to make sure she really was sitting in the restaurant at Harrods, waiting to listen to one of the great ladies of the beauty world.

Jane had arrived early and selected a table discreetly screened by an enormous potted palm. Although her appearance had changed beyond belief, she still couldn't quite shake off the plain Jane image that had formed her inner personality, so she was thankful that she'd been spared the curious glances aimed at the exquisite creatures who arrived later.

Her thoughts soon wandered to the man who had made it all possible. Paul was right, she was beholden to him. A year ago she had been jobless, and if Paul hadn't taken the picture editor of London's newest glossy magazine to lunch *and* if he hadn't remembered to tell his sister about the vacancy in the beauty department before he went back to America, Jane knew she wouldn't be sitting here now. Even though she had worn her latest 'New Look' suit for the interview, with its long, straight skirt, and little peplum flaring from the waist, she hadn't expected to be seriously considered, but when the magazine editor heard about her advertising experience and the beauty course, Jane was offered the job, to her surprise and delight.

She still found it difficult to believe that Paul West, a photographer of debutantes, film stars and models, could be in any way interested in such an ordinary person as Jane Harrison, even though she was now the Assistant Beauty Editor of *Lady Fair* magazine. The two months since the wedding had whirled by in Paul's exhilarating company. He had escorted her to Frank Sinatra's London debut; film premieres; and introduced her to cinema clubs that screened avant garde French films. 'La Ronde' and 'Les Enfants Terrible' were certainly different, but Jane wasn't quite sure that she preferred them to a good British picture, like 'The Mudlark'. Not that it really mattered, not when her companion was holding her hand and stroking her fingers in the most sensuous way imaginable.

Smiling at delicious memories, Jane leaned back in the velvet-covered chair and reflected on her new lifestyle of taxis, fashionable clothes, a car of her own and an invitation from Paul to join him in France. His next assignment was to take the stills for a French film company. The thought of Christmas in Paris was breathtaking. Last Christmas had been so dreary, she had made up her mind she would go anywhere rather than stay at home this year — but Paris? What would her mother say? Probably nothing. When Jane had excitedly shown her family the gorgeous coat she had bought in the sale, her father and Grandad had beamed, Kathleen had begged to try it on, even though it swamped her, but Mrs Harrison had merely said, 'Thought you were trying to save up', and switched the Hoover on again. Jane hadn't shown her mother the other clothes, but had treated Kathleen to a private viewing in the bedroom. Poor Kathleen. She would have a miserable Christmas if Jane went to Paris.

Christmas, Paris and Paul. A dangerous essence of romance. Despite Paul's assurances that it would all be very proper, Jane wasn't sure that she could trust her own feelings if he attempted to seduce her. Many times she had longed for him to go just that little bit further than spine-tingling kisses and caresses — but an inbuilt fear had been stronger than her passion. A fear that he might lose his respect for her; fear that once he possessed her she would be discarded for a new conquest; and — most important of all — fear that she might find herself in the same predicament as Rose.

A little flurry of clapping brought her back to the present. The great lady had arrived. Although perfectly groomed and with impeccable make-up, she wasn't the glamorous beauty Jane had imagined, nor could she truly be described as handsome, like Helena Rubinstein. But what a personality! Her eyes photographed the audience as her toothy smile greeted them.

'Well, hullo there! I guess I'm not quite what you expected — English ladies are no better at hiding their feelings than the girls back home in New York, but I won't let it worry me if you don't. Now, girls, let's get downa to this business called b e a u t y.' She pronounced each letter individually, paused for effect, then continued, 'It really is all in the eye and ear of the beholder, you know.'

Proving her point, Madame Rose Laird went on to explain that even the plainest person had something going for them. 'One good feature is all it takes. Maybe hair; eyes; a neat figure. And even if you've drawn the short straw on all the physical attributes, you can develop a genuine smile, good deportment and a pleasant speaking voice. That's what I did.' She leaned on the lectern, giving the impression of taking the audience into her confidence. 'It became a real drag, being the wallflower, so I decided I'd go sit with the other ugly ducklings and see if I couldn't make them feel better about themselves.' Her gaze scanned the room. 'I can still flush out the girls with low self-opinion — they'll be sitting behind the biggest darned plant they can find.'

Jane found herself blushing and sharing an embarrassed glance with a woman sitting at another secluded table as the guest speaker left her podium and confronted them. First she summed up the other woman. 'Just because you're short-sighted, doesn't mean you can't wear eye make-up,' she observed.

'But I can't see to do it without my glasses,' the young woman argued.

'There are tricks — I'll tell you about them later. And go get new spectacles, throw those in the trash can. Your eyes will look really swell with blue mascara and eyeshadow.'

Madame Rose Laird swung around to face

Jane. 'Good bone structure,' she commented, 'and great hands. So why are you hiding?' Jane remained silent while being appraised. 'Could it be that you were more Jane Withers than Shirley Temple as a child?' Jane nodded. 'Then it's your head that needs improving more than your face. Just keep telling yourself you're not a plain kid any more but a very elegant young lady. Say it enough times and you'll believe it. If you believe it, so will the rest of the world.' She smiled around the tables. 'I bet there's not one of you here that doesn't think I'm a very attractive lady by now.' They laughed. 'Sure you do, and you know why? Because I don't think of myself as an overweight old gal. I feel good about myself, because I've found my assets and made the most of them and I'm going to show you how powerful that feeling can be.' She looked back at Jane. 'I'd like to focus on those cheekbones, then demonstrate some neat little mirrors for gals who wear glasses.'

Such was the compulsion and charm of the speaker, by the time she had finished, Jane felt as though a door had been opened: one that might change her whole way of thinking and behaving. When the other beauty and fashion editors complimented Jane on her appearance, she was able to thank them

149

graciously without feeling over-awed by their presence.

Clutching her bag of purchases, Jane left the store on a wave of well-being. About to hail a taxi, she remembered that she hadn't heard from Miss Dawson for some weeks, and decided to walk around the corner to the little flat. The spinster was delighted to see Jane, but a trifle downhearted.

'Nothing in particular, my dear. I haven't been able to find suitable employment, and it is a little depressing to be rejected merely because one is fifty years old.' She glanced around the room. 'Four walls are somewhat confining when one spends too much time alone. In fact, I am seriously contemplating moving to Devonshire. My sister has said I may share her little cottage if I wish, and I would be able to visit your aunt more frequently.'

'That sounds like an excellent idea, although I shall miss our visits to the Albert Hall.'

'So shall I, my dear, so shall I. However, you have a new life now and I shall look forward to hearing about it. If I may say so, Jane, I have never seen you look so charming. Is it possible that you are in love again?'

On the way home, Jane thought about Paul — and about love. Bernard claimed he loved her, but was it really love or a rebound attraction only lingering because it was not reciprocated? The difference between true love and infatuation was a very fine line indeed. On reflection, she realised that what she had felt for Olaf had been adolescent first love. There had been stirrings when Sandy danced with her at her birthday party, but that was out of the question. Jane pushed the memory back into the recesses of her mind and concentrated on Paul.

His kisses were mature and exciting. Just thinking about them brought a rush of blood to her face. He claimed he loved her, but did his love mean 'until death us do part' or just until another woman caught his eye? His sister had expressed her doubts as to his ability to be faithful to one woman — but perhaps he only needed a different kind of woman. He had actually told Jane that he was tired of girls with brains in their bums, and it was a great relief to have an intelligent conversation with a woman. Sisters didn't always know everything about their brothers.

That brought her thoughts back to her own brother. Betty's drinking was becoming a serious problem — Jane had paid off one very aggressive money-lender, threatening to tell her brother if it happened again, but how could she? It was apparent that Jack's inner fury was not far beneath the surface — a volcano waiting to erupt. It was putting his job at risk, and it could destroy his sanity. She was also pretty certain that Sheila Green's feelings towards Jack were more than those of the 'girl next door' type of friendship. And if Jack felt the same way, where would it all end? With Betty selling off bits and pieces of furniture and Johnny not progressing well, a 'happy ever after' ending was hardly guaranteed.

When Sheila drove her mother over to the Harrisons the following week, Jane watched her friend closely, but she was interested in Jane's work, as was her mother.

'You've certainly come up in the world a bit, Janey, since I last saw you. What do you do exactly?'

'Oh, I go to beauty demonstrations if Belinda is busy, check on new products and their stockists, liaise with the advertising department — they like the Beauty Editor to say something nice about a product that is being advertised. Then there are the special promotions for samples.'

'Like that one last week for a free jar of skinfood? I sent off the coupon but it hasn't come yet.'

Jane laughed. 'We had three thousand coupons, so I think it might take a little longer, Mrs Green. But it's worth waiting for, believe me.'

'Oh, good. I thought it was lost in the post. Do you meet any really interesting people, Janey?'

'Last week I saw Diana Dors — in the cloakroom, of all places.'

'Really?' Mrs Green gasped. 'I thought she was ever so good in *Here come the Huggets*. What is she like, and what did she say to you?'

'She's very nice, but she was meeting our Executive Editor for lunch, so she just asked me if her seams were straight and said 'thank you'.' Jane laughed. 'I'm quite small fry really. Mostly I answer lots of readers' letters about their beauty problems.'

'Fancy that! We always thought Rose would be the one . . . ' Mrs Green cast an anxious glance at Mrs Harrison, then quickly changed the subject. 'I hear you have a little car of your own, just like Sheila. Don't you use it for work?' She peered curiously out of the window.

'Not every day. Generally it's easier to take the train — I rent a lock-up garage around the corner.' Jane stood up. 'Would you like another cup of tea?'

Sheila followed Jane back into the kitchenette. 'I'm glad I brought Mum over,' she said.

'She'd got so into the habit of not going out when Dad was ill, she's hardly left the house since the funeral.'

Jane nodded. 'It must be lonely for her without him, but it's early days yet. Bring her over again, it's good for Mum as well. She doesn't see many of her old friends.'

'Talking of old friends, have you heard from Sandy?'

'No. But I wasn't expecting to.'

'So you didn't know he was in the army medical corps?'

'Mum might have mentioned something. She sees Mrs Randall at the hospital sometimes.'

'Jack said there's a chance he might have to go to Korea if the situation gets any worse out there.'

Jane felt a sinking feeling in her stomach. Although she never wanted to see Sandy again, she couldn't bring herself to wish him harm.

Sheila was still talking. 'We had some good times together in the old days, didn't we?' She was pensive. 'I wish you had met Tim, although . . . ' She gazed out of the window. 'When I think of him I can't always remember his face. Makes me wonder whether the marriage would really have worked if he had lived.' She turned to face

Jane. 'Does that sound crazy to you?'

'It was a crazy world for five years and we grasped what happiness we could, when we could.' Although Jane was reflecting on Rose, her thoughts turned to Olaf. 'I know I was much too young to think of marrying and settling down.'

'We were all too young.' Sheila's smile was a little tremulous. 'But we grew up pretty quickly, that's for sure.'

'True.'

Sheila helped Jane set out teacups on the tray. 'The awful thing is not only the lovers who were killed, but losing a love through stupidity, and then finding out it's too late.' Her expression told Jane more than the words.

When their guests had gone home, and Jane had carried the tray back to the kitchenette, she thought of the many chances of happiness that had been lost: Aunt Grace, whose fiance had been killed in battle; Uncle Len, who adored Laura Marshall; Desmond, now in the army, but dreaming about a student in Exeter; Bernard Berwick, with an ex-wife in America and an unrequited love for Jane. Even her father was so consumed with guilt over his daughter's death, he could not find his way back to his wife's heart.

With her thoughts turning full circle and

returning to herself, Jane wondered about her own chance of happiness. If things had been different, it might have been with a certain young doctor. But that was before Rose, and before Paul.

Perhaps her future happiness lay with Paul? Now that was an exciting thought.

8

The Eiffel Tower soared into the December sky, its top level obscured by clouds. Resisting an urge to sing and dance, Jane remembered Eunice's warning that she might find the magic of Paris more intoxicating than champagne.

'Happy Christmas!' she cried.

'It's still only Christmas Eve.' Paul hooted with laughter. 'But in Paris, every day is like Christmas Day.'

'Have we time to look at the shops again? I've never seen such window displays, and I must buy a souvenir for Mum — she hasn't forgiven me for deserting them.'

A dainty brooch, the Eiffel Tower studded with marcasites, caught her eye before they strolled around the artists' colony in Montparnesse. Jane snuggled her chin deeper into the fur collar as she admired a small painting of the Ile de la Cité. Suddenly, she became aware of the soulful eyes of the artist, who told her that he greatly desired to paint the beautiful mademoiselle — if monsieur would permit? Answering haltingly in his own language, she thanked him but regretted there was no time. However, if he could tell her the price of the watercolour? It was more than she could afford and she was about to walk away when Paul intervened, bargaining rapidly with the man. Eventually, agreement was reached upon a sum only half the original figure and the painting presented to Jane by the artist, who bowed low as he kissed her hand, murmuring, 'Au revoir, mademoiselle. My heart is broken that I cannot paint your portrait.'

'I suppose he says that to all the tourists,' Jane commented as they walked away. 'But he said it so beautifully.' She chuckled. 'The closest I've come to it before was a wolf whistle from a barrow boy — not the same thing at all.'

'The French are masterly when it comes to flirtation.' Paul took the painting so she could tuck her hands into the muff. 'You must always haggle in Paris — never pay the asking price.'

'I bow to your knowledge of the world.' She thought again about the painting. 'I hope Miss Dawson likes it. It's not in quite the same class as her Turner, but it's something else of her own to hang in her sister's cottage.'

'A genuine painting by Turner? You're kidding!'

158

'Cross my heart. The family fortunes took a dive after the stock market crash and a bomb destroyed their other treasures, but the Turner has a charmed life.'

'Well, I hope she has it insured, it must be worth thousands.'

'Priceless, I should imagine. Now, just something for Kathleen, then I'm all yours.'

'If only . . . ' he teased, but waited patiently while Jane chose a 1951 calendar with a reproduction of a Toulouse-Lautrec painting. Then he steered her towards a bridge. 'I want to show you the Champs Elysees.' They strolled along the handsome boulevard, took photographs of the Arc de Triomphe, rode on the metro, bought postcards in Montmartre and gazed at the Basilica of the Sacre Coeur.

'Is it like you imagined?' Paul asked.

'No, it's better. Much better!' Jane swivelled on her three-inch heel, admiring every aspect of the view. 'Thank God these beautiful buildings survived the occupation.'

'Only because Hitler's orders to destroy Paris were ignored.'

Appalled, Jane stared at him, then she shivered.

'Come on.' Paul tucked her hand back inside the muff. 'Time for an aperitif to warm us up.'

When they left the cafe, it was almost dark

and the lights were breathtaking, outlining the distinctive sails of the Moulin Rouge. Eunice was right, Jane thought. Paris defied description. You had to be there to feel the magic. It had even eclipsed the excitement of her first flight. From the moment that Paul had met her at the airport and driven her to the hotel, she had known what Cinderella would have felt like as she was whisked away to the Ball — except that midnight held no fears for Jane Harrison. Her Prince Charming would escort her home — and perhaps this would be the night when he would propose marriage?

Bringing her mind back from fantasy to reality, Jane wondered whether they would be able to take in a nightclub or theatre. 'Eunice told me the Bluebell dancers are performing at the Lido. I suppose there's no chance of getting tickets?'

'On Christmas Eve? No chance.' Slowly, Paul reached inside his overcoat. 'Anyway, I already have tickets for a show called *Enchantment*.'

'I'm sure it will be lovely. Where is it on?'

Paul peered closely at the tickets, then held them at a distance. 'I must get my eyes tested,' he said. 'Here, you read it.'

After a moment, Jane gasped. 'It's at the Lido! You're wonderful, and I can't thank you enough.' She kissed his cheek. 'How did you know I wanted to see it?'

'I guessed. And that's not much of a thank-you. Come here.' His kiss was long and intimate — very intimate.

Eventually, she pulled away. 'Paul!' She was quite breathless. 'Not in the street. People are looking.'

'My darling Jane, this is Paris, and Parisians are quite accustomed to lovers. Look at the couple in that doorway.'

Her eyes widened as she watched a man slide his hand inside the woman's fur coat and expose her naked breast. 'She's not wearing anything underneath!' she exclaimed.

'How else can she display her wares?' Paul laughed. 'Oh, Jane darling, you are so naive. I do believe you're still a virgin.'

Her voice was low as she looked at the pavement. 'I don't see anything wrong with that, so please don't make fun of me.'

His hand lifted her chin until her face was level with his. 'I would never make fun of you, Jane,' he said. 'One of the things I love about you is your innocence. It's a commodity in rare supply these days.'

'You really are making fun of me.'

'No, and I won't do anything to spoil that innocence, I promise you.' He kissed the tip of her nose. 'Now we must hurry back to the hotel and change. I told the others we'd meet them at seven.'

About a dozen people from the film crew joined them for another aperitif. They were friendly and lively, if a little eccentric. They also seemed immune to the effects of liberal quantities of wine. When they moved on to the Lido, Paul ordered champagne with the meal. Jane was shocked at the prices but fascinated by the hubbub, the closely packed tables and the decor. An older man with a slightly jaded expression sat on the other side of Jane. He shook his head mournfully as Paul downed his drink in one gulp. 'A glass of champagne should be approached like a beautiful woman,' he commented. 'All the senses should be feasted first: eyes; ears; and especially, the touch.' Stroking the slender stem, he held the glass high, listening to the gentle fizz of the bubbles. 'Then, and only then, my dear Paul, you put the glass to your lips and take a little sip, no more. It should be an intensely slow and pleasurable experience.' Charles Boyer could not have spoken the words with more passion, Jane thought.

Laughing, Paul refilled his glass. 'I agree with you on one point, André,' he said. 'A glass of champagne can be compared to a beautiful woman — but watch this.' He raised the glass and drank the contents without pausing for breath. Then he glanced at Jane and smiled. It was a wickedly mischievous smile. 'You see, just as much intense pleasure — but quicker.' Again he reached for the champagne bottle.

André whispered in Jane's ear. 'Do not let him drink cognac, *ma cherie*. Champagne keeps him happy, but cognac . . . ' He shrugged his shoulders expressively.

'What do you mean?' Jane laughed, mimicking his gesture.

André tapped his nose. 'You have heard of Doctor Jekyll and Monsieur Hyde, no?'

Before she could answer, the floor show began. The dancers towered over the tables, their long legs kicking high in perfect unison, smiles never faltering. How Rose would have loved this, Jane thought.

Then the showgirls appeared. Jane had expected semi-nudity, and the girls had obviously been selected for their firm breasts and gorgeous legs. As for the costumes, the effect of mountains of plumes, fur and sequins adorning such nakedness was stunning. At one point, Paul tilted her chin back to close her mouth.

The evening whirled to a close and they meandered slowly towards the River Seine, joining the throng called by the bells of Notre Dame. Several of the film crew wished to celebrate Mass, and Jane asked if she would be allowed to go into the cathedral. 'I am not a Catholic, but it would be a perfect end to a perfect day.'

The others shrugged their Gallic shoulders and propelled her up the steps. 'Just stay with us,' one advised, 'but do not take the sacrament.'

Mesmerised by the splendour of the great rose windows, Jane clung to Paul's hand, her senses reeling from the impact of the music, the incense and the feeling of spiritual unity as hundreds knelt in prayer. Their companions halted by an array of candles, each lighting one and placing it into a holder. Filled with a desperate urge, Jane put some francs into the box and took a candle. 'For Rose,' she murmured, as the flame flickered into life.

The first hour of Christmas Day had barely passed when they emerged. Parisians wished each other '*Joyeux Noel*', and Jane was kissed soundly on both cheeks many times before Paul was able to lead her away towards the hotel. His room was next to hers, but he just opened the door, handed over the key and kissed her lightly upon the lips as she tried to stifle a yawn.

'You do not need to send signals.' He smiled ruefully.

Disappointment at her own fatigue swept over Jane. 'I'm dreadfully sorry, Paul, but everything seems to be catching up on me. It has been a wonderful day, but I really am exhausted.'

'Then sleep, perchance to dream, my sweet Jane. Tomorrow is another day. Correction! Today is another day. Happy Christmas.' Swaying slightly, Paul turned towards his own room and blew her a kiss from the doorway.

Despite her genuine tiredness, Jane felt a slight pang of regret.

★ ★ ★

It seemed strange to be eating warm croissants in a French cafe on Christmas morning, instead of helping to stuff a turkey and prepare masses of vegetables in the kitchenette back home. Jane could not help feeling a little guilty when she thought of her mother, and Kathleen, but the gaiety of Paul and his colleagues soon dispelled any gloomy thoughts as they strolled through the city, greeting other friends until quite a large party gathered for the inevitable aperitif before a lunch of the most delicious crusty bread Jane had ever tasted, with chunks of cheese and paté. The conversation, food and wine lasted well into the afternoon, when the others dispersed to take a short rest before meeting again for dinner. Jane would also have welcomed a nap, but Paul insisted on driving her to see where he worked.

The industrial area on the perimeter of the city was desolate. Not a light pierced the approaching dusk. They bumped across a gloomy yard and pulled up outside a large, shabby building.

'It was a warehouse once and had been empty for years,' Paul explained, as he ushered her in through a metal door and locked it behind them. 'Just the job for a film set, out of the way of sightseers, but accessible — ' He threw a piece of wood at a furry shape which squeaked and scuttled into a corner. 'We'll have to put some more rat poison down.' Paul pulled a face. 'Can't stand the little monsters.'

Jane shivered as she looked around at the sections of scenery, cameras and vast lights with miles of cable. 'How long will you be working here?' she asked.

'A few months yet. They've got two more films on line, and I have some other projects on the go as well as the stills. Come up to the projection room and I'll show you. It's warmer up there.'

She followed him up a rickety flight of wooden stairs, into a room equipped with chairs, tables and a small cinema screen. Paul switched on the electric fire before he opened a cupboard and took out a bottle and two glasses.

'Here, this will warm you up until the fire gets going.'

'Only a little for me, please. I'm not keen on brandy.' She remembered André's warning at the Lido and hoped Paul would merely have one drink. As she watched him gulp down the second, she had to say something. 'Paul, perhaps you should not drink any more.'

'Why not? Has someone been talking to you?'

'You had quite a lot of wine at lunchtime, and you have to drive us back in a minute.'

'Christmas is a time for drinking,' he said. 'We can always leave the car and take a taxi.' His smile wore a little thin at the edges. 'Don't nag, darling, it's so boring. And take off your coat, it's warming up in here.' Paul unlocked another cupboard and ran his fingers down the stacks of circular tins until he found what he wanted and slotted a film into the projector. 'Sit back and relax.'

The film was set in a school for teenage girls. An older man wearing a mortarboard and black gown came into the classroom, tapping a cane lightly against the palm of his hand. He walked up and down the rows of desks, stopped by one and viciously slapped the cane down upon it. As the camera came into close-up Jane recognised the man — it was André — and the schoolgirl looking up at him with such a frightened expression had also been one of their companions at the Lido. When the headmaster followed the girl upstairs and into a dormitory, still holding the cane, Jane began to feel uneasy.

Suddenly the girl stopped shrinking backwards and held out her hand for the cane, watching as the man removed his trousers and bent over the bed. The girl smiled seductively, whacked the man twice across the buttocks and undid the shoulder buttons of her gymslip.

Turning, Jane realised that Paul was watching her, not the screen. Icily, she asked, 'Is this one of your other projects?'

He nodded. 'There's a lot of money in these. Don't you think the bit where the girl becomes the aggressor is exciting? Perhaps you will prefer this one — don't move.' He pushed her back onto the chair. 'Just tell me what you think.'

At first, Jane didn't know what she was looking at, then realised it was three naked bodies at close range. A man and two women. Angrily, she jumped to her feet. 'Please take me back to the hotel,' she said.

Grabbing her coat from the back of the chair, Paul threw it onto the floor. 'I love it when you're pretending to be a tease,' he said. 'It really gets me going. Come on, darling, the film looks much better from a horizontal position.'

'I'm not pretending anything. How could you possibly think I'd be interested in blue movies?'

'Everybody is — they pay good money for them. Why should you be any different?'

'I don't want to talk about it. I just want to leave.'

The cognac was beginning to take effect on Paul. He gripped her arms tightly and forced her down onto her knees. 'Not yet, my darling. Not yet.'

As he attempted to kiss her, Jane turned her head and struggled to free her arms, but he was stronger. She shouted at him to stop, but he just laughed and tightened his grip.

'You don't really want me to stop. When we kiss, I know you want me to go on and on.'

'Not like this, Paul! Never like this. It's — '

'Rape? There's no such thing, my darling. Every woman fantasises about this. Go on, admit it.'

Her screams were loud, but his chilling laughter silenced her.

'Scream away. Who will hear? Some drunk living rough? Will he come to the rescue? No, my sweet little virgin, there's no one — and you knew it when you came here.' He shifted his position and felt for her breast.

Jane knew she had to talk her way out of this before he overpowered her.

'You promised,' she pleaded. 'You said I had nothing to fear from you.'

'I have never made anyone pregnant yet . . . ' He was breathless, and his humourless laughter became almost manic. 'So far as I know.' He pushed her back onto her coat and forced his open mouth onto hers. Jane thought she would choke. There was only one way she could breathe.

As he brushed his hand across his mouth, Paul stared at the smear of blood where she had bitten his lip. Suddenly, his mood became angrier and he tore at the neck of her dress. She remembered what her dinner companion had said about Jekyll and Hyde. Oh, Lord, it was true!

'You bitch!' Paul muttered through clenched teeth. 'You knew what it was all about when you agreed to come.' He ripped her dress and petticoat to the waist. 'So don't think you can come the holier than thou little innocent with me.' His weight pinned her to the ground as he fumbled with the belt of his trousers. Although Jane was almost as tall as her aggressor, she couldn't match Paul's strength, made even more powerful by the alcohol.

Through the haze of ineffectual struggling, she heard Rose's voice telling her what to do. For a brief moment, she relaxed completely, then brought her knee up sharply. Instantly Paul doubled up in pain, just enough for her to push him away. It wasn't enough. As she staggered to her feet, he grabbed her ankle, pulling her back down to her knees. His face was brutally ugly.

'You want to play rough? I'll show you what rough really means!' He struck her hard around the face and grabbed her by the throat. Again she tried to jab her knee into his groin, but he swung her sideways and again struck her around the face. Then he dragged her to her feet and flung her across the room, her head hitting the cupboard so hard, the reels of film spilled out onto the floor.

As she struggled to hold on to consciousness, Jane realised she was in mortal danger. The cognac had turned Paul into a monster — obsessed with a blood lust as well as sexual desire. She had to get away. But how?

The moaning and heavy breathing from the screen formed a bizarre sound effect while Paul watched her from across the room, fists raised as though daring her to defy him. Her own fists would not be enough. She needed a weapon. As though guided by some helpful presence, her hand touched metal. Trying to remember every instruction she had been given years ago by the gym teacher, Jane hurled the heavy film can as though it were a discus. It spun through the air, hitting right on target!

Not delaying a moment, she rushed downstairs and was struggling with the lock of the outer door when Paul shouted at her from the top of the stairs. Screaming obscenities, he lurched forward and grabbed the flimsy handrail. With an ear-splitting crack, it broke under his weight.

Jane watched in horror, knowing she would never forget the sight of Paul's body, almost in slow motion, hurtling to the ground. The silence was terrifying as she waited for him to move. Carefully, she approached him. He lay on his side, one leg bent under and an arm stretched out — so terribly still. His eyes were closed, his skin a strange colour, the blood gushed from the wound where the can had struck his forehead. There was no doubt. Paul was dead!

For a moment, she remained transfixed, staring at his body. She had planned to take his car and flee to safety, but that was out of the question now. What should she do? Who could help? The film crew? She did not have their telephone numbers, and if she waited all night, they would not come looking for her and Paul. No one knew they were here.

The police? Was her French good enough to explain; and would they believe her? After all, she had been alone in a remote film studio with the man — a studio that made pornographic movies! Thoughts of questions and suspicions raced through her mind as panic threatened. She had to get away and give herself time to think.

She had unlocked the door before she remembered that her coat and bag were still upstairs. Fighting back waves of nausea, she stepped over Paul's body and went back for her belongings, leaving everything else as it was, the film still whirring in the projector.

Once outside, panic took over. What if there were down-and-outs sheltering nearby, the way they did on the Thames embankment? Supposing she had been seen and could be recognised? She ran as fast as her shaking legs could manage, across the waste land and along a street of derelict houses with windows boarded up. When she could run no further she crouched under a barren tree, panting. On the corner of the street was a telephone booth. She was too terrified to phone the police, but she couldn't leave Paul to the mercy of the rats.

Jane dialled the operator and asked for an ambulance, trying to remember the location, and saying she had found a man lying on the floor of a warehouse. When they asked her name she hung up. Then she skimmed through the torn pages of the directory and phoned a taxicab service. The ambulance made its noisy way along the street before the taxi arrived to take her to the hotel.

Safely back in her room, she began to tremble as she realised the enormity of what had happened. Her flight wasn't due to leave until the next day, but she couldn't stay here. Eventually his friends would come looking for him.

Still shaking from head to foot, she washed and changed, thrusting the torn garments into her suitcase. Bruises were beginning to discolour her face and neck, so she brushed the dirt from her coat, pulled the fur collar high and tied a scarf over her head before she paid her bill and left. The concierge had obviously also supped well throughout the day and appeared quite indifferent when Jane murmured that she would be sleeping elsewhere that night. Keeping to the shadows, she walked aimlessly for hours, jumping every time she saw a gendarme.

174

'*Combien de, mademoiselle?*' A well dressed man raised his hat and smiled at her. Not understanding at first, she stared, until he repeated his question. Shaking her head, she hurried in the opposite direction.

A blister pained her heel and she needed to sit down, but not somewhere she might again be mistaken for a prostitute.

For the second time in two days Jane lit a candle at the Notre Dame. This time it was for Paul. As she huddled at the back of the great cathedral, the tears eventually came. She wept quietly throughout the evening Mass, until the last worshipper left.

An elderly priest hesitated by her pew. 'Mademoiselle? Are you ill?' he asked, in French.

'No, just tired — thank you. I will leave now.'

He waited by the door, watching as she slowly walked down the steps.

Jane was not hungry but her mouth was parched and she had to find somewhere to stay the night. The run-down cafe where she had ordered coffee had one room vacant — mademoiselle was indeed fortunate. As she lay shivering on the grubby bed, feeling the bugs attacking her battered body, Jane listened to the sounds of Paris through the shutters.

This was supposed to have been the Christmas that changed her life for ever. But not like this! She had been in love with Paul, trusted him. Her fantasies had been of the look in his eyes when he saw her in a bridal gown, but he had left her with memories of brutal rage. The bruises would fade, but not the images. How could someone from such a loving, caring family be so different?

For the first time, Jane thought of Laura. Dear God! What could she say to her friend — Paul's sister?

9

'Ta!' Johnny was not an eloquent child, but the pleasure showed in his expression as he unwrapped the sketch pad and box of paints.

Betty pulled a face. 'Don't you go making a mess with that lot. You know what Nan's like.'

'I'm sorry, I didn't realise.' Sheila hesitated, then turned to the boy. 'If you put a piece of newspaper on the table in the kitchenette you won't make a mess, will you, Johnny?'

'No mess. Paint now?'

Mrs Harrison smiled. 'Not now, Johnny — we've got to have tea first.'

His lip quivered and his chin drooped onto his chest. Oh, dear, Jane thought, another tantrum. But Sheila saved the situation.

'As soon as you've blown out all ten candles on your lovely birthday cake, I'm sure Nan will let you paint.'

Mrs Harrison nodded, and Johnny frowned for a moment, then put the paints to one side and opened the next present.

As they were cutting the cake, Mrs Harrison said, 'Mustn't forget to keep some back for Desmond and Kathleen.'

'What film have they gone to see?' Sheila asked.

'That one with Jean Simmons, about the girl who goes to Paris and her brother disappears.'

'*So Long at the Fair*? It's quite scary.' Sheila handed Mrs Harrison another plate. 'Can you imagine being in a situation like that where you're in a strange country and can't make anyone understand what happened?'

Jane understood only too well, but Paris was the last place she wanted to discuss.

Her mother flashed a glance at Jane — full of meaning. 'I can't understand why anyone would want to go to Paris anyway,' she said. 'You never know what might happen in those foreign places.' She put another slice of cake into a greaseproof bag and handed it to Sheila. 'Give this to your mum, and tell her I hope her cough's soon better.'

'Thanks. To be honest, I don't think the cough stopped her coming. It was her first Christmas without Dad and . . . I know he could be difficult, but she misses him. She's got no one to look after now.'

'Whoever would have thought that someone as big and strong as Wilf Green would become an invalid.' Nell Harrison sighed. 'Like our Jack. Thirteen stone and the picture of health before the war. Now look at him.' Jack still hadn't regained his old weight.

Grandad held out his hand for the plate. 'Thanks, Nell. I like that nice soft icing. I won't have to put my teeth in.' His mouth full, he went on. 'Mind you, I'd have put them in if Laura had come. She's a real lady, and she treats me like a gentleman.' He wiped the crumbs from his chin. 'Why did she have to scarper at such short notice?'

'Don't know, Dad. I had a note from her this morning, sending her apologies. Something to do with her brother.'

'The one down in Devon?'

'I wouldn't think so or Peg would have mentioned it — she popped a letter in with her postal order for Johnny.' Knife poised, Mrs Harrison paused for a moment. 'She said Grace has a bad cold, and she seemed a bit concerned about the underpinning not being finished yet, but she didn't mention Robert.'

Mr Harrison wiped his sticky fingers on his handkerchief. 'Len said Nobby was fed up to the teeth with the builders when he telephoned on Christmas Eve. The workmen only turned up when they felt like it and kept making excuses about the weather.'

'Well, I hope they finish it soon, Fred. Grace has quite a few early bookings, I believe.'

Grandad looked troubled. 'They promised I could go down next month and stay till Easter. It's a lot warmer down there, and they don't get the peasoupers.'

Jane was glad the conversation had veered away from Laura. 'I'll phone Aunt Grace on Monday from the office,' she said, 'and try to find out what's happening.'

Sheila followed Jane into the kitchenette and picked up a tea towel. 'I've been meaning to ask; how was Paris, apart from falling bum over tip? Meet any rich, handsome Frenchmen?'

Jane's reply was non-committal. The family had been told that Christmas in Paris was an assignment from the magazine. Paul had not been mentioned and, to keep up the pretence, it was essential that nobody else knew. Not Sheila; not Kathleen; and not Laura — especially not Laura.

The last few days had been a nightmare. She'd flown back to London on Boxing Day and sat in a newsreel theatre until late evening, delaying the inevitable questions at home. To account for the bruises she had concocted two stories: a nasty tumble down the steps of the Paris metro for the family; and a patch of ice outside the back door for her colleagues at the office, who thought she had spent Christmas at home.

Belinda, the Beauty Editor, asked if she wanted a couple of days off but Jane preferred to be at work, anything to keep the dreadful memories at bay. Fortunately, as always, there was a huge pile of readers' beauty problems so she was able to immerse herself in work for the next three days and lose the evenings in preparations for the January show at the Winter Baths.

When she had first told Bernard she was going to France on business, he looked so dejected Jane actually agreed to go to a masked ball with him on New Year's Eve, but his concern about the bruises gave her the perfect excuse to cancel the date.

No mention was made in the national newspapers of a British photographer having been found dead in Paris, but somebody had obviously identified Paul and contacted Laura. Night after night Jane lay awake, thinking about the lies and deceit created from her panic. It was too late to go to the police and there was no way she could tell Laura how her brother had died, nor could she pretend that all was normal. Losing Laura's friendship would be heartbreaking.

For the first time Jane understood how Rose had dug a hole for herself, deeper and deeper, until it was impossible to climb out.

Once the washing up from Johnny's tea

party was finished, Jane spread a newspaper across the table in the kitchenette, half filled a jam jar with water and found an old piece of rag for cleaning the paint brushes. Reluctant to join the rest of the family in the living room, she decided to work on her notes for the concert at the other end of the table, while Johnny tried out his new pencils and paints, encouraged by Sheila. Usually the girls talked non-stop, but since she returned from Paris, Jane had been unable to maintain a conversation with anyone for any length of time. She felt defensive, almost expecting to be asked, 'What happened to Paul?', and was grateful for Sheila's rare gift of understanding that, today, Jane was not in the mood for idle chatter.

For an hour, the two friends sat in uncharacteristic silence, one quietly guiding a little boy with his first painting, the other trying to concentrate on her notes, wondering how she could restore her energy before the show, and desperately wishing she could confide in her companion.

The peace was disturbed by Mrs Harrison. 'I'll have to tear Johnny away from his painting, I'm afraid, Sheila. Never known him to take to anything so much. But it's getting a bit late, and Jack wants to make a move soon. He's rather tired.'

And he wants to get Betty away from the remainder of the Christmas drink, Jane thought.

Head still down, Johnny said, 'Not done, Nan.'

Mrs Harrison looked over his shoulder and smiled. 'That's very good, dear,' she said. She sounded as though she meant it. 'Who are the people?'

'Mum. Dad.' Johnny remained completely absorbed in his task.

'Of course.' Mrs Harrison watched him for a while longer, a thoughtful expression on her face. Then she said, 'Another ten minutes, then you'll have to go home.'

Finally, his first painting was complete.

'Look, Auntie Jane!' His face was the picture of pride as he held the piece of paper aloft. 'Christmas.'

'It's just like a Christmas card!' Amazed, Jane studied the picture. Johnny had painted a room festooned with paper chains, a boy opening presents beneath a Christmas tree, a blazing fire and a table laden with festive food. Seated at the table, a smiling man and woman pulled a cracker. Johnny's dream family. Full of details, it was good by any standard. 'It's quite wonderful, Johnny,' she said.

'You're right, it is wonderful.' Jack was

standing behind Jane, gazing at the painting. He smiled warmly at Sheila. 'It's the first time he's shown a real interest in anything,' he said, 'and it's all thanks to you.'

Colouring a little, Sheila said, 'I had a feeling he might have a natural talent when I watched him colouring with his crayons, but this is exceptional for his age.' She picked up the painting carefully by the corners. 'Let's show it to Mummy, shall we?'

Grabbing it from her hands, Johnny raced into the living room and excitedly waved the painting in front of his mother, who was reading her mother-in-law's *Home Notes* magazine. 'I'm trying to finish this story,' she said, pushing his arm away.

Johnny must have realised that the only way his mother would look at his creation was to put it on the open pages of her magazine. 'Mum! Look at picture,' he demanded. 'It's you!'

'Careful!' Sheila cried. 'It's still damp.'

Her warning was unheeded by child or mother. As she saw the multi-coloured smudge from the back of the painting blur the last paragraph of her story, Betty's expression changed from irritation to fury. 'Now look what you've done!' she shouted. 'You stupid little . . . ' Jumping to her feet, she shoved him out of the way and, before anyone realised her intention, Betty had screwed up the painting and tossed it into the fire.

For a brief moment, the room was still. Again Jane felt the deep horror she had experienced in Paris, when she knew something dreadful had happened, and worse was to come.

Johnny was the first to move. With a fearful shriek, he hurled himself at the fireplace, trying to reach over the fireguard to his precious work of art, now being consumed by hungry flames. Then he sank to his knees, sobbing uncontrollably, beating his fists on the ground and screaming, 'No! No! No!' over and over.

Oblivious to the damage she had caused, Betty tried to push past Jack, who blocked the doorway. 'Let me through, Jack. If I don't clean this off straight away, I won't be able to read the end.'

Jack snatched the magazine from her hand and gave it to his mother. Then he dragged Betty over to the fireplace and pointed at the flames. 'That was your son's first painting,' he shouted above Johnny's screams. 'I can buy Mum another magazine, but nothing can ever replace his work.'

As though realising, for the first time, that she had antagonised the whole family, Betty looked from face to hostile face. She began to bluster. 'All this fuss over a silly painting. He can do another one.' If she had left it at that, Jack might have calmed down but Betty, being Betty, didn't have the intelligence to apologise, or to shut up.

Jane knew her sister-in-law was going to make matters worse when she saw her eyes flicker towards Sheila.

'It's all her fault,' Betty blurted out. 'If she hadn't bought him the bloody box of paints, it wouldn't have happened. It'll only be a nine-days wonder, anyway. He's too stupid to stick at anything.'

'Johnny is not stupid!' Jack's fists clenched and unclenched. 'And at least Sheila is prepared to spend some time with him. You don't even help him with his speech, or his leg exercises.'

'What's the point, when everyone knows he'll never talk properly, or run around like normal kids. I'm sick and tired of his noise and tantrums. He ought to be in a loony bin, and I'm going to make sure he goes into one before he gets much older.'

Jane was kneeling by Johnny, trying to pacify the child, when Jack moved towards Betty. 'Over my dead body!' he shouted. 'Or it could be yours.'

With a little yelp of fear, Betty backed into

a small table, knocking it over. 'Don't you threaten me, Jack Taylor.' Her voice was shaky, but she ploughed on into even more disaster. 'Just because you're trying to impress your lady friend.'

Jack's head swivelled towards Sheila, who looked uncomfortable as she picked up the table.

Mrs Harrison placed a hand on her son's arm. 'Don't, Jack,' she warned. 'You'll only make yourself bad, and she doesn't know what she's saying.'

Jane feared that her brother was too angry to heed his mother, and the door opening was a welcome intrusion. Desmond and Kathleen were back, their faces concerned. They must have been aware of the fierceness of the quarrel the moment Kathleen opened the front door.

Jack took a deep breath, then stepped back. 'Sorry about that,' he apologised, then sank down onto the nearest chair. His hand trembled as he lit a cigarette.

The atmosphere was so tense and Desmond looked so embarrassed, Jane felt she should say something — anything. 'Did you enjoy the picture?' she asked.

'Er — yes.' Kathleen unbuttoned her coat. 'I was on the edge of my seat right to the end, wasn't I, Desmond?'

As Mrs Harrison lifted the crying child from Jane's arms, and took him into the kitchenette, Jane noticed for the first time how Desmond had changed. She had always thought of him as a sensitive and gentle boy, but somewhat immature in the way he clung to his mother. Now, he acted the perfect escort, taking Kathleen's coat and hat, and picking up on the need to lighten the atmosphere.

'But you guessed the ending long before I did.' He hung the clothes on the hallstand and turned to Jane. 'Haven't seen you since I came home on leave,' he said. 'And Kathleen tells me you went to Paris.'

Oh, God, Jane thought. He's going to say something about Paul. Frantically, she tried to think of something to say, some diversion, but her mouth was too dry, so she just nodded. Thankfully, before Desmond could say any more, her father spoke.

'How's life in the army then, son? Settling in all right, are you?'

'It was a little strange at first, but yes — I am settling in fine now, thank you.'

Recovering a little of her composure, Jane murmured, 'I'll put the kettle on', and escaped to the kitchenette, leaving behind her a bizarre tableau of Mr Harrison, Desmond and Kathleen holding a polite conversation as though nothing had happened, Grandad staring into the fire, Sheila looking as though she wished the floor would open up and swallow her, Betty sulking in the corner, and Jack silently smoking his cigarette. Who knew what thoughts were going through his tortured mind?

In the kitchenette, Mrs Harrison had managed to quieten her grandson a little, but he still quietly sobbed in her arms. Deep in her own thoughts, trying to work out what she would say if Desmond mentioned Paul, Jane silently filled the kettle and set the cups out on a tray. Her mother didn't speak either. After a few minutes, Desmond put his head around the door.

'I have to be off now, Mrs Harrison. Promised Granbea I'd call in on my way home, so don't want to miss the train.'

Mrs Harrison nodded. 'Goodnight, Desmond. Sorry you had to hear our argument.'

'Oh, don't worry.' He smiled. 'It happens in the best of families.'

'I suppose so. But I don't like rows, never have.' Mrs Harrison sighed. 'When do you go back?'

'Tomorrow. So I'd better wish you both a happy New Year now. Wonder what nineteen-fifty-one holds in store for us all?'

After they heard the front door close and

Jane poured the tea, Mrs Harrison suddenly said, 'I meant to ask him why Laura had suddenly gone away. Oh, well, I suppose she'll tell us when she gets back.'

Jane was relieved, but curious as to why Desmond hadn't mentioned his uncle. Perhaps he didn't know. He only had a forty-eight-hour pass and Laura might have left before he came home. But surely Bea Marshall would have said something? It was possible, of course, that Laura hadn't wanted to worry her so had just made some excuse and gone quickly to Paris to find out the details. Oh, hell, what a mess. And it wouldn't go away. At some time or other, Laura was going to put two and two together, and ask questions. What on earth can I say to her? Jane thought.

By now, Johnny had cried himself to sleep, so Mrs Harrison carried him upstairs. Sheila said she would go home as soon as she had drunk her tea, and Jack took his cup without a word. Kathleen tried to resurrect some sense of normality by asking Sheila what presents she had received for Christmas.

'Lots of toiletries — I like those. Chocolates from my boss and — ' Sheila fumbled at her neck, 'this from Mum.' She lifted the pendant so that Kathleen could examine it.

Jane said, 'I noticed it earlier. It's very pretty.'

'I love it. Mum bought it in that funny little shop at Manor Park — the one that sells antique and second-hand jewellery.'

'I remember. We used to laugh at the old boy with his yiddish accent and black skullcap.'

'He's still there. I went back there today to get the clasp fixed.' Sheila tucked the pendant back inside her blouse. 'And guess what? He had another one, almost identical to the one Bernard bought you for your birthday. Even had your name engraved on the back.' She laughed. 'If I didn't know better, I'd have thought you'd hocked it!'

Sick with apprehension, Jane carried the tray back to the kitchenette and began washing up the cups. After a few moments, Sheila came into the room, wearing her outdoor clothes.

'I'll take the cake for Mum, if I may,' she said.

Jane felt compelled to say something. Someone should apologise on behalf of the family. 'I'm sorry, Sheila' sounded terribly inadequate.

'I know, but it wasn't your fault. Perhaps I shouldn't have tried to help Johnny. The last thing I want is to come between

191

husband and wife.'

'For goodness sake! The rift was already a mile wide. Oh, Sheila, if you knew how I wish . . . '

'So do I, Jane.' Sheila really didn't need to use words. The pain was in her face. Silently they hugged. Then Sheila broke away. 'I must go,' she said. Her eyes were moist.

As soon as Sheila had left, Jane rushed up to her room. The slender jewellery case was in the dressing-table drawer, but the gold pendant and chain was not nestling amongst the satin lining. Only one person would have taken it.

Too angry to be discreet, Jane stormed downstairs and confronted Betty with the empty jewel case. 'My gold pendant was in here a few days ago. Today it's for sale in a jeweller's shop at Manor Park.'

Betty opened and closed her mouth, her face a picture of guilt. 'You don't know it's the same one,' she blustered.

'Sheila gave a pretty good description, even to my name engraved on the back.'

'Might have known Miss Goody-goody would have something to do with it,' she said.

'Never mind that. I want the truth, and I want it now!'

'Are you trying to say I stole it?'

'Not trying, I know you stole it, Betty. It

couldn't have been anyone else, so you might as well own up.'

'All right! All right! I took the rotten thing. You've plenty more where that came from, so why all the fuss?'

If Jane had been watching Jack's face, she might have seen the danger signals, but her eyes were blurred with angry tears, and he'd grabbed Betty before she could stop him, shaking her like a rag doll and shouting, 'You drunken slut! You're nothing but a rotten little thief!'

Before Jane and her father could drag Jack away, he suddenly flung Betty back onto the settee and stood over her, his fists clenched. Betty stared up at him, looking too terrified to cry.

For the first time, Mr Harrison spoke. 'Let it go, Jack. Let it go now, before things get out of hand.'

After a long moment, Jack nodded. Very quietly, he said to his wife, 'Get out of my sight.' The icy hatred in his voice was something that even Betty couldn't argue with, although she made one last feeble effort.

'And where am I supposed to go?'

'Up to the pub. Anywhere.'

'I haven't any money.' Her voice was sullen.

'Put it on the slate. It won't be the first time.'

'The landlord won't let me have any more on the slate.' Deflated, Betty began to whimper.

Jack rummaged in his trouser pocket and pulled out a handful of coins, throwing them onto the table. 'It's all I've got. Take it and drink yourself stupid.' As Betty grabbed the coins and thrust them into her handbag, Jack moved away to the far side of the room. It was as though he couldn't bear to be near his wife. 'And first thing tomorrow, you'll get that locket back.'

'How can I do that?' Betty grizzled. 'I've spent the money.'

'I don't care how you do it. Sell yourself on the streets if you want. You can't sink any lower.' Shaking his head, he went on, 'You've never been much of a wife, and you're not fit to be a mother.'

Tearfully, Betty raised her head. 'If I'd known I was going to have to live with two cripples, I'd never have married you in the first place.'

Mrs Harrison's hand raised in horror and Kathleen gasped as Jack moved swiftly across the room. But their fears were unfounded. Dragging back the chenille curtain protecting the room from draughts, Jack flung open the door. 'Just get out,' he said, his voice devoid of emotion. 'To be honest, I don't care if I never see you again.'

As soon as Betty had sidled past him, Jack closed the door and drew the curtains back into place. A few minutes later, the front door slammed.

Jack broke the long silence. 'I'd better take Johnny home now, Mum,' he said.

'Oh, no. He's sound asleep in Janey's room, on Rose's — on the other bed. Leave him for tonight — and tomorrow, if you like.'

Jack looked too weary to argue. 'If you're sure you don't mind? Thanks, Mum, that will be a help. I really don't fancy leaving him with her while she's like this.' He looked at Jane. 'I'm sorry about your locket, Sis, but I will get it back, I promise.'

'Don't worry. It's not your fault.'

'That doesn't make it any easier.' Jack looked at the calendar on the wall. 'I had hoped that we could make a fresh start for the New Year, but now . . . ' He shrugged.

'Jack,' Jane said tentatively, 'I read an article recently about a group called Alcoholics Anonymous. They started in America, but now have come over here. Apparently they're very good with people like Betty.'

'What do they do? Put them in one of those clinics, or something? I couldn't afford

195

that, unless it was on the National Health.'

'No. I think they just talk, in groups. The main thing seems to be to get them to admit they have a problem in the first place.'

'I can't see Betty doing anything like that, can you?'

'I'm not sure, but it might be worth a try. Actually, I left the article lying around in the hope she might read it. Would you like me to talk to her about it?'

'It beats me why you want to help her in the first place after what she's done to you.' Jack's smile was wan. 'But give it a try if you think it'll do any good.'

'OK.' Jane squeezed his arm. 'But I'll be honest, I'm doing it for you and Johnny.'

Mr Harrison began to roll another cigarette. 'Do you think I ought to go up to the pub, make sure she gets home all right?'

'No — thanks just the same. I reckon she'll go over to her dad's afterwards. He lives right opposite the pub.'

Grandad looked up from his musings. 'Why didn't Mr Kennedy come to Johnny's birthday party, then?'

'He never does, Dad.' Mrs Harrison began plumping up cushions, putting the room straight as she usually did before bedtime. 'It's the anniversary of the night Mrs

Kennedy was killed in that bad raid — don't you remember? He's never been able to accept it — or get over it. And that's Betty's problem, as well.'

'Oh, yes, I remember now.' Grandad searched back into his long memory. 'That was the night when the whole of London was on fire, and Betty was screaming her head off behind the piano.'

Mr Harrison frowned. 'Are you sure she'll be all right, Jack? I know she's behaved badly, but she was in a bit of a state.'

Jack stood up. 'She's spent the night at her dad's before when we've had a row.'

Eyebrows raised, Jane and Kathleen glanced at each other. This was certainly news to Jane.

'She'll be all right,' Jack went on. 'Usually she creeps home some time the next day, a bit worse for wear, and promises not to get drunk again . . . until the next time.'

'Who looks after Johnny when she stays out all night?' Mrs Harrison asked.

'I do, Mum. If it's a weekend it's not a problem, but during the week it does mean I have to have time off work and the manager's not very happy about it.'

'Oh, Jack.' Mrs Harrison's voice was tearful. 'Why didn't you tell us?'

'I was too ashamed.' He shrugged. 'And

you've got enough problems without being lumbered with mine.'

'That's what mothers are for, you silly boy.' Mrs Harrison blew her nose. 'And if it happens again, you're to let me know so I can take care of Johnny. Promise?'

'Thanks, Mum. But I'm going to have a very serious talk with her tomorrow. It's bad enough when it's just us, but when it involves other people . . . I really can't take much more.' He went through the hall and took his overcoat from the hallstand. 'I'd better get back just in case she decides to come home and apologise, although I doubt it. Goodnight, Mum.' He kissed her cheek. 'And thanks for keeping Johnny here. I'll come back for him tomorrow, when I've sorted everything out with Betty.'

No one said very much as they cleared up and prepared for bed. It was almost midnight by the time Jane undressed and sat at her dressing table, creaming the make-up from her face and listening to the gentle snuffling and snoring from Johnny. The events of the evening had pushed the memories of Paris slightly into the background, but they had been so disturbing she felt it would be impossible to sleep, despite her tiredness. She had to decide how she would approach Betty about Alcoholics

Anonymous. If the truth were told, she didn't hold out much more hope than Jack, but at least she could try to make her sister-in-law see sense.

The loud rat-tat-tat of the door knocker made her jump, and she ran down the stairs just ahead of her father.

Her mother called down from the landing, 'Who can that be at this time of night?'

'Probably Betty, Mum. Go back to bed.'

'Don't be stupid, Janey. She wouldn't come back here.'

Mr Harrison put a hand on Jane's arm as she was about to open the front door. 'Leave it to me,' he quietly said. 'You don't know who it might be.'

It was a uniformed policeman. 'Sorry to disturb you, but I'm trying to find the address of Mr Jack Taylor. The landlord of the Three Bells didn't know his current address, but claims he used to live here.'

'That's right, officer. But he went home about an hour ago. What's the . . . ?'

Before he could say any more, Mrs Harrison pushed past Jane. 'Has something happened to Jack?' she cried. 'I'm his mother — tell me what's happened.'

'No, it's not Mr Taylor.' The policeman shifted his weight from foot to foot as he pondered. Then he went on, 'He'll probably want you to be with him, anyway.' He looked at their faces, as though assessing their reaction. 'It's his wife. I'm very sorry, but I'm afraid I have bad news.'

10

The coroner listened carefully as the bus driver stated that the deceased had stepped straight out in front of him. He'd braked hard, but it was too late. It had been such a terrible shock, he hadn't been able to return to work since that dreadful night.

While the coroner wrote his notes, Jane wondered what sort of inquest would be held in Paris, and who would give evidence. Paul's colleagues? They would be wary, because of their involvement with the illegal film. Would they mention that 'the deceased' had left the cafe on Christmas Day with his English girlfriend? Probably. Oh, God, what an awful expression to use for Paul — or Betty. She shuddered at the thought of two young people, who should have been in the prime of their lives, being referred to as 'the deceased'.

Now it was the turn of the publican to give evidence. He explained that on the night of Saturday, 30th December 1950, he'd had occasion to refuse to serve Mrs Taylor. Why? Because she ran out of money and had already run up a fair amount on the slate. No, he wouldn't go so far as to say she was very intoxicated when she left his premises, although she seemed to be slightly the worse for wear when she arrived. Funny thing was, she seemed to sober up after a while. Yes, she did drink regularly, and rather heavily. With an embarrassed glance at Jack, the publican continued. In fact, only that night she had said something about having a row with her husband and not wanting to go on like this any longer. He had thought she meant the drinking, because she'd once asked him whether he knew anything about Alcoholics Anonymous. Said she had read something about them in a magazine but didn't want to phone them in case they were cranky, like some of those American religious outfits. No, she never met anyone else so far as he knew. Usually, Mrs Taylor just sat in the Private Bar by herself, drinking until closing time. Her behaviour on the night in question? Well, she did seem a bit down in the dumps. Muttered something about wishing she was dead, but a lot of people say that if they're feeling sorry for themselves. It had never occurred to him for a moment that she might really be thinking of doing herself in, or he would have sent a message to Mr Taylor.

A bus passenger had noticed the young woman standing outside the public house, as if waiting for the bus to pass. As she stepped off the pavement, the poor girl was crying. Perhaps that was why she didn't see the bus, sir? the emotional passenger suggested.

Given the circumstances, the coroner could not be sure whether Mrs Taylor had intended to take her own life or was too distressed about the quarrel to notice the bus. An Open verdict was recorded and arrangements made for Betty to be laid to rest in the family grave beneath the memorial headstone to Mrs Kennedy. Mr Kennedy did not attend his daughter's inquest or funeral. He said he had 'flu and couldn't leave the house. Jane was concerned about her mother, as it was almost six years to the cold January day that she had wept by a graveside in the same cemetery, and buried her daughter.

When Laura arrived, Aunt Grace and Nobby Clark moved to stand with her and Jane was thankful. She really couldn't face her friend. As soon as the last respects were paid, Jane turned towards Rose's grave, then slipped away while Laura was deep in conversation with Aunt Grace.

Eventually, Jane was cornered at home, brewing yet another pot of tea.

Laura kissed Jane's cheek. 'You must be worn out, with one thing and another.'

Nervously rattling the teacups, Jane murmured, 'It has been rather hectic.'

'Where is Johnny?'

'Next door with the Arkwrights.'

'How is he taking it?'

'He doesn't seem to realise his mother isn't around. Just wants to paint all the time.'

After an uncomfortable silence, Laura said, 'I was sorry to miss his birthday party, but I had to go to France. Have you heard about Paul?'

This was the moment Jane had dreaded. She couldn't just say, 'Yes, please accept my condolences.' Nor could she deny all knowledge, not after her mother had mentioned Laura's letter.

Kathleen saved the day by putting her head around the door. 'Jack is taking it very badly, Jane. I'm wondering if you should go up and give your mam a hand? She's pretty upset as well — remembering, you know . . . '

Jane nodded. 'I'll put a drop of brandy in their tea. Excuse me, Laura.'

She knew Laura was watching as she carried the two cups upstairs. She also knew the situation would have to be faced sooner or later — but not today. Today she could only think about her brother. Consumed with guilt, as his stepfather had been when Rose died, Jack searched his soul.

'Why didn't I listen to her, instead of shouting?' he appealed to his mother. 'It can't have been easy for her, with me away all those years and Johnny like he is. But I never really tried to understand. All I could think about was myself, and what *I'd* been through.'

'Shush, son.' Mrs Harrison dried her own tears and patted his hand. 'Don't forget, you were very ill when you came back from that awful place.'

'That was four years ago, Mum. I could have made a bit more effort. There had to be a reason why she turned to drink.'

Jane drew the curtains against the January dusk. 'We all have different ways of dealing with our problems. Some turn to a bottle for comfort, some to religion — '

'And some can't take any more,' Jack interrupted. 'It's the Open verdict, the not knowing, that's getting to me. If only it had been Accidental Death, I think I could handle it better.'

'Ah, if only!' Sheila stood in the doorway. 'The saddest words in the English language, and the most useless.' Sheila's eyes reflected her own sadness as she gazed back at Jack.

Jane recalled a similar conversation with her brother, many years ago. 'Jack, do you remember when my schoolfriend was killed at the beginning of the war?' she asked. 'You told me to forget the *if onlys* and remember the friendship.'

'That's the trouble!' he cried. 'Betty and I were never friends, just lovers for forty-eight hours here and there.' He drew a deep breath. 'We were married for eleven years, and the only good times I can remember are when I was with my mates and flying gliders.'

Laura was waiting by the front door when Jane took the empty cups downstairs. 'I have to go, but I do need to see you, to talk about Paul. Can we lunch together soon?'

Rapidly, Jane thought, then nodded. 'Of course, but I can't say when until I check my desk diary. Belinda is off to America tomorrow, and I have to cover her appointments as well as my own. I'll ring you.'

'Please do. It is important.'

As she went back into the living room, Jane remembered that she had a message for Aunt Grace. 'Miss Dawson said if you have time while you're here, would you like to take tea with her. She's not moving until Easter, and expects you will be too busy with your visitors to see her for a while after that.'

Aunt Grace's smile was wry. 'How I wish that were true.'

'Surely the builders will be out by then?'

Uncle Nobby shook his head. 'They demanded half the money in advance, and now they've done a moonlight!'

'That's awful! Can't you prosecute?'

'If we could find them we might — along with half a dozen other hotels. We could also prosecute the surveyor who said the extension wouldn't affect the structure of the old building, but that will take time and money for legal fees. We can't even honour bookings to get the money for another builder because the place isn't safe. In fact, we've had to refund their deposits and that's the last of our capital gone.'

'Have you tried to get a bank loan?'

'There's not much collateral in a building that's subsiding and no chance of any income until it's fixed.' Uncle Nobby looked sad. 'When I was a kid in the orphanage, I used to dream about a home of my own. This was my dream home, even though I shared it with others. Now it's all going down the drain.'

After a moment's quiet calculation, Jane said, 'I have about two hundred pounds savings. Would that help?'

Tears filled Aunt Grace's eyes. 'It's good of you, dear, but we couldn't take your savings. You've been trying so hard to get a little place of your own.'

'But I won't do anything for another two years — Kathleen and I have decided to look for something we can share when she graduates.'

'But you never know when you might need it.'

'Nonsense. I earn good money and I've more than enough for my present needs. Regard it as a loan if you like, but do take it. Please — you know you'd do the same for me.'

Reluctantly, they agreed. Jane knew it wasn't enough, and racked her brain as to where she might be able to raise more money for them. She even contemplated asking Bernard. He had told her his business had flourished over the Christmas period, and she knew he would lend her whatever money he might have available. But it would put her under an obligation, and she didn't really feel it would be a wise move.

Given different circumstances, she might have approached Laura, but now she could only make excuses to avoid meeting her friend. The excuses were genuine enough. Each day there were conferences about the special supplement for the Festival of Britain, and evenings were filled with discussions and meetings with local amateur dramatic and musical groups. To his delight, Bernard had been asked to mastermind an impressive outdoor pageant, with the help of Eunice and Jane.

Despite that, Jane would have made an

effort to slip out for a quick lunch with Laura, if only she had the time to plan what she would say.

Eventually, Laura brought matters to a head by arriving in Reception. 'I apologise for interrupting your work, Jane, but I have an appointment at the French Embassy this afternoon and really do need to speak to you first.'

The evil moment could not be put off any longer.

'Let's go to a little Italian restaurant I know,' suggested Laura. 'I haven't booked, but it shouldn't be too difficult to get a table.'

The restaurant was packed, and they were lucky to find a table for two in a secluded alcove. As soon as they had ordered, Laura came straight to the point.

'Were you with Paul at Christmas?' she asked.

Taken aback, Jane could only nod.

'I thought so.' Laura fiddled with the menu, then went on. 'I spoke to some of his colleagues in Paris, and they said they had last seen him with an English girl. They couldn't remember her name, but the description fitted you.' She raised her eyes and quietly asked, 'Why didn't you tell me?'

Taking a sip of water, Jane tried to regain her composure. 'To begin with, I hadn't told my mother. You know she has preconceived ideas about that sort of thing.'

'Dirty weekends in Brighton?'

Jane nodded. 'So I thought it best not to tell anyone. I hated lying, but it was kinder for her to think I was there on business than with a man, even though it was all perfectly innocent.'

'Innocent? Hardly a word I would use to describe my brother, not after some of the things . . . ' Laura didn't speak again until the waiter had left the steaming bowls of pasta, then she went on, 'From what I hear, Paul may have been making pornographic films. Did you know?'

Miserably, Jane nodded.

'Oh, Jane!' Laura's voice filled with dismay. 'However did you get mixed up with all that?'

'I wasn't mixed up in it! In fact, I didn't know anything about it, until . . . '

Quietly, Laura said, 'I think you'd better tell me the truth, exactly as it happened.'

Let the dead keep some secrets, Jane thought, for the sake of the bereaved. The attempted rape was the only omission: she told how she'd been shocked at the film and left. Paul had followed her, lost his footing and fallen down the stairs.

Laura stared at Jane across the table, a puzzled frown on her face. 'So far I can understand what happened. What I do not understand is why you did not telephone me. I would have come on the next plane, Christmas Day or no Christmas Day!' Her voice was anguished.

Lowering her gaze, Jane felt the flush of shame rising to her face, but she did not answer.

Laura's voice was calmer, but hostile. 'After Paul had fallen down the stairs, what exactly did you do?'

This was worse than Jane had ever imagined, and Laura was persistent.

'I was afraid, and there didn't seem to be anything I could do — so I just ran.'

'Nothing you could do?' The couple sitting at the next table looked up sharply at Laura's raised voice. 'You could have telephoned the police!'

'My French is not that good. I didn't think they would believe me, not with those films . . . '

'So you ran around like a headless chicken, while my brother lay in that dreadful place. If a stranger had not telephoned for an ambulance, he could have been there for another two days!'

Jane could not allow her friend to think she had done nothing at all. 'I was the one who telephoned,' she whispered.

Taking a deep breath, Laura looked at the ceiling. 'I see,' she said. 'And then you calmly checked out of your hotel, came home and went back to work, as though nothing had happened.'

'It wasn't quite like that.'

'I think it was exactly like that. You did not even telephone the hospital to find out how badly Paul had been injured.'

Stunned, Jane stammered, 'B — but he was dead!'

'Dead?' Laura looked as shocked as Jane felt. 'If you had examined him more closely, you would have realised he was not dead. Badly injured, yes, but alive!'

'Oh, my God!' Jane closed her eyes. 'I really thought Paul was dead — he didn't move.'

'Of course he didn't move.' The contempt in Laura's voice was almost more than Jane could bear. 'With a leg broken in three places and severe concussion, he was incapable of moving. As a matter of fact, it was thirty-six hours before he regained consciousness.'

'Is — is he going to be all right?'

'He's out of danger, if that's what you mean. But it's a little late for you to be showing concern about his welfare. I really cannot believe that you left him there for dead. How could you, Jane?'

For a moment, Jane was tempted to tell the

whole story, rub away the layers of pancake that disguised her fading bruises, tear away the scarf that hid the marks on her neck, and let Laura Marshall know what her brother was really like when drunk. But whatever the excuse, Laura was right — Jane should have telephoned the police, and she should have contacted Paul's family.

Laura's voice was cold. 'At least Paul had the decency to keep your name out of it.' She pushed away her untouched plate. 'Now I must talk to the embassy officials.'

'What will you tell them?'

'I'll think of something.' Laura put some money on the table and snapped her handbag shut. 'My brother has been a fool, but I really do not want his career prospects ruined by wretched publicity about blue movies. Perhaps I can convince them that the suspect films were made by someone else, and he merely called in at the studio to pick up his camera.' She looked pointedly at Jane. 'You needn't worry — I shan't mention your involvement.'

Jane couldn't think of anything to say. 'Thank you' would have been too facetious.

'More lies. More deception,' Laura went on. 'I'm not even sure that I believe you did not know he was making those dreadful films.' Her anger was apparent. 'But I shall never be able to forget that you left Paul, and . . . ' Choking on her words, Laura stood up and pushed through the crowded restaurant, leaving the unspoken words ringing in Jane's head.

'I will never be able to forgive you!'

11

Ruefully, Jane surveyed the pile of letters on her desk. Only a few hours left to decide who should be invited to the studio for the 'before' photographs. As the winner of the *Festival of Britain Lady Fair*, the successful reader would be escorted around the South Bank Exhibition by a current heart-throb and auditioned by a top model agency. Rose would have revelled in the opportunity.

Belinda's secretary dumped another sack of mail on the floor. 'That'll wipe the smile off your face,' she grinned. 'When you cooked up the idea, I bet you never realised you'd have to deal with it all by yourself.'

Horrified, Jane protested, 'We can't read all those today! Where's Belinda?'

'Good question. She said she was going out to lunch, and didn't know when she'd be back. But fear not — I've seconded two of the typists from fashion to give our girls a hand. They can throw out those without photos for a start — and those in the wrong age group.'

'Trish, you're a gem. What would we do without you?'

'Have a nervous breakdown — or find

215

another brilliant secretary. Now, how many have you short-listed so far?'

By lunchtime, they had narrowed it down to twenty.

'This one might be possible — listen.' Trish read from a letter. ' 'I used to be slim and attractive, but as a busy vicar's wife it is difficult to find the time to eat properly and I tend to snack throughout the day. Needless to say, I have gained weight and after five children my breasts have sagged dreadfully. I can't afford to have my hair cut properly any more, and now I wear glasses I can't see to make up my eyes, which used to be my best feature. My husband doesn't seem to notice, but I hate looking at myself in the mirror. Please help me.' '

Jane munched a sandwich. 'How old?' she asked.

'Twenty-six.'

'And five children. She's a brood mare.'

'Looks it too — here's the photograph.'

The woman could have been any age from thirty to forty-five and certainly needed help. 'We couldn't shift all that weight in a month.' Jane studied the snapshot more closely. 'Has she written to us before?' she asked Trish.

'Don't recognise her. Why?'

'There's something vaguely familiar.'

Trish turned the letter over. 'No, I'd have

remembered the name — Isabel Montmercy-Smythe. Now there's a handle to be lumbered with.'

Isabel? Could it be? Jane peered even more closely at the photograph of the frumpish matron, forcing her memory back ten years. The Isabel Wallis she remembered had been the school glamour puss, with her sexy green eyes and sleek black hair cut into a vampish bob. At one time she had narrowly missed being expelled because of her wild behaviour. Rose and Isabel had been arch enemies, tossing cutting remarks backwards and forwards with expert swordsmanship, and Isabel had always referred to Jane as 'the ugly sister'. It would have been poetic justice to select her but, tempting as it was, Jane couldn't do it. The confrontation would really be too cruel.

'Send her our diet sheet, breast firming exercises, hair care — oh — let her have all the leaflets, and details of the hinged mirror for eye make-up,' she instructed. 'My money's on the Welsh farmer's wife. She's quite photogenic, has three children, four dogs and umpteen cats. Right now she's tired out with hand-rearing a clutch of newborn lambs and the poor soul has never been outside the valley. A deserving case if ever I saw one.' Jane handed the letter over to Trish.

'If Belinda's not back by four, Megan Jones will be on the cover of our May the second issue.'

Trish had just finished typing the letter of congratulation when Belinda returned and called Jane into her office. She looked flushed, and Jane suspected she'd had more than one glass of wine with her prolonged lunch. When she spoke her voice was breathless, but she came straight to the point. 'I'm going to work in America!'

'America?'

'Yep. Last month I met a publisher at a cocktail party. Today he flew over from New York to offer me a post as editor of a totally different type of magazine and he's flying back tonight! Can you believe that?'

'That's going some. Tell me about the magazine.'

'It's called *New Woman*. Jane, I can't tell you how stimulating it is. No knitting patterns, no cookery, no cosy fiction. A magazine full of intelligent features about intelligent women. Don't you think it sounds marvellous?'

'Well, America is always way ahead of the field.'

'There's an enormous untapped market of readers who want to know about women who've escaped from the kitchen sink. It'll

218

take a bit longer before British women are quite ready for such emancipation, but it will come one day. You wait and see.'

Jane knew she would miss Belinda, and wondered who would replace her. 'Have you told Kay?' she asked.

'Not yet, I wanted to speak to you first.'

'Oh?'

Belinda sat back from the desk and studied her assistant. 'If you want my job, I can put in a good word for you.'

Speechless, Jane could only stare. Of course she wanted the job — then doubts began to filter through her mind. 'I'm not twenty-three until April. Won't Kay think I'm too young?'

'Don't see why. She's often said you're more mature than most girls your age.'

'Maybe she will have someone else in mind?'

'I doubt if there's anyone else who could do the job better.' Belinda counted the plus points on her fingers. 'She was very pleased with the features you wrote while I was away and you get on well with the girls — and the advertisers. You have good creative ideas too; Kay knows the Festival Reader was your dream child . . . ' Belinda grabbed the desk calendar. 'Oh, my God! The deadline's today.'

'It's all right. I've picked out the winner,

with Trish's help, but there's time for you to look through the short-list and make your own choice.'

'No, I trust your judgement — and thanks for stepping into the breach.' Belinda took a cigarette from the box on her desk. 'If Kay agrees that you're the best person to be my successor — and there's no reason why she shouldn't — you will need an assistant. Anyone in mind?'

'Trish is an obvious choice. But she's such a good secretary, she will be difficult to replace.'

Thoughtfully, Belinda blew smoke rings towards the ceiling. 'She could be promoted to personal assistant and do both jobs,' she suggested.

'Nice idea, but too much work for one person.'

'Not if we take on a new junior and promote one of the typists to help Trish.'

★ ★ ★

By the time Jane had moved into Belinda's office, rehearsals for the local pageant to coincide with the Festival of Britain were well under way. The ambitious event was to take place in the old manor house, now council offices, and would present a dramatic historical extravaganza, opening with a Viking invasion sailing around the moat — an opportunity seized with gusto by the local boy scouts. Every amateur dramatic and musical group in the area agreed to take part, their leading ladies eager to play Queen Elizabeth I making her entrance on horse-back, riding side-saddle, and delivering the dramatic speech to her troops at Tilbury before sending them off to battle. As musical director, it was Jane's responsibility to audition soloists and choirs and select appropriate music for each episode, a painstaking and time-consuming task.

There were times when she longed to drop everything and escape to the peace and calm of Devonshire, but she could not get away until Megan Jones had been pampered by beauticians and hairdressers, handed over to the Fashion Editor, then posed for the 'after' photographs. Poring over the new and expensive colour transparencies left Jane with sore eyes and a headache, and she still had to write the final feature. Two things made it all worthwhile: the glow on Megan's face, and seeing her own photograph in the magazine for the first time as the new Beauty Editor.

It took a little while before Grandad could understand why the name underneath Jane's photograph was Helena Beaumont. Patiently,

Jane explained more than once that the beauty Editors were always called Helena Beaumont, whether their real names were Belinda Prescott or Jane Harrison. After digesting the information, Grandad nodded and thanked her once more for the celebration gift of a double-sized birdcage on a chrome stand, and talked about trying to breed some love birds again.

Jane wanted to buy her parents something special, but hadn't had time to shop around. Perhaps she would find something suitable in Torquay. Now the special beauty issue had been despatched to the printer, and the pageant music arranged, she could at last take a few days off.

* * *

After the long drive, Jane was ready for a tray of tea and chat with Aunt Grace. 'I shudder when I think how close you came to losing all this,' she said, looking around the comfortable sitting room. 'How long before you can have paying guests again?'

'Another couple of weeks. All the structural work has been done, and Nobby has started on the painting and decorating and Robert and Yvonne come over to help when they can. I told you she's given up nursing to work with Robert?'

Jane nodded, then commented, 'The builders have left the garden in a bit of a mess.'

'I know, but Miss Dawson insists she can create a rockery. She's here straight after breakfast every morning, works on the plans with Joe, then starts sorting through the rubble. Nobby has quite a job persuading her to go home in the evening.'

Jane spluttered into her teacup. 'You're joking!'

'Oh, no. She may look frail, but Augustine Dawson has hidden depths. The way she baled us out was nothing short of a miracle.'

'What happened exactly? It was a dreadful line when you telephoned.'

'Well, when we visited her in January, we told her about our problems. Of course, we never dreamed she could do anything to help.'

'So what did she do?'

'Telephoned an art expert, her banker, and her solicitor. Then she offered us a business deal.'

'Really?' Jane laughed. 'I can't imagine Miss Dawson making deals.'

'That's precisely what she did — offered an investment into the guest house, in return for a working partnership.'

'As your gardener?'

Aunt Grace smiled. 'That's just her new hobby — but she has taken over the bookings and accounts. There's plenty for me to do, and Peg has her hands full in the kitchen, so it's a great help, I can assure you.' Pouring another cup of tea, she went on, 'What's more, Miss Dawson has written to all our previous guests and placed advertisements in *Dalton's Weekly* and *The Lady*, with the result that we're fully booked until the end of October. Which reminds me — ' Aunt Grace took an envelope from the bureau. 'We agreed that yours would be the first loan repaid. Thank you very much, dear.'

'Are you sure?'

'Quite sure, thank you.' Aunt Grace smiled as two tiny bundles of black and white fur pushed open the door, golden eyes like saucers fixed upon Jane. 'You haven't met our latest residents, have you? Courtesy of the cat next door and a midnight assignation with an unknown gentleman prowler.'

'Oh, they are gorgeous!' Jane scooped up a kitten with each hand. 'What are they called?'

'The one with the black smudge on the nose is Winnie. She's mine, and Clementine actually belongs to Miss Dawson, but her sister won't allow any pets in the cottage, so they both live here. Hopefully they will become good mousers, but at the moment they are more intent on disrupting the gardening. Ah, that sounds like Miss Dawson back from the nursery. Let's go down and see what she's been up to.'

Miss Dawson was unloading a box of plants from the carrier of a rather ancient bicycle. 'Such a nice gentleman,' she enthused, after she had greeted Jane. 'I really do not know what I should do without his expert advice. These are called alpines and will grow quite happily in rock crevices.'

The old-fashioned coiled plaits of the twenties had been replaced with a cropped bob more reminiscent of the thirties, and Jane watched in amazement as her ex-colleague picked up a trowel with hands that showed evidence of her manual labour. 'Do talk to me while I work,' she suggested. 'I want to get these settled in before supper.'

They discussed Jane's new job, Johnny's paintings, the Festival of Britain — and Miss Dawson's new hairstyle.

'So much easier to look after with all this outdoor work,' she said, ramming a rather battered straw hat onto her head. 'And one must keep abreast of the times.'

Resisting a strong urge to laugh, Jane brought the subject back to Miss Dawson's business venture.

'Well, it made sense, my dear.' A plant was tenderly placed. 'And the bank had a healthy collateral in the painting, so they were not at risk.'

'But weren't you afraid you might lose your precious Turner?'

'Goodness me, no. I knew I would recover my investment eventually.'

Such faith, Jane thought. A gift of true friendship. 'What made you decide to take such an active part in the running of the place?' she asked.

Squatting back on her heels, Miss Dawson peered up at the blue sky. Frowning slightly, she said, 'As children, Adeline and I were always told what to do by Arabella, even though she was the youngest.' Her lips twitched slightly. 'Cook always called her Little Miss Bossy-boots. And, of course, as a headmistress she is used to giving orders.' Miss Dawson gently prevented Clementine from digging up a saxifrage. 'I admit I had certain reservations when I agreed to share her cottage, but now I have found a little niche of my own we live quite happily together.' She smiled up at Jane. 'It has given my life a purpose, as has my furry friend here.' She stroked the kitten until it became restless and tumbled out of her arms to seek more mischief.

Later that evening, Jane recalled the words. Ever since that ill-fated trip to Paris there had been a void in her life. As she unpinned her chignon Jane realised that, until Christmas Day, Paul had given her life meaning, albeit for a short while. He had been an exciting companion, knew how to thrill with a glance or a caress. Olaf was inexperienced, but his youthful kisses had brought about the transition from child to woman. Both had desired Jane and, to her surprise, she had enjoyed being desired.

As a child, Jane had been conditioned that her destiny was to be the old maid of the family and she was content to fit into the mould. Watching men lusting after Rose had successfully suppressed any budding feelings of sexuality on Jane's part until she met Olaf.

But Paul had reawakened more than romantic dreams. These thoughts and dreams were not so easily put to rest. For a while, she had thought she could never bear a man to touch her again, but Paul's dreadful behaviour must have been due to a reaction to the cognac — he had not shown any signs of violence before. Gradually, she had come to accept that the reaction was an illness, a disease.

Now, Jane wanted to be loved again, but with tenderness, not brutality. The role of virgin spinster no longer sat comfortably upon her shoulders. Most of her friends and colleagues were married, engaged, or had 'an arrangement', as Trish referred to her dalliance with a married man. Even Belinda was happily living in sin with her American publisher. So why was Jane Harrison so desperately lonely?

A solitary tear tricked down her cheek as she gazed at her reflection. Not a pretty reflection, like Rose's, but she had developed a certain style that was not unattractive. Perhaps it was her personality that lacked the magic something that attracted men. Rose had it; Isabel Wallis had it once; Laura still had it. But the 'it' was beyond definition, and without 'it', Jane Harrison didn't have a chance of attracting any healthy young male worth his salt. A brief vision of a tall young man with hair like thatch and an engaging smile intruded, but was promptly pushed into the background by thoughts of Bernard.

Bernard had a slight limp and he was not particularly young, but he was kind, generous, devoted — and honourable. Not unlike her father. Although not overly demonstrative, Fred Harrison had been affectionate towards his wife before Rose was killed, and they had seemed happy enough together.

Jane's thoughts wandered to her grandparents: she tried to imagine them making love. They had created quite a large brood, so something must have happened. But her imagination failed to turn the old folks into young lovers. Jack and Betty had not had a passionate marriage either, but they had stayed together, just like Mr and Mrs Green, the Arkwrights next door — Uncle Joe and Aunt Peggy.

Perhaps that was the norm for most people, with passion fading soon after the honeymoon, to be found only in the pages of romantic fiction. Was that why poor Betty had avidly devoured so many cheap magazines, searching for her own lost passion? The reality seemed to be that marriage was something people settled into afterwards and, in the long term, the best partner was a thoughtful, kind person. As Jane reached for the astringent lotion she wondered, for the first time, what it would be like to be married to Bernard.

★ ★ ★

Before she went home, Jane lunched with Kathleen in Exeter. Now she was twenty and had been at university for two years, the childlike quality had been replaced by a

229

maturity that came from being allowed to stretch her mental abilities to the utmost. She was contented and wise beyond her years and, as Jane had predicted, stunningly beautiful. As soon as they had ordered, she asked after Jack.

'He seems to have withdrawn into his shell again, like he did when he first came home.'

'Has he ever told anyone what really happened in the prison camp?'

Jane shook her head. 'And now he has this guilt thing about Betty, he just sits staring into the distance. None of us can get through to him.'

'Not even Sheila?'

'No, and it's breaking her heart, seeing him so tormented.' Jane shook her head briskly. 'Do you mind if we talk about something else? Tell me about university.'

'I love it all,' Kathleen told Jane. 'There is so much to learn, and I'm always wishing there were forty-eight hours in every day so I could learn even more!'

Jane threw her head back and laughed at the joy in her friend's face. Then she asked a mischievous question. 'And what about young men?'

Kathleen grinned. 'And why should I be telling the likes of you about young men? Sure, and it's you that should be telling me whether you have met Mr Right yet.'

Jane was thankful that Kathleen had not lost her soft Irish brogue. 'I asked first,' she insisted.

'Oh, well, that's all right then . . . ' Kathleen crumbled a piece of roll on her plate as she reflected. 'I've had a few dates, and mostly they're nice lads, but would you believe that some of them still think that girls should not be learning so much.'

'Really?'

'It's true. And one of the tutors actually told me that if I intended to be a wife and mother, I might as well not waste my time and his by wanting to be a solicitor.'

Jane pulled a face. 'Will they never learn that this is nineteen-fifty-one not eighteen-fifty-one?'

'It seems that we have a choice between love and a career, but we can't have both. Not yet, anyway. Maybe in some distant future men won't control the world and make all the rules.'

'We might even have a married woman with children running the country.'

'And pigs might fly.'

Both girls dissolved into fits of laughter. Then Kathleen asked, 'What about your own prospects, Jane? How high can you go in publishing?'

'I could become an editor, I suppose, like Kay.'

'And if the elusive Mr Right came along and asked you to give it up, would you?'

Truthfully Jane answered, 'Years ago, I told cousin Peter that I would never let any man dictate what I should do with my life. I haven't changed that opinion.' Dipping her fingers into the wine, she slowly circled the rim of her glass. 'But I'm a realist, Kathleen, and I don't believe in Mr Right any more than I believe in fairies.' A ringing tone filled the air as she continued to tune the glass. 'One day I might think about settling down with a nice Mr Average.' With a wry smile, Jane looked up at her friend. 'But I haven't quite made up my mind — not yet.'

12

At last Jane felt she had found the perfect gift. Not mink, like Laura's, that was way out of her price range, but it was almost identical to the coat her mother had admired in the same *haute couture* window near the harbour in Torquay — was it really ten years ago? When Rose was innocent and Nell Harrison had smiled; Jane fantasised about placing a good fur coat around her mother's shoulders.

The stylish box on the passenger seat was patted frequently on the journey home, as Jane anticipated a look of pleasure on her mother's face.

For a long moment, Mrs Harrison held the last layer of tissue in her hand as she gazed at the sable, her face expressionless. Then she dropped the tissue back into the box, murmuring, 'Thank you, although I don't know when I'm ever going to wear it.'

Even Grandad was astonished. 'Aren't you going to try it on, girl?' he asked.

'There's no need. I can see it's my size.' Mrs Harrison put the lid back on the box and turned to leave the room, but the sharpness of her husband's voice stopped her at the door.

'What on earth's the matter with you?' he demanded.

'Nothing.' She paused, but didn't meet his angry gaze. 'There doesn't seem much point trying on a fur coat at this time of year, that's all.'

'The point, Nell, is that Jane has gone to a lot of trouble to buy us all smashing presents, as well as having the telephone put in.'

'She only had it put in because she needed it for her new job.'

Grandad wagged a finger. 'Be fair, Nell. You used it to call the doctor when I was bad — and to order the coal.'

'We'll all use it, but Jane's paying the bill,' Fred Harrison pointed out. 'She could have bought a new car. Instead, I've got a greenhouse on order and you've got a fur coat that most women would give their eye teeth for — and you can't even be bothered to try it on. It's an insult to her!'

His wife coloured at the tone of his voice, but she still averted her eyes. 'I didn't mean to insult anyone, I'm sure.' Her voice was more petulant than contrite. 'And I expect Janey understands, even if you don't.'

'No!' Finding her voice through the

overwhelming disappointment, Jane contradicted her mother. 'I can't understand how any mother could deliberately hurt her daughter the way you do.'

'How dare you say I do it deliberately? Is it my fault if you're too sensitive?'

'I'd need the hide of an elephant not to be hurt, and I really don't see why I should pretend it doesn't matter.'

'If you don't like the way I talk, you might as well leave. You can afford to live anywhere you like, so there's nothing to stop you.'

The shocked silence lingered until Jane asked, 'Is that what you want? To be rid of me?'

Mrs Harrison's eyes flickered towards Jane and away again. 'I really don't care much, one way or the other, and I haven't got time to stand here talking all day.'

Trying to control her voice, Jane said, 'You always found time to talk to Rose.'

'She's right, Nell.' Grandad looked sternly at his daughter. 'You'd have tried the coat on quick enough if Rose had bought it.'

The flush drained from Mrs Harrison's face as she looked from one to another. Then she turned and left the room.

Nobody spoke for a minute or so until Grandad murmured, 'Sometimes I can't make Nell out.' He popped a Devon Cream

Toffee into his mouth. 'Do you think it's the Change?' he went on, his cheek bulging.

'No, Grandad,' Jane said. 'It's been going on far too long — as long as I can remember.' She looked earnestly at her father. 'I asked Gran once why Mum didn't love me, and she hinted that it had something to do with my birth. You must know about it, Dad.'

Mr Harrison shook his head. 'It was a long time ago, Jane. Leave it be.'

'I can't. Not any more. For years I've heard rumours and whispers, but no one has ever told me what really happened when Rose and I were born.' Her father remained silent, but Jane persisted. 'It obviously has some bearing on why Mum treated us so differently, and I've a right to know.'

For a long moment, Fred Harrison stared at Jane. Then he nodded, and reached for his little cigarette machine. 'Rose was born just after midnight — a tiny little thing, less than six pounds.' He was obviously reluctant to explain. 'Trouble was, when the midwife realised there was another baby, she thought it was the same size, but she was wrong.' Again Jane waited while her father lit his cigarette. 'You were much bigger, and the wrong way round. It was hours before the nurse sent for the doctor. They should have got Mum into hospital for a caesarian, but left it too late, so he had to use forceps.'

Grandad pulled a face as he chewed at his toffee. 'Nell was bad for a long time,' he mumbled. 'Just like Betty — only she didn't make such a song and dance about it.'

Fred Harrison nodded. 'We thought we were going to lose her, then she began to recover, but she wouldn't look at you. Gran and I made up your bottles.'

'What about Rose?' Jane asked. 'Who fed her?'

Her father looked uncomfortable. 'The nurse wanted to put Rose on a formula as well, but your mum insisted she could feed one herself, even though it left her so weak. I suppose that's why she was so close to Rose from the beginning.' He shook his head. 'I shouldn't have let it go on for so long, but I took the easy way out. I'm sorry, Jane.'

'It wasn't your fault, Dad.'

'I've always made allowances for her, but no more! What Nell said just now was unforgivable — and she's ruddy well going to take it back.'

'I've been thinking about getting a place of my own for some time. It may be the only solution.' Jane put a hand on her father's arm to still his protests. 'There's only one way to find out.'

Mrs Harrison was in the dining room,

standing by the sideboard with Rose's framed photograph in her hand. 'You were always jealous of her,' she accused.

'No, Mum. I loved Rose too much to be jealous. But I did envy her ability to get what she wanted without having to try very hard.'

'When she smiled, you just couldn't say no.' Mrs Harrison replaced the photograph. 'With her looks and talent, she would have been a film star if she'd lived.'

Jane knew her mother would never accept the truth that Rose had lost her dreams long before she lost her life.

Moving the vase of flowers closer to the photograph, Mrs Harrison continued to reminisce. 'As soon as they placed Rose in my arms I knew she was going to be the perfect daughter I'd always wanted.'

'But you only wanted one daughter, not two.'

'Yes.' Mrs Harrison's mind went back through the years. It was as though Jane wasn't in the room. 'Even when I was married to Jack's father I dreamed of a blue-eyed, golden-haired little girl. One I could dress in pretty clothes, send to dancing classes . . .'

'Instead of which, you had a son more interested in football than ballet.'

Still far away, Mrs Harrison said, 'When

they told me I had a daughter at last, I thought I'd gone to heaven.'

'But the second daughter sent you to hell.'

Mrs Harrison nodded.

'Why didn't you tell me about the problems, Mum? It would have helped me to understand why you resented me so much.'

'I couldn't talk about it — and I didn't want anyone else to talk about it. I just didn't want to be reminded of the hours of terrible pain — and I was badly torn inside. It was months before I could walk properly. All I wanted to do was nurse my beautiful Rose. You weren't a bit like her.'

'No, I was the plain one.'

'It wasn't just that.' Mrs Harrison sat down. 'I didn't know I was carrying twins. We didn't have anything ready, or much money.' She fidgeted with the table runner. 'Rose was a good baby, whereas you were grizzly. I was too ill to cope with you.'

Perhaps I wouldn't have been so grizzly if I'd been cuddled sometimes, Jane thought. But she waited for her mother to go on.

'When you were both growing up, Rose turned out exactly as I'd dreamed, but you — you were different. I couldn't make you look nice, no matter how I tried.' Mrs Harrison picked up a magazine lying on the table, and flicked the pages until she stopped at Jane's feature. 'Who'd have thought you would finish up as a Beauty Editor.'

'I hoped you would be proud of me. Dad was.'

'Well, he would. When you were naughty, he always stuck up for you.'

'I needed someone on my side.' Jane's voice was quiet.

For the first time, Nell Harrison looked straight into her daughter's eyes. Then she said, 'I know you shouldn't have favourites, but I suppose we all do it. Gran always had a soft spot for Len.'

'Favourites I can understand. What I've never been able to understand is your attitude to me since Rose was killed. As though you wished I was dead, too.'

Her mother's eyes dilated as she stared back. 'When Rose died, part of me died with her. But you didn't understand.'

'Of course I understood! Part of me died too. But I didn't hate you because Rose was dead.'

'I didn't hate you, I just couldn't . . . '

'Love me? Is that the word that sticks in your throat?' The silence was unbearable. 'You've never been able to love me from the time I was born, have you?'

Mrs Harrison shrugged. 'I can't help the way I feel.'

240

'But you can help the way you talk. You once told me you couldn't bear to look at me because I reminded you that Rose was gone. How could you be so cruel?'

'Cruel! You don't know the meaning of the word.' Mrs Harrison's voice was hard with anger. 'When you've lost a husband and a child, then you'll understand what cruel means.'

'Oh, I understand only too well.' Jane found it difficult to control her own anger. 'Your indifference is cruel; telling me to leave home is cruel; and the most cruel thing of all is that you don't care whether I leave or stay.' Jane desperately wanted her mother to deny the accusation, but she remained silent. 'I have to know, Mum. Do you want me to leave?'

Mrs Harrison stood up and fiddled with the vase of flowers on the table. 'You're of age,' she mumbled. 'It's up to you.'

Frustration raised Jane's voice. 'I'm not talking about me! It's you. What do you want?'

There was no indifference now in her mother's face as she swung round to face Jane. 'I'll tell you want I want.' Her voice was tearfully passionate. 'I want my Rose back! She was the only one who understood me. The only one who cared.'

'You're wrong, Nell.' Mr Harrison stood in the doorway, holding a tray of teacups. 'Jane was the caring daughter, not Rose.'

'Keep out of this Fred, It's nothing to do with you.'

Fred Harrison stood his ground. 'I should have spoken up years ago when I saw the way things were going. It was Jane who worked hard at school and helped around the house, while Rose did as little as possible. You never gave Jane one word of thanks, but Rose — well, anyone would have thought the sun shone out of her backside as far as you were concerned.'

'How dare you speak ill of the dead like that!' Mrs Harrison's face was contorted with rage.

'Because it happens to be true, but you won't face up to it. I loved Rose, but I watched her twist us all around her little finger — and she's still doing it.'

'That's a wicked thing to say, Fred! Wicked,' Mrs Harrison cried. 'Just like the wicked things you said to Rose the night she was . . . ' Tears replaced words.

Mr Harrison bit his lip and turned to Jane. 'Do you really have to see Bernard and Eunice tonight?' he asked.

'I should, there's so much to discuss. But I want to know where I stand first.' For a moment, the image of her mother quietly weeping, her face buried in her hands, cut through Jane's anger.

Her father nodded. 'Let's take the tea into the other room first. Perhaps we need a breathing space.'

Miserably, Jane followed him into the living room. She had hoped the discussion might clear the air, but it appeared to have gone around in a circle. Her mother did not seem to want her to stay or leave — she really did not care one way or the other. Although Jane had thought about leaving home, her plans had centred around sharing a flat with Kathleen, who still had another year to go before she graduated. Financially, it would be very difficult for Jane to leave home just now — most of her savings had been spent on the family gifts.

Grandad broke the long silence. 'Well, Janey. Are you leaving or staying?'

'I really don't know what to do for the best, Grandad.'

Dunking his biscuit, he said, 'Seems a bit daft, moving out when you've a perfectly good home here.' Noisily he sipped his tea. 'But Nell was a bit rude about the coat. Reckon she owes you an apology.'

'Oh, you do, do you?' Nell Harrison came into the room and took her cup with an unsteady hand. 'And what about the things Janey said in the other room? Don't I deserve an apology from her? And Fred. If he hadn't lost his temper, Rose wouldn't have gone out in a huff and been . . . ' She reached into her apron pocket for a handkerchief.

Noticing the anguished expression on her father's face, Jane quickly said, 'Dad wasn't to blame. Rose was determined to go out and it wouldn't have made any difference what anyone said.'

Mrs Harrison seemed determined to fuel her husband's guilt. 'Rose only wanted to borrow some money,' she sniffed. 'That was no reason for your father to call her those dreadful names. He made out she was some kind of slut, but she was a good girl. As for you — ' Mrs Harrison switched the attack to Jane. 'You don't even take a bunch of flowers to her grave. That's how much you care for your sister's memory. I'm the one who scrubs the headstone and puts fresh flowers in the vase every week — never miss going. Not like you and your precious father!'

Jane knew it was useless trying to explain that she could not feel any closeness to Rose in a cemetery, watching over a grave concealing a coffin that had once held her sister's finger — all that had remained to bury. She felt closer to Rose in the garden, or looking through an old photo album in their bedroom, or just sitting quietly with her memories.

Barely pausing to draw breath, her mother continued, 'And you weren't there the night your father drove your sister out of the house, Janey, so what do you know about it?'

Grandad took another biscuit. 'I remember the row. That was the night my poor Rosie got in a state when she found someone had taken her little nest egg.'

Nell Harrison's voice was sharp. 'Nobody took Gran's money, Dad. It was in her handkerchief sachet all the time.'

'Well, something funny was going on. Rosie always kept her money in the vase, not the hankie sachet.'

Wearily, Fred Harrison stirred his tea. 'We know that, Dad, but she was bothered by the rockets and sometimes people get a bit confused when they're getting on a bit.'

A rare flash of anger crossed Grandad's face, as he retorted, 'Not my Rosie! She had all her marbles, right to the end.'

'I didn't mean — '

'Anyway,' Grandad went on as though he hadn't been interrupted. 'I saw her counting it out only the night before. And I saw her put it back in the vase. More than eleven pounds there was. So somebody must have taken it — and somebody must have put it back in the wrong place, deliberately, to make us think Gran was going ga-ga. Which she wasn't!' His glare defied contradiction.

Mr Harrison tried to reason with his father-in-law. 'But who could have taken it, Dad? Betty was in Torquay and none of us here would touch it.'

'Rosie was convinced it was young Margaret Arkwright from next door. I always liked the girl, but — who else could it have been?'

Tight-lipped, Mrs Harrison snapped, 'What does it matter? Gran got it back, didn't she?'

'I'd still like to know what was going on.'

'Oh, for goodness' sake, Dad, shut up! I've been listening to Fred and Jane telling the most awful lies about Rose, and I couldn't care less if it was Margaret Ackroyd or the King of England who touched the stupid money!'

Something in Jane snapped. For half an hour she had listened to her mother extolling the virtues of Rose and now the truth had to be told — or some of it.

'It was Rose who took the money,' she said, 'and I put it back. Margaret had nothing to do with it.'

All heads turned towards Jane, mouths

open. Her father was the first to speak. 'Are you sure?' he asked.

Before Jane could answer, her mother hurled the remains of her tea straight into Jane's face, then rained a barrage of painful blows with her fists, knocking Jane's head backwards and forwards, all the time screaming, 'Stop it! I won't listen to such lies! My Rose would never do such a thing!'

It took some little while before Mr Harrison was able to pull his wife away. Trying to catch her breath, Jane cried, 'It's the truth, and I can't let you all go on believing it was Margaret.'

Grandad looked perplexed. 'But why did Rose need the money?' he asked.

Jane knew the real reason, but the truth would be too much for the family to bear. 'Rose told me she'd seen a coat she liked but it was expensive,' she lied. 'Also, she wanted to go to the pantomime and she couldn't borrow the money from Mum or Dad so she — borrowed Gran's money. I expect she intended — '

'Get out of my house!' Nell Harrison's shaking finger pointed to the door. 'You asked me if I wanted you to leave. Well, I do. Pack your things and go tonight!'

Fred Harrison looked from his daughter to his wife. 'You can't ask her to leave tonight,' he protested. 'Not like this.'

'After all the terrible things she's said about Rose, I couldn't bear to have her under my roof another night. She's evil!' Nell Harrison was quite hysterical as she began another tirade against Jane. 'I want you out tonight — and don't ever come through that door again unless you own up that you're a rotten little liar.'

'It's all right, I'm going. It's probably for the best, anyway.' Jane hoped her legs would support her to the top of the stairs. She had almost finished packing her overnight bag when her father knocked on the bedroom door. He looked distraught.

'What can I say, Janey? She won't listen to reason.'

'I know.' Jane closed the lid of the case. 'I'll come back for my other things as soon as I've found somewhere to live.'

Mr Harrison looked too exhausted to think properly as he asked, 'Where will you go, love?'

For the first time, the reality struck home. Where would she go? Even if she had to book into a hotel for a few nights, she would need something more permanent in the long term. 'Don't worry.' Jane tried to reassure her father with a hug. 'I'll find something — I'll telephone you.' She hurried down the stairs, thankful the living room door was closed, although the silence was almost tangible.

Not until she had reached the lock-up garage and was sitting behind the wheel of her car did Jane allow herself the indulgence of tears.

13

Jane wasn't sure exactly how long she sat in the garage, weeping, but when she finally glanced at her watch she realised that if she didn't do something soon, she would probably have to sleep in the car! The only place she knew that provided bed and breakfast would be full with contractors working at local factories, and hotels in London were too expensive. She would have to drive further out into Essex. Bernard had taken her to one or two that had restaurants . . . oh, heavens! Bernard! Jane had promised to talk to Bernard and Eunice tonight about the choral arrangements for the pageant. If she didn't turn up, he would probably drive round to her home, to see if everything was all right. But she really couldn't face him, not with such tear-stained eyes. She would phone him — there was a telephone box near the station.

It was difficult to keep the emotion from her voice as she tried to explain briefly that she would have to postpone their meeting until the following night — and could Bernard remember the name of the hotel just outside Brentwood where they had that nice meal?

For a moment there was silence, then Bernard quietly asked, 'What's wrong, Jane?'

'Nothing,' she lied. 'I just need the name of that hotel, that's all.'

'That's not all — I can tell from the sound of your voice. Have you quarrelled with your mother?'

She gasped at his perceptiveness. 'Why — what makes you say that?' Her voice faltered.

'Because, dear Jane, I have seen it coming for a long time. In fact, I'm surprised it hasn't happened sooner.'

Jane couldn't answer, the tears had begun to flow again.

'And you are not going to stay in a hotel all by yourself,' Bernard said. 'Where are you now?'

'Near the station,' she sniffed.

'Then you are to drive straight here. You can sleep in the spare room.'

Jane made a token protestation. 'Eunice might not like the idea of an unexpected guest.'

'Leave Eunice to me. We'll have the bed made up by the time you get here. And, Jane . . .'

Her voice was a whisper. 'Yes?'

251

'You don't have to tell me about the quarrel — unless you want to.'

Bernard really is a kind, thoughtful man, Jane thought. And she was too weary to argue any more.

★ ★ ★

After the opening by King George VI, the public flocked in their thousands to see the vast exhibition built on a bomb site near Waterloo Station. They 'oohed' and 'aahed' at the Skylon and danced in the park in the evenings, regardless of the rain, but raised their eyebrows when asked to pay ninepence for a cup of coffee. Megan Jones trembled with excitement when introduced to film actor Anthony Steel, who said she was even prettier than her cover photograph. When Jane finally escorted the ecstatic young woman to her carriage at Paddington Station, she was certain that Megan would float all the way home to the valley.

The next main event would be the opening of the Battersea Pleasure Gardens at the end of May. Jack had promised he would take Johnny, and Fred Harrison took advantage of the trip to meet his daughter.

'Hope it's a bit warmer than this when you have your pageant,' he commented as they waved to Johnny, tucked safely between Jack and Sheila on the Big Wheel.

'So do I, Dad, but that's the risk you take with English summers.'

'How's it going?'

'Fine, thanks.' Jane knew her father wanted to discuss more important things than the weather, but had to wait until they had queued at the refreshment kiosk and found an empty table. Even then, it took some throat-clearing and tea-sipping before Fred Harrison voiced his worries.

'This arrangement you have with Bernard and Eunice — is it likely to go on much longer?'

'Bernard has said I can stay for as long as I wish.'

'What about his sister?'

'Eunice agreed and it is his house, so I don't think it's a problem.'

'Couldn't you have shared with someone else? Someone from work?'

'They either have tiny bedsits, or live with their parents.'

'Sheila has her own flat.'

'I would have liked that, Dad, but she only has one bedroom and I really didn't fancy sleeping on her little settee.'

Mr Harrison nodded, but his expression was no happier. 'It's just that . . . '

'Just what?'

'Well — ' His voice sounded as uncomfortable as his words. 'Do you think you are being fair to Bernard?'

For a moment, Jane could not answer as she tried to follow her father's drift.

'He's very fond of you,' Mr Harrison went on, 'and he might see this in a different light.'

'I'm only lodging there for a few weeks while I look for a place of my own. What could he possibly read into that?'

'He might — ' Mr Harrison cleared his throat again. 'He might think you're leading him on.'

'Dad! Bernard knows very well where we stand, and I insisted on paying rent. We're only sharing a house, not a bed!' The expression on her father's face brought a quick apology. 'I'm sorry, that wasn't meant the way it sounded.' Jane tried to be more reassuring. 'Bernard understands it is only a temporary measure.'

'Are you sure?' Mr Harrison looked searchingly into her face.

'Of course. What's really bothering you about it?'

'Oh, Janey. You may be educated and have secretaries and so on, but you're still a child in many ways.' Mr Harrison took out his cigarette case, half filled with ready-mades

— his wife thought it common to roll cigarettes in public. 'Bernard wants to believe you are in love with him,' he went on, 'so he will clutch at any straw — and the fact that you have agreed to share his home may well be all the proof he needs.'

Now it was Jane's turn to look troubled. It was true that Bernard had been more attentive since she had moved in, but she had thought it just part of his sympathetic nature. Or perhaps she had fooled herself into thinking that was the reason?

Slowly, she answered her father. 'I hadn't realised it might . . . ' She drew a deep breath. 'Bernard is a very nice, caring man, and he has asked me to marry him, several times. Would it worry you very much if I said yes?'

At the next table, two young lovers held hands under the table, smiling into each other's eyes. Mr Harrison nodded in their direction as he softly said, 'That's what it should be like for a girl of twenty-three, Jane. Not settling down with a man approaching middle age, a divorced man at that.'

'He's not forty yet, and surely age doesn't matter if people really love each other?'

'Ah! That's the point, dear. Does Bernard really love you or is he just searching for true love? Even more important, do you really love him or are you just looking for security?'

Unable to answer truthfully, Jane watched the young couple, envying their mutual adoration. 'Bernard would be a very good husband.' She evaded a direct answer. 'And I'm sure I could make him happy.'

'I'm sure you would, but could you keep him happy? No — don't interrupt. Supposing you marry Bernard, then one day you fall deeply in love with someone of your own age?'

'Oh, come on, Dad. You know me. Once a vow is made, it's made for life.'

'It isn't always that simple. Delia didn't intend to hurt Bernard, but she couldn't pass up the chance of happiness with another man. You may not be able to, either, and even if you did, what sort of life would you have, staying with a man out of duty?'

'Listen, Dad. I know the risk and, believe me, I would never ever hurt Bernard after all he went through in that prison camp and then coming home to find Delia wanted a divorce. I would put him first, no matter what happened.' She covered her father's hand with her own and forced a smile. 'Anyway, I haven't come to a decision yet.'

As Johnny limped towards them, Fred Harrison stood up. 'Why don't you come home, Janey?' he pleaded. 'I'm sure Mum would forgive and forget if you just say you made a mistake about Rose.'

'But I didn't make a mistake, Dad, and I won't lie about it. I'm sorry.'

★ ★ ★

The last night of the pageant was fine and dry, and they played to a capacity crowd sprawled on lawns the other side of the moat. A few minor hitches — the scouts sinking one of the Viking longboats and a wheel coming off the stage coach — seemed to add to the enjoyment of the audience. Once she had conducted the massed choirs at the end of the evening, Jane had only to play the recording of Elgar's *Pomp and Circumstance* during the firework display which brought the week-long pageant to a close.

The joint casts presented Bernard with an engraved silver tankard, Eunice with a hand-carved figure of a ballerina, and Jane with a book on English composers. Bernard's speech was amusing and beautifully phrased, concluding with two gifts: a bouquet of mixed flowers and a kiss on the cheek for Eunice; a dozen red roses for Jane, bestowed with an affectionate hug and kiss on the lips. After she had made a brief speech of thanks, Jane pushed her way through the crowd of artistes and their friends and relatives. She was pleased her father had come with Jack and surprised to see Uncle Len.

'Wouldn't have missed it. Well done, all of you,' he said. Then lowered his voice, 'I was sorry to hear you've left home, although I can't say I'm really surprised.'

'Oh?' Jane waited for him to explain.

'Perhaps I shouldn't take sides — Nell is my sister, and she's had more than her share of rotten luck — but she's never really appreciated you, Janey.' He slipped his arm around her shoulders. 'I don't blame you for walking out, but I'm sure Nell will be glad to have you back when things have cooled down a bit.'

'I didn't walk out — I was thrown out. And Mum made it quite clear she didn't want me back, ever.'

'Oh, dear! I didn't realise.' Uncle Len's expression was sad. 'So what are your plans?'

'I've looked at a few places in town, but they charge the earth for a poky bedsit with hardly any furniture, and there's key money on top.'

He nodded thoughtfully, then said, 'I reckon Laura would let you have a couple of her rooms now that both the boys are gone. She'd probably be glad of your company.'

If only that were possible, Jane thought.

Laura was the one person she would dearly love to talk to, but they had been avoiding each other for the past six months.

'Have you seen Laura lately?' she asked.

'No.' Uncle Len looked into the distance. 'Nell told me she went to tea the other day and Desmond has been called up for his national service — it'll do him good.' He looked back at Jane. 'Why don't you ring her when she gets back from Naples? You never know your luck.'

'Naples? Is she visiting her mother's family?'

'From what I hear, it's something to do with that scallywag young brother of hers. Got himself into a spot of bother with the police.'

At the mention of Paul, Jane's heart flipped a beat and she turned away, wondering what the wretch had done this time — more blue movies, Italian style?

'Anyway,' Uncle Len was still speaking. 'I expect Laura will tell you all about it when she gets back.' He shook his head. 'You'd never think he was their brother, would you? Robert is so level headed, and no one has a stronger sense of duty than . . . ' His voice trailed off.

At that moment, a whirlwind of flying black hair and long college scarf hurtled across the grass and into Jane's arms. 'The train was so late, I came straight here, and there were so many people I couldn't see your folks, and I had to wait over there and all!' Kathleen was quite out of breath. 'And wasn't it the grandest show you've ever seen?' She turned to Uncle Len. 'Aren't you the proudest uncle ever? That singing at the end was quite glorious!'

'I couldn't have put it better myself.' Grinning, Uncle Len kissed his ward, then held her at arm's length. 'And you are still the prettiest colleen I've ever seen.'

'Oh, away with you. You're making me blush.' Kathleen linked arms with both of them. 'I can't tell you how good it is to be home again.' Her face saddened a little as she turned to Jane. 'Your mam's not here, so I guess you're still at Bernard's house?'

Jane nodded.

'I shall miss our wee chats at bedtime, Jane.' Kathleen frowned, then flashed her beautiful smile. 'Never mind, I've got until October with nothing to do except enjoy myself with my dearest friends. And that includes my guardian, of course.'

'Good.' Uncle Len smiled across at Jane. 'We can both do with cheering up, love, can't we? And I reckon Kathleen is just what the doctor ordered.'

260

Kathleen was the best tonic Jane could have wished for. They made plans to look for a small flat next summer, after Kathleen's finals. Already she had been provisionally offered a job with a firm of solicitors in the city. Her 1951 exam results were first class, so her future looked promising. Although she did not complain, Kathleen must have found the atmosphere with the Harrisons somewhat strained, and Jane felt it wise to take heed of her father's advice and not spend quite so much time with Bernard while her mind was in such a quandary. So the girls spent most weekends together, joining the multitudes of tourists exploring London during the daytime, on to the latest film or show during the evening.

On the rare days when the temperatures were a degree or two warmer, they packed a picnic and drove out to the countryside or down to the coast, giggling like schoolgirls as their tensions eased. It was Jane's idea to spend the last week of Kathleen's vacation in Torquay. Because the guest house was full and Miss Dawson was visiting her older sister in Scotland there was little opportunity for a heart-to-heart chat between aunt and niece until the last day, when Jane was packing.

As Jane explained the dilemma about Bernard, Aunt Grace neatly folded Jane's dresses in layers of tissue, a thoughtful expression on her face. Finally she said, 'I usually say 'follow your heart', but you do not seem to know where your heart is leading.' She handed Jane another garment. 'And no one else can tell you.'

'I know, and that's the problem — can you do the striped cotton one next, please?'

Aunt Grace slipped the dress from the hanger. 'There is only one piece of advice I can give you, dear.'

'Anything! I've tried writing everything down in two columns, and the pros and cons are equal. So now I'm clutching at straws.'

Smiling, Aunt Grace said, 'It may sound a strange anomaly, but if I am in doubt about buying anything — say a frock like this — I have a little saying that helps.' She carefully straightened a pleat before she continued, 'When in doubt — don't. I call it my personal family motto.'

'Oh.' Jane was disappointed. 'How does that help?'

'If you think about it, it makes sense. When something is absolutely right, there are no doubts.' Aunt Grace looked around the bedroom. 'I knew it was right for me to take on this venture with Nobby, just as I knew it would be wrong for us to marry.' Her face clouded a little as she said, 'Edgar was the only man for me, and after he was killed I knew I could never truly love another man.' The tissue rustled as she folded the sleeves. 'That does not mean you will not learn to love Bernard but, until you know for certain that you truly love him, it may be wiser to do nothing.'

Aunt Grace was probably right, Jane thought, but was it fair to Bernard?

As they locked the suitcase, Aunt Grace said, 'And don't forget, if it all becomes too much, my offer is still good. You are welcome to live here — if you can put up with these monsters.' Winnie and Clementine, quite grown but still playful, chased each other around the empty wardrobe.

Reaching across the suitcase, Jane squeezed her aunt's hand. The offer was attractive: a congenial atmosphere; Aunt Peggy's cooking; the friendship of Miss Dawson; two lively cats; and Jane had always loved Babbacombe.

After she had dropped off Kathleen at her lodgings in Exeter, Jane only had her confused thoughts for company on the long drive back to London. With Kathleen in Devonshire, she had no excuse to avoid Bernard — but did she really want to avoid him? He was intelligent, quietly witty and very romantic. His kisses were not youthfully sweet like Olaf's, nor breathtaking like Paul's, but she did not find them unpleasant and it was refreshing to be courted with such old-fashioned graciousness. Really, she could not imagine anyone else she would be prepared to partner for the rest of her life, and they had a solid basis of friendship which would outlast all the romance and passion.

As she drove through the heart of London, Jane realised that there was no one else she could turn to for advice. Sheila had her own problems — Jack seemed reluctant to make another commitment. The only other person who might have listened was Laura.

Mulling over her own feelings and Aunt Grace's words, Jane was no nearer a decision when she parked Little Mo outside Bernard's house. The only thing she was certain of was that she wanted to stay in London. Right now her job was the most satisfying part of her life.

* * *

As Jane sifted through the pile of post and messages that had accumulated during her week away from the office, Trish put her head around the door.

'Only the top two are really urgent — coffee?'

'Please. Trish, do you know why Kay wants to take me to lunch? Are there problems?'

'Nope.' Trish grinned. 'But you're going to have to wait and see.'

'Why do I put up with you?' Jane pulled a face at her assistant, then stared at the second message. Laura wanted to see her as soon as possible.

When Trish brought in the coffee, Jane questioned her about the message. 'When did Mrs Marshall telephone?'

'Last Tuesday. She said it was important.'

'Did she give you any clue as to why she wants to see me?'

'Not really.' Trish turned back a few pages of her shorthand notebook. 'I suggested a lunch appointment, but she said that wouldn't be private enough, and she would be grateful if you could go to Westcliff one evening after work. When I told her you would probably work late most of this week and it might be Saturday, she seemed disappointed.'

Jane was too curious to wait until Saturday, but her conversation with her editor over lunch made it impossible for her to get away from the office on time until Wednesday.

Laura looked solemn as she opened her

265

front door. Feeling awkward, Jane did not know what to say, or whether to politely offer her hand. The older woman took the initiative.

'Thank you for coming,' she said and stood back, still holding the door.

It was many months since Jane had sat in the comfortable lounge. 'I'm sorry I couldn't get away sooner.' Jane knew her voice sounded high-pitched. 'Did Trish explain?'

'She said you were busy with a new project, but she didn't say what it was.' Laura's voice was just as strained.

'Well, actually, they've asked me to write a book.'

This is ridiculous, Jane thought. I've been asked to come here, obviously to discuss something in particular, and we are making small talk.

'Oh, what sort of book?'

Perhaps Laura needed a warming-up conversation before she came to the point?

'I have to interview personalities and compile their beauty secrets into a book.'

'Sounds interesting — film stars?'

'Yes. And debutantes.'

Laura nodded, her mind obviously on something else. She stood up. 'May I offer you coffee, or a drink?' She seemed anxious to have something to do.

'Coffee would be fine, thank you.'

While Laura was in the kitchen, Jane wandered over to the window and admired the display of chrysanthemums in the garden, remembering how Uncle Len had once pretended a fondness for gardening as an excuse to visit. It was eleven years since Laura Marshall had been widowed but she was still alone in this big house, while Uncle Len remained in his lonely room at the Seaman's Hostel. Jane's mind went back to the conversation with her uncle after the pageant. Had he spoken to Laura about her spare rooms, unaware of the rift between the two women? Was that the reason behind the summons? It would explain the reluctance to get to the point.

Laura interrupted Jane's reverie by returning with the tray. After she had poured their coffee she began. 'This is incredibly difficult, but I have to ask . . . ' Laura put down her coffee cup and looked directly at Jane. 'Last Christmas — did my brother attack you?'

The cup rattled in her saucer as Jane stared back at Laura. This was not what she had expected, and she hedged. 'What makes you think that?'

Laura took the cup from Jane's shaking hand. 'This, for one thing; your expression for another, and certain things I heard in Italy.'

267

'What sort of things?'

A frown crossed Laura's face as she answered. 'One of the Italian film extras accused Paul of attempted rape. She said he became quite violent when she resisted.'

'Oh, no!'

'At first I thought it was a confidence trick because Paul admitted he had drunk rather a lot of cognac and remembered little of the incident.' Laura took a cigarette from a box on the mantelpiece. 'He was in a police cell when I arrived. The conditions were not good and he was in quite a distressed state, but something he said made me wonder.' Jane remained silent while Laura lit her cigarette, then went on, 'At one point he became rather emotional and said he was sorry if he had hurt the girl. Then, out of the blue, he asked if you were all right — and I wondered why he should ask that?'

No words came to Jane, as Laura searched her eyes for the truth. Finally, as the first tear escaped, Laura sighed a deep sigh and whispered, 'So it is true. Oh, my dear, why didn't you tell me?'

'How could I? Would you have believed that your brother could do such a thing?'

Laura shook her head. 'I didn't want to believe it, but now I have to. Can you bear to tell me what happened?'

Retelling the sordid tale unleashed such a flood of tears that Laura gathered the girl into her arms and rocked her like a child until the sobs died away. 'I am so ashamed — for both of us,' she murmured, her own eyes moist. 'And for once in my life, I don't know what to do.'

'I think Paul needs help.' Jane blew her nose. 'Medical help. One of his colleagues warned me not to allow him to drink brandy.'

Thoughtfully, Laura poured two more cups of coffee. 'You could be right,' she said. 'His Italian lawyer pleaded medical evidence, but it was too technical for me to understand.'

'Was there a trial?'

'Thankfully, no. We made the girl a settlement out of court.'

'Where is Paul now?' Jane hoped he would not return to England.

'In Persia.' Laura smiled wryly. 'I thought a spell in a country where alcohol is forbidden would do him good. However — ' She frowned. 'It might be wiser to look for a specialist who can help him. I believe there are clinics in America.'

'Do you think he would agree to such treatment?'

'He doesn't have any choice.' Laura's voice was grim. 'After what he did to you and that girl, I shall threaten to break his other leg if he doesn't do exactly as I say. When I think of the dreadful things I said to you — '

'It's over.' Jane touched Laura's arm. 'And I can't tell you how relieved I am. I really missed your friendship.'

'So did I.' After they had hugged, Laura looked at the clock. 'Have you eaten?' she asked.

'No, I came straight from work.'

'Neither have I, and I'm starving. Come and talk to me in the kitchen while I rustle up something.'

Over a glass of Italian red wine and a spaghetti dish with a delicious sauce of bacon, tomatoes and garlic, they caught up on the news about their respective families. Jane mentioned the quarrel with her mother and subsequent events only briefly — there would be plenty of opportunity for intimate chats about Bernard later. For now she was content to enjoy this evening of restored friendship — and to fit one or two arrows into Cupid's bow, just to test the reaction.

'Uncle Len came to the last night of the pageant,' she said casually, watching Laura's face.

There was the slightest hesitation before Laura answered. 'That was nice. How is he?'

'Sad — and lonely. I'm not the only one who misses you!'

The dark eyes widened and a hint of colour touched Laura's cheeks. 'Nonsense!' she protested. 'Len has a very full life running the hostel, and he must have many other activities.'

'Oh, yes. He reads a lot, sometimes he goes to the cinema with a colleague, and he visits Mum from time to time. Does that sound like a full life to you?'

Laura arched her eyebrows. 'What are you trying to say?'

'You can work it out for yourself, Laura. It only needs a telephone call.' Dramatically, Jane looked at her watch. 'Gosh! Is that the time? I must be going!'

'But I wanted to talk to you about your mother — '

'Sorry, Laura. Must dash, or Eunice will be wondering what has happened to me.' A quick kiss on Laura's cheek and Jane was running down the path. As she put the car into gear, Laura waved from the window. Her expression was quite bemused.

The book was so time consuming that several weeks passed before Jane was able to see Laura again. This time the invitation was for Sunday lunch, but the table in Laura's dining room had four place settings. It was good to see Auntie Bea looking remarkably well in spite of her advancing years. The fourth guest was a complete surprise.

'Uncle Len!' Jane cried. 'I didn't expect to see you.'

'Obviously not.' He looked like the proverbial Cheshire cat. 'Any more than I expected to receive a phone call from Laura after all this time — but you know all about that, don't you?'

'Me?' Jane's face was a picture of innocence. 'How could you think such a thing?'

He kissed her forehead. 'Whatever you did or said, I'm glad. And we have some news for you.'

It wasn't quite what Jane expected.

'We've bought a pub.' Uncle Len's grin stretched from ear to ear.

'A pub! You and Laura?' Jane could not quite picture Laura pulling pints.

'Why not? All sailors finish up with a pub — or a garden,' he teased. 'But our pub will be different.'

'In what way?'

'Ours will provide proper food, not just crisps or a cheese roll. It was Laura's idea to look for a pub that had the potential to add on a restaurant, and we've found the perfect place, haven't we, Laura?'

'That's right, an old inn near Upminster Common.'

'The Coach and Horses?'

Laura nodded. 'The location is ideal, on the road to Southend, and it has loads of character.' She smiled. 'I've often thought about running a restaurant, but couldn't do it on my own.'

When Uncle Len reached across and took Laura's hand, Jane knew this was the news she had been expecting. The smile hadn't once left his face, and Auntie Bea beamed with pleasure.

'So we're getting married at Christmas.' His laugh was joyful. 'We've wasted too many years already, so no point in waiting any longer.'

Jane dashed around the table to hug and kiss the happy couple. 'That's the best news I've had in ages!' she cried. 'I can't tell you how delighted I am.'

'You're not the only one.' Uncle Len kissed Laura's hand, then held the chair steady while she sat down. 'The boys don't know yet — but Bea has given her blessing.'

Laura's radiant smile spoke volumes as she looked at Jane. 'And I'd like you to be my maid of honour,' she said.

As they toasted the happy couple in champagne, Jane hoped and prayed that her mother's reaction to an estranged daughter would not mar the wedding.

* * *

As Jane had feared, her mother had delivered an unpleasant ultimatum over the wedding. If Jane was present, Nell Harrison would not attend. Not even the combined pleading of Laura and the family could change her mind.

The reopening of the refurbished Coach and Horses had to be delayed until January and Laura insisted that Jane be part of the celebration, as she had missed the wedding. When she had driven to her home to collect her father and Grandad, her mother had shut herself in her bedroom, not answering when Jane called up, 'Happy New Year, Mum. Can we talk?'

Uncle Len still looked as though he couldn't believe his luck, and when Laura smiled back at him, nobody could doubt her affection. Jane had wondered how Desmond would respond to the union but he had been smiling and relaxed, a very young army officer, chatting confidently to Kathleen.

'When I think of all the time I wasted,' Laura had confided, 'I could kick myself, Jane. The only thing Desmond was bothered about was that he might be sent overseas before Christmas. And Bea hasn't stopped saying, 'I told you so'.'

Jane laughed. 'People can say what they like

about national service. It's certainly broadened the outlook for quite a few young men. Where might he go?'

'Cyprus.' Laura's gaze moved to her elder son, talking to his new stepfather. 'I'm so glad Lawrence was home for the wedding. You can never tell with the navy. He's off to foreign waters again next week. It was nice to have all the family here. Well, almost all the family.'

Jane knew why Laura's face clouded slightly. She hesitated, then asked, 'Do you ever hear from Paul?'

'Not since he started his treatment. He was never much of a letter writer at the best of times, and he knows he's fallen from grace.' Laura shrugged her shoulders. 'Occasionally I see one of his photographs in *Life* magazine or something like that. He's good, there's no doubt about it.' She was thoughtful for a moment, then took Jane's arm. 'Enough of that. It's time you had another glass of champagne.' Laura glanced across the room to where Bernard was settling Auntie Bea comfortably by the fire. 'He has quite a way with the ladies, doesn't he?'

As Bernard looked up, Jane returned his smile. 'He really is very sweet,' she said. 'I don't know what I would have done without his support.'

Laura looked into Jane's eyes, as though

trying to read her mind. Then she quietly said, 'I'm glad you had a friend when you needed one, but don't confuse gratitude with love.'

Jane was surprised at the observation — she hadn't had a suitable opportunity to talk about her own love life to Laura. But she had made up her mind to tell Bernard her decision after the book was launched.

14

'A conference, Jane. In half an hour.' Kay's secretary sounded harassed.

'Right.' Jane shifted the telephone to her other hand and picked up a pencil. 'Will we have to reschedule more than one issue?'

'Afraid so. I've been on to the printers and asked them to hold the cover for March twelfth. I suppose you don't know what make-up she uses?'

'As a matter of fact, I decided to do a chapter on both princesses for my book, so I've quite a comprehensive list on file.'

'Thank goodness for that. Kay's worried sick about not being ahead of the field. We can get the black and white stuff out in three weeks, but the colour holds us up for another two, and that's with scrapping the issue we scheduled yesterday.'

As Jane replaced the telephone, Trish rushed through the door. 'Isn't it sad?' she said. 'Such a dreadful shock for her, poor thing. Imagine being all those miles away in Africa and getting news like that!'

Jane shuddered at the thought. 'It's bad enough being told you've lost your father, but to be thrust into affairs of state at the same time . . . '

Trish leaned over Jane's shoulder to read the black-edged front page of a newspaper, ' . . . 'peacefully at Sandringham'. Wouldn't like to be in her shoes, would you?'

'No, and I don't suppose she expected to be such a young queen. He was only fifty-six.' Jane opened her desk diary. 'I won't have time to keep my lunch appointment with the plastic surgeon tomorrow. Will you postpone with my apologies? I'm sure he'll understand.' She sighed. 'God knows when I'll be able to get back to him with all this reshuffling.'

Three weeks later, Jane was proof-reading the feature of Elizabeth Taylor's marriage to Michael Wilding when Trish came into the room. 'The consultant you were going to see is too busy now, so they've sent an SHO, whatever that might mean.'

'What's his name?'

'Dr Clive Randall.' Trish rolled her eyes. 'And he can reshape my body any time he likes.'

'I'll give you my considered opinion after lunch.' Jane laughed. 'Show him in, Trish.'

'How do you do, Miss Beaumont — ' The young man with straw-coloured hair stopped, his hand outstretched.

It took some moments for Jane's stomach to lurch back into its rightful place. Dr Clive Randall — Sandy! The penny just hadn't dropped. Of all the rotten luck.

He was the first to break the stunned silence. Grabbing her hand, he pumped it up and down. 'Is it really you, Jane?' he cried. 'I can't believe how you've changed.' She tried to withdraw her hand, but he was having none of it. 'I thought I was going to meet a bottle-blonde with a smile cracking under layers of make-up.' He shook his head in disbelief as he stared at her. 'And just look at you — you're a knockout! How long is it since your birthday party?'

Would he never let go of her hand? If she didn't do something quickly, she would find herself smiling back at him. Oh, God, why did you send him back into my life just as I'd forgotten all about him?

'Nearly three years,' she murmured. 'And I expect we've all changed a bit in that time. Do sit down.' She felt safer with her desk between them.

'What happened to Helena Beaumont?' He was still grinning broadly. 'Are you her assistant or something?'

'I'm Helena Beaumont. It's a pseudonym.'

'So you're the Beauty Editor! Well done, Jane. Didn't realise you were so ambitious.'

'You're pretty ambitious yourself, aren't you?' She shifted her tensions into thoughts of Rose and the reason why she hated him in the first place. Keep remembering how much you hate him, she reminded herself.

He didn't rise to the sarcastic tone of her voice, just said, 'It was hearing Laura talk about the skin grafting operations on her brother's face that first aroused my curiosity. The work that Archibald McIndoe was doing at East Grinstead was quite fantastic. Then, when I had to decide which branch of medicine to follow, I looked more seriously at plastic surgery. Saw the need for it when I was doing my national service. I expect you heard I was in Korea?'

'No,' she lied. Jack had mentioned it after he'd bumped into Mrs Randall at the hospital, and told Jane that Sandy was a lieutenant in the RAMC.

'It was quite an experience, working under those conditions, and I won't deny I'm glad to get back to civilisation and a well equipped hospital. I'm at jolly old Kings College again, but this time as an SHO' He obviously felt he had to explain. 'That's Senior House Officer to the uninitiated. So — ' He leaned back in his chair and smiled. 'Here I am, as your adviser. But tell me, how's life treating you? Haven't had a chance yet to get together with

Jack or Bernard and catch up on all the news.'

The last thing she wanted was to discuss his army career — or her private life. All she really wanted was to get rid of him. But she had a job to do. Best get on with it as quickly as possible.

'Have you been briefed on what I need for my feature on cosmetic surgery?' she asked.

This time Sandy appeared to notice her lack of warmth. Frowning slightly, he stared at her across the desk, glanced out of the window, then said, 'Perhaps this time it's because it's raining. Or could it be something about me that brings out the worst in you?'

Unable to meet his eyes, Jane stared silently at her notebook, pen poised, until Sandy lifted a bulging briefcase onto his lap.

'I was just asked to bring this file of recent case histories and take it from there.' He took out a thick book. 'You may not think these are suitable for viewing over lunch.' The laughter was gone from his voice. 'They're quite explicit.'

Even though warned, Jane was not prepared for the stark photographs. The patients photographed before and some time later were no problem. It was the pictures taken immediately after surgery that caused her sharp intake of breath.

Sandy was still speaking. 'We don't usually let them near a mirror for a few days. Nose jobs always give the patients black eyes, and you can see the stitches on those who have jowls lifted and skin tightened around the eyes. Breasts are at the end of the file.' He leaned forward to turn the pages.

She closed the book quickly. 'I'll study them later. Excuse me a moment, I must speak to my assistant.' Seething, Jane left the room. He'd deliberately tried to shock her, she thought, and he wasn't going to get away with it.

As usual, when Jane wanted somewhere quiet to talk, Trish had booked a table at Rules. 'Give them my apologies again, will you,' Jane said. 'I've thought of another place. No need to book.'

'OK.' Trish peered into Jane's face. 'Are you all right?' she asked. 'You look a bit pale.'

'I'm fine, thanks.' Jane turned away, then remembered. 'Don't look at that file on my desk before lunch,' she said. 'It'll put you off your ham sandwiches for life!'

In the taxi they sat silently, deep in their own thoughts. Jane's were quite evil. At school, Sandy had often mentioned that he disliked the noisy atmosphere of the dining room, and having to wait when he was hungry. He'd been a fussy eater, only choosing plain food and never trying anything different, especially if it had a sauce. He would hate Mario's. It was always crowded, and they would have to queue.

'Italian food? Wonderful!' His face brightened. 'Discovered it when I was in Birmingham. Well worth waiting for.'

It was like a game of chess. As fast as she tried to outwit him, he confused her with another move. With a tantalising smile, he asked after her parents. He expressed his sympathy about Betty — his mother had told him — and he asked how Jack was getting on. Then, one at a time, he asked after Grandad, Johnny, Aunt Grace, Kathleen, Bernard — even Laura and her family. Her brief replies were just about polite, and his eyes never left her face. She didn't tell him she had left home, or that Laura and Len were married. He may have heard things from his mother. He might be testing her. She didn't care, but she did feel uncomfortable.

Jane ordered a main course liberally enhanced with garlic. Sandy ordered the same dish, asked for additional Parmesan cheese, used the fork and spoon adeptly, Italian style, drank chianti and ate with great relish. Round one to Sandy.

Suddenly, he changed the subject, and his mood. He was the professional medical man, asking relevant questions about the planned feature and giving the exact information she required. His shoulders dropped a little as he warmed to his subject and Jane listened intently, writing shorthand notes as he answered her questions. Then the moment was ruined. His voice serious, he commented, 'It's worthwhile if you can improve the quality of even one person's life.'

Snapping the rubber band around her notebook, Jane signalled the waiter. Normally, if her guest was a man, she would sign the bill and arrange for Trish to pay later. Not today. Slowly and carefully, she counted out the notes and small change, adding the correct amount for the tip. She hoped he squirmed. No inconvenience, no humiliation, was too great for this monster who believed he was helping mankind but had coldly and deliberately abandoned her sister for the sake of his own career.

'I had thought of asking you out for a drink one evening,' he said, as they waited for the receipted bill, 'to talk about something other than birthmarks and broken noses. But I'm sure your calendar is full — with new friends.'

If he thought she was going to be drawn, he was mistaken. 'Actually, I'm in the final stages of writing a book,' she said. 'But thank you for the thought.' She nodded graciously.

Outside the restaurant he paused. 'You're not the Jane Harrison I remember,' he observed. 'And I don't mean just your appearance. That's an improvement.'

Jane couldn't think of an answer that was as cutting, so she hailed a taxi. 'I have another appointment so I'm afraid I can't offer you a lift,' she said. 'I'll get my secretary to telephone you when I've looked through the file. Thank you for your time.' She extended her hand.

His voice was equally cool. 'And thank you for the lunch.' Then his parting thrust. 'I notice that you're still not wearing a ring. Is that because you're afraid of men?'

That was definitely below the belt. But she was ready. 'Not at all,' she answered. 'I just can't imagine wanting to spend the rest of my life with one of them, that's all.' Checkmate!

As the taxi pulled away, she was furious to realise that her shaking fingers tingled from Sandy's handshake.

★ ★ ★

'It's like hitting my head against a brick wall, Jane.' Sheila drew deeply on her cigarette.

'Does Jack know how you feel?'

'He ought to. I've dropped enough hints.' Sheila picked up the coal shovel from the

285

hearth. 'Do you think he still feels bad about Betty?' she asked.

'No. He told me the other day that he's sad things didn't work out, but he doesn't brood about it any more.' Jane watched as Sheila stoked the fire. 'I know he's not happy that Mum has to look after Johnny again after school — he feels it's a bit of an imposition.'

'But wouldn't you think that would be even more reason for him to seriously consider getting married again?'

'Especially as you and Johnny get on so well together.' Jane sighed. 'One thing I do know. He's fed up with his job. Because of the problems he had with Betty and his health, he didn't get the promotion he wanted, and his mates have all left him behind. That's why he's helping Laura and Uncle Len at weekends — he needs the extra money.'

Sadly, Sheila nodded. 'He said once that he had nothing to offer Johnny. Perhaps he feels the same about me.' She looked into the past. 'When I was engaged to Tim, he offered me the moon. His family had pots of money.' Sheila blinked back the tears. 'But when he was shot down, I realised none of that mattered. And I'd marry Jack tomorrow, if only he'd ask me.'

There didn't seem to be an answer. Jane was pretty sure that Jack's real problem went back to the prison camp.

As if reading her mind, Sheila went on, 'The psychiatrist said there's a part of his memory that might always haunt Jack but never be fully released.' She looked appealingly at Jane. 'There must be a trigger somewhere, surely?'

'If there is, I don't know what — unless it's a mule?'

'A mule?'

'The glider he moved heaven and earth to fly was carrying mules,' Jane explained.

'Jack's never mentioned mules. In fact, he won't talk about what happened at all.'

'Even the doctors haven't managed to get much out of him. You know he trained the Americans to take the gliders into Burma?'

Sheila nodded.

'Well, we think Jack persuaded one of them to let him take his place. He thought the glider was carrying troops, or weapons, but . . . ' Jane sighed deeply. 'Jack's life wasn't torn apart by a bullet, but a load of mules.'

'What a stupid waste.'

'I know. If Jack had been badly wounded in action, he might have accepted it better. And he's blocked out everything from the moment he was captured, so looking for a trigger is a bit like looking for a needle in a haystack.'

Sheila moved closer to the fire to warm her

hands. 'I'm nearly thirty-three, Jane. With these odds, I'll be drawing my old age pension instead of my family allowance.'

Sheila would make a wonderful mother, Jane thought, but it was highly probable that Jack would not make a move until he felt he was a whole man again.

★ ★ ★

Reflections of Great Beauty was published the week of Jane's twenty-fourth birthday. The cocktail party was well patronised by contributors, editors, publishers, photographers — and one Senior House Officer. As he walked through the door of the Board Room, Jane grabbed her assistant's arm.

'Steady on,' Trish protested. 'I've got a tray of drinks here.'

Jane kept her voice low. 'Whose idea was it to invite him?'

'Who?'

'Him.' Jane jerked her head.

'I can't interpret neck exercises.' Trish glanced around the room. 'And I can't see any gatecrashers. You'll have to point him out.'

Jane cringed into the corner. 'Over by the door.'

'Dr Randall?'

'Yes,' Jane whispered angrily. 'He wasn't on my list.'

'Kay asked me to phone him yesterday. Didn't I tell you?'

'No, you ruddy well didn't. And why should Kay invite him?'

Before Trish could answer, Sandy was standing at her side. 'Ah, my favourite tipple.' Trish gazed longingly up into his eyes as he helped himself to a glass of champagne. 'Thanks.' He raised a slightly cynical eyebrow at Jane. 'Congratulations, Miss Beaumont. This is quite a splash. Hope you don't mind my joining the elite company, but your editor was very persuasive.'

Jane was furious but, aware of Trish's presence, she smiled back with her mouth and spoke with a tone of pure honey. 'Not at all. Is there any reason why I should mind?'

He sipped his champagne before answering. 'Only that I have nothing whatsoever to do with your book launch.'

'That's true.' Curiosity nudged instinct. 'But I'm sure Kay has her reasons.' Oh, dear. That was a mistake. And he pounced upon it.

'Hasn't she told you why she invited me?'

Trying to stifle murderous inclinations towards her boss, Jane broke her golden rule of drinking very little alcohol until the last guest had gone, and reached for another glass of champagne. Not until the glass was half empty could she bring herself to speak. 'Kay and I have been frantically busy for days.'

'Of course.'

He still wasn't going to tell her, and she certainly wasn't going to ask. 'Excuse me.' She forced the sweet smile back onto her lips. 'I have to circulate.'

Despite her best intentions, she couldn't resist glancing in his direction from time to time as she moved among the guests. Trish, obviously besotted, introduced Sandy to the Managing Editor, a television presenter, and the Queen's beautician. In no time at all, the group of guests questioning the magazine's astrologer, resplendent in his Romany costume, had drifted towards and around the young doctor, who talked about his work with great charm and confidence. Not once did he look in Jane's direction.

'Such an attractive young man, don't you think?' Kay handed Jane a glass of champagne.

'Do you think so?' Jane downed the drink in one and wondered what her editor would think if she knew the heart of stone beneath the doctor's charm. 'Why didn't you tell me you had invited him?' Her voice sounded calmer than she felt.

'Didn't I? Sorry. I didn't think you'd mind, especially as you are old friends.'

'We just happened to go to the same school, years ago.'

'Oh. Dr Randall gave me the impression . . . well, anyway, it's nice to renew acquaintances, and I expect he told you about my idea.'

'He assumed I already knew.' Jane's voice was brittle. 'But I didn't, of course.'

Kay flashed her a quick glance, then apologised again. 'I had hoped we could get together today, but it was impossible.' She turned to greet someone who had just arrived. After the book critic had gushed her congratulations, Kay turned back to Jane. 'So, what do you think?' she asked.

This really was too much. Jane struggled to retain her composure, but lost. 'If someone would tell me what I'm supposed to know,' she shouted, 'I might be able to give an opinion.'

Suddenly, the room was intensely quiet. Jane was aware that everyone was looking in her direction, and she found it difficult to focus and impossible to speak.

Sandy excused himself from his audience and took her arm. 'I should have realised that she was over-tired,' he murmured to Kay. 'After all, I am a doctor.'

'Don't you dare patronise me!' Jane glared at him.

'What you need is a cup of black coffee and one of my magical pills.' He looked at Kay. 'Is there somewhere quiet where Jane can rest for a while?'

'My office.'

Jane felt like a prisoner being escorted to a cell. The coffee did not stop the room from spinning around, but the pill worked after a while. 'Just something to calm you down,' Sandy soothed.

Eventually, Kay's office reappeared out of the fuzz. God, what a spectacle she had made of herself.

'I'm so sorry,' she apologised to Kay. 'What must you think of me?'

'Don't worry. We've pushed you pretty hard for the last few weeks. And it was my fault, really. In all the confusion, I thought I'd told you about my idea. But we don't have to talk about it tonight . . . ' Kay hesitated. 'Unless, of course, you want to.'

Jane knew she wouldn't sleep until she had found out what it was all about. 'I'm fine, now. Honest.'

'Well, if you're sure.' Kay refilled Jane's coffee cup and sat down. 'As you know, I've always been conscious of my lopsided nose. So I've decided to do something about it, and use it as a running feature in the magazine, with photographs. No holds barred.'

'That's very brave of you.'

'Dr Randall is arranging for the operation to be carried out by a senior consultant, with his assistant. And he will be writing all the medical notes for the feature.'

Still slightly dizzy, Jane didn't realise the full implications until Kay went on, 'So you'll be working quite closely together for the next few months.'

15

The only thing that made life bearable for Jane during the next week or so was a brief visit from Aunt Grace. Over an excellent dinner in Laura's restaurant, Aunt Grace questioned Jane closely about her book, then said, 'My friend who runs the bookshop wondered if there was any chance of you coming down for a book-signing.'

'In Torquay?'

'Yes. She's read the excellent reviews, and is sure her customers will be interested in reading what make-up the Queen uses and things like that. She has a contact on the local paper, so you'd get publicity, but it's up to you, dear.'

Jane thought for a moment. 'I suppose I could manage something next month. It would have to be a brief overnight stop, though. I've just started the series on plastic surgery with Sandy.' As soon as the words were out of her mouth she regretted them. Hopefully Aunt Grace wouldn't put two and two together. But she was quite capable of adding up to four.

'Wasn't he your old school chum —

the medical student?'

'Yes.' Please don't ask too many questions, Jane silently pleaded.

'Very pleasant boy, as I remember. Glad he's done so well. It must be nice for you to be able to talk over old times.' Aunt Grace peered over her spectacles at Jane. 'Are you still keeping Bernard dangling on a string?'

Shocked, Jane raised her eyes. Was this how her behaviour appeared? Her father had hinted at it last summer, and it was now a year since she had shared Bernard's home: three years since he had first proposed. It really wasn't fair to keep him waiting any longer.

Not until she'd finished dictating her feature to Trish the following morning was Jane able to review her thoughts on marriage.

What were the alternatives? Even if she found a flat to share with her best friend, it was unlikely that Kathleen would remain single for long. Then what? To live her life as an unbedded bachelor girl, with her home becoming more of a prison than a refuge? Perhaps that was the real crunch of the matter. The thought of one day showering Kathleen with confetti and returning to the lonely existence of a spinster, with no mother to comfort her, a father who would visit whenever he could sneak out, and no children

295

of her own — only a career. Was that enough? And if she didn't marry Bernard, who else might ask?

She glanced at the doodles she'd scribbled around the blotting pad; circles; dots; patterns; squiggles; and a single word.

Startled, she stared at the name: *Sandy*. Why should he intrude into her private thoughts, when she made such an effort to keep him out? Why did she remember so vividly the touch of his handclasp, his enthusiasm as he described his work, his wide grin as he joked with Kay, the golden hairs on the back of his hand as he sketched a nose?

Dear God, Jane prayed, please don't let me fall in love with him. The mere thought of loving someone she despised was too awful to contemplate — and Jane was certain the contempt was mutual. There was no doubting that Sandy grabbed every opportunity to humiliate and embarrass. Even when Kay had mentioned that Jane was to talk about her book on Woman's Hour, he had raised an eyebrow, waited until Kay had left the room, then asked Jane which voice she proposed to inflict upon the interviewer. Sweet? Or sour?

Tearing the sheet of blotting paper into shreds, Jane thought again about Bernard. He would never behave like Sandy. Bernard was an honourable man, kind and considerate, with a good sense of humour and a shared interest in music and theatre — an easy man to learn to love.

* * *

Bernard's face was a picture of happiness. 'Are you sure?' he asked, his eyes searching her face for any sign of doubt.

'I'm sure.' Jane laughed. It was like watching a child who had not been sure whether Santa would bring him the train set he'd longed for, and when it finally arrived he couldn't believe it actually had his name on the label.

'Oh, my dearest!' He cupped her face in his hands and kissed her lips, then gently pushed her down onto the armchair. 'Please — just wait there.'

Jane guessed why he hurried upstairs. When he returned, Bernard held a small box in his hand, which he lovingly placed into her palm.

'Please tell me if you don't like it. I can easily change it for one you do like, and if it doesn't fit I can have it altered and . . . ' His words were rushed as he slipped the sapphire and diamond ring onto the third finger of her left hand, then he paused and gazed anxiously at her face.

'It's beautiful — and a perfect fit.' The more Bernard kissed her, the more Jane felt she had made the right decision.

As if reading her thoughts, he said, 'You won't regret this, my dearest. I shall love and take care of you for the rest of my life. And I want the whole world to know how happy I am — beginning with an announcement in the paper.'

Pulling slightly back from his arms, Jane said, 'Bernard, dear, could we keep our engagement between ourselves for just a little while?'

'Oh.' He looked disappointed. 'Is there any particular reason?'

'Don't you think it would be nice for us to share our secret a little longer? And there's the publicity.'

'Publicity?'

'Well, I am becoming a little bit known because of the book and going on radio and so on — and newspaper reporters might ask questions and want interviews and . . . ' Jane knew she was rambling, just as Bernard had when he gave her the ring.

Laughing, he stopped the flow of words by covering her lips with his finger. 'And I shall tell them that I am the luckiest man in the world to have such a clever bride,' he declared. 'So it really doesn't matter, does it?'

'Not when you put it like that. But — once this series on plastic surgery is over, I'll have the time to concentrate on our plans for the future. I really would rather wait before making an announcement. Do you mind?'

Suddenly, Jane knew her true reason for delaying the announcement. She wanted Sandy out of her life before any mention was made of her engagement to Bernard. She just couldn't face whatever sarcastic comment he might feel compelled to make.

Still looking slightly crestfallen, Bernard nodded. 'If that's what you really want. It's just that I have waited so long for this moment, and I want to shout it to the heavens.' His kisses became more urgent, more passionate, his hands more exploring. Then he lifted his head. 'You're not planning a long engagement, are you?'

Smiling, she touched his cheek. 'You have been so patient. Could you bear to wait another year?'

'Just about — although I had hoped it might be sooner.'

'I would love to be a June bride, and — ' Her face clouded a little. 'Perhaps within that time I might be able to reconcile with my mother.'

For a moment, Bernard held her close, then he asked, 'Will you tell your family yet?'

'No, but I will tell them before anyone else.'

Bernard hesitated before he said, 'I really would like to tell Eunice when she comes in.'

'Oh, but — '

'To be honest, my dearest girl, I don't think I could keep it from her. She'll guess as soon as she sees me.'

It was true. No one could possibly look at Bernard and not realise that he was bubbling over with joy.

'You're right.' Jane smiled, although she was a little apprehensive about his sister's reaction. 'But no one else, please.'

Bernard's sigh had a happy sound. 'No one else,' he agreed. 'On one condition.'

Curious, Jane waited while he fetched the diary from the telephone table.

'I'm going to write it down and hold you to it.' Beaming, Bernard turned the pages of the calendar for the following year. 'You can pick any date you like for your wedding day — as long as it is in June 1953!'

★ ★ ★

As Jane parked her car outside Sheila's shop, she wondered again what was behind the cryptic telephone message left with Trish. Nothing to worry about, but Sheila needed a friend. Could Jane call in after work on Friday?

Sheila was waiting by the private entrance. 'I heard your car,' she said.

'Ah, yes.' Jane turned towards the staircase. 'It needs a service, but I haven't had time to — what are you doing?'

Putting a finger to her lips, Sheila had grabbed Jane's arm, bustled her along the corridor and through the rear entrance into the garden. Jane followed her friend under the arch, covered with pale pink roses just in bud. Sheila waited until they reached a rustic seat in a secluded arbour before she spoke.

'Say a prayer for me, Jane,' she pleaded. 'And Jack.'

'I often do.' Jane smiled. 'Anything specific in mind?'

'Oh, Jane!' Sheila covered her face with her hands. 'I hope I've done the right thing. It would be too dreadful if I made matters worse.'

'Just tell me from the beginning.'

'Well.' Sheila lowered her hands. 'I kept remembering what you said about the mules, so I contacted the Red Cross, then the Airborne Division.'

'And — ?'

'They suggested I get in touch with one of the Chindits who'd written to them after the

301

war, thanking them for getting supplies through. So I did — and Captain Harlow's with Jack now!' Sheila licked her lips and drew a deep breath. 'That's why I'm so frightened. Supposing it goes wrong? I'd never forgive myself.'

For a moment, Jane was speechless. Such love. Such courage. It had to work. She took Sheila's hand and held it tightly. 'What is he like?' she asked.

'A lovely man, not much older than Jack. He was one of General Wingate's officers. I'm just hoping and praying he can make Jack see it wasn't a waste.'

'You did the right thing, Sheila. It's worth — ' An anguished cry cut short her words. It came through the open upper window like the wail of a tortured soul. Just one cry. Then silence.

'Oh, my God!' Sheila jumped to her feet. 'What have I done?'

'It may not be as bad as it sounds.' Jane wished her words carried more conviction. As Sheila began to run towards the house a young man in uniform appeared in the archway.

'He's asking for you, Miss Green,' he said, then looked at Jane. 'I'll wait here, if I may?' His face was strained and he took a cigarette case from his pocket, but quickly replaced it.

'Do sit down,' Jane said. 'And smoke if you wish.' She shook her head at the proffered cigarette case, then asked, 'Is Jack all right? That cry . . . '

'I'm sorry you were distressed. It was something he remembered.'

'Captain Harlow,' Jane hesitated, 'will you tell me what my brother has remembered? It might make it easier for us to help him — and his doctors will want to know.'

He looked directly at Jane, as though summing up her strength. 'I should warn you, it is not pleasant.'

'Please . . . '

After a moment, he told her that Jack's life had been saved by two Americans who had carried him through the jungle after they were captured. Conditions in the camp were bad, the guards were savage, and prisoners beaten for the slightest misdemeanour. Captain Harlow slowly paced the arbour, as though comparing the scene.

'Early in nineteen-forty-five, your brother had a severe bout of dysentery and one of his friends was caught stealing medicine.'

The silence was so long, Jane had to ask, 'And he was punished?'

'He was beheaded.' As she gasped, the young officer turned. 'I'm sorry. There's no easy way to recount this.'

Jane took a deep breath. 'And that was the memory that he blocked out for all these years.'

'Yes. And the beatings and torture.'

For some time, the silence was only broken by the intermittent buzz of a bee gathering pollen. Then Jane asked, 'What happened to the other American?'

'He was so weak through malnutrition, he died before they were released, despite your brother giving him most of his own rations.'

'Oh, no.' Jane was close to tears at the thought of her brother, alone in that hostile camp, trying desperately to survive. 'Now that he's talked about it, will Jack get better?' she asked.

'I hope so, but he felt responsible, so it may take time.' He smiled gently. 'Hopefully, I may have helped him to realise that prisoners were killed for the slightest provocation. My brother was executed for stealing a handful of rice.'

Unable to speak, Jane closed her eyes against the tears. It must have taken tremendous courage for this young man to talk to Jack, opening up his own grief again. Eventually, she said, 'I really can't thank you enough for coming.'

'If it helps your brother, it will have been worthwhile. At least he accepts that the mules were as vital to us as weapons. Nothing else could travel through that territory.' A faint smile illuminated his face as he noticed the label on one of the rose bushes. 'Peace,' he read aloud. ' 'One of the last new species to come out of France before the occupation'.'

'Sheila's neighbour created the rose garden,' Jane explained. 'He took part in the D-Day landings and wanted something beautiful as a memorial to his friends.'

'Much wiser than bitterness.' Captain Harlow shook hands.

★ ★ ★

On the drive home, Jane recalled every word the captain had said. She had thought her own war was bad enough, with losing their home and her sister. Olaf's war had also been tough — his country occupied by the enemy, and his brother killed fighting with the resistance movement. But nothing compared with the deprivations of the prisoners of war, cut off from their loved ones and civilisation.

She thought of Bernard. The Red Cross had kept him in touch with England, but he had been deprived of love for almost the whole of the war. Only his dreams of coming home to his wife sustained him, and plans to renew their dancing partnership. Both were cruelly taken from him, one by an American sergeant, the other by a freezing German winter, which cost him the loss of two toes.

Fighting back the tears, Jane hurried back to Bernard, anxious to hug him, give him the love he had lost. Never again, she vowed, would he feel forlorn and lonely. She would spend the rest of her life trying to make him the happiest man on earth. He deserved it.

It was almost dark when she reached Bernard's house, and she was surprised to find Eunice sitting alone in the kitchen.

'One of Bernard's friends from the prison camp phoned,' she explained. 'They've gone up the road for a drink.'

'Shall I switch on the light?' Jane asked. 'Or do you have a headache?'

'I hadn't realised it was so dark — just sitting here with my thoughts.' Eunice blinked at the glare of the light. 'Can you imagine what it must have been like for Bernard, being shut away in that dreadful place for five years?'

'No.' Jane's thoughts went back to Captain Harlow. 'But I am so thankful he wasn't in Burma. At least he didn't have to endure beatings and torture. Not like . . . ' As the tears began to fall, Jane put down the kettle and groped for a handkerchief. She had hoped to weep in solitude for her brother and his companions, but Eunice was surprisingly sympathetic, making tea and listening intently as Jane recounted Captain Harlow's horrific story.

When it was over they sat quietly, staring into their cups, until Eunice commented, 'Sheila must love him very deeply, to go to such lengths.'

'Oh, she does. And I hope Jack soon realises that she would make him a wonderful wife.'

Raising her eyes, Eunice said, 'And how about you, Jane? Will you make Bernard a wonderful wife?'

Shocked at the bluntness of the question, Jane stammered, 'Of, of course I will try to be the best wife I can.'

For a long moment Eunice stared back, then put down her cup. 'You are so much younger and, in many ways, still so innocent, Jane. I'm not sure you understand the real meaning of betrayal — no, let me go on — I have been wanting an opportunity to say this since Bernard told me of your engagement.' Her eyes wandered to Jane's left hand. 'In my book, not wearing his ring is an act of betrayal.'

'How dare you call it that? We just want to keep it to ourselves a little longer, and I always wear the ring when I am here. I

307

haven't been upstairs yet, that's all.'

Eunice poured herself another cup of tea. 'Listen, Jane,' she said. 'War brings to the surface every kind of betrayal under the sun, and the opposite of the coin — loyalty. Miss Bluebell was loyal to her girls and risked her own life to hide her husband.' She lit a cigarette. 'But there were many women in the occupied countries who slept with Germans in return for extra rations and comforts. That was just as much an act of betrayal as those who gave names to the Gestapo — and they deserved their punishment.'

Jane recalled newsreels of women who had collaborated being dragged through the streets of France and humiliated.

Eunice was still speaking. 'I have no regrets that I helped uncover some of the bitches from their hiding places. And to be honest, if I had known in time, I would have tied Delia to a chair out in this street and personally shaved every hair from her head!'

Like a fly trapped in a web, Jane watched her companion, wondering when she would pounce.

Noting Jane's horrified expression, Eunice shrugged. 'Even that is not a harsh enough punishment for betrayal.' She sighed. 'I am not suggesting that you will follow in Delia's unfaithful footsteps, but — ' Eunice drew deeply on her cigarette. 'I am concerned that you may not be the kind of wife my brother needs.'

Regaining some of her composure, Jane protested, 'As long as Bernard is happy, I really don't think you have anything to be concerned about.'

'In other words — mind my own business?' Eunice raised her eyebrows. 'Bernard and I have both been victims of betrayal, and I intend to protect him from any more suffering.' Deep in thought, she wandered over to the window and drew the curtains. 'I was in love with a Frenchman. He was my contact with the Maquis and we planned to marry after the war. Then one day he wasn't at our meeting place and I only just managed to escape. Later, I found out that he had been captured and tortured until he gave away all the names of our lines of contact — including mine.'

'Oh, no,' Jane whispered. 'How dreadful for you.'

It was as though Eunice hadn't heard. 'They shot him, of course, once he'd fulfilled his usefulness.' She turned around. 'So you see, Jane, there is little I do not know about betrayal or loyalty, and — ' She stared straight into Jane's eyes. 'I will not allow it to happen within this family again! I hope you

309

understand what I am saying.'

Jane understood only too well. The fanatical expression on the face of her future sister-in-law was more explicit than her words. And it was terrifying!

16

Thursday, 1st January 1953. The page on Jane's desk diary was blank. A transient virgin, like its owner. As Jane picked up her fountain pen, the light caught her engagement ring, now sparkling on her finger for all to see. Neither diary nor owner would be 'returned unused'. With the Coronation planned for this summer, Kay was planning bumper issues covering everything from protocol to female dignitaries, and Jane had been briefed to find out what cosmetics were likely to be used by the ladies in waiting to withstand the arduous period in the Abbey.

As for Jane's own great day — she had set her heart on a church wedding, but three rectors had shaken their heads when Bernard mentioned he was a divorcee — so she would have to be content with a brief ceremony in a registry office. Bernard had suggested Caxton Hall, to make it a little special. But she would have no bridesmaids, just two witnesses. No mother to shed a tear. Nell Harrison was relentless. And no breathtaking bridal gown with billowing veil. Better make an appointment for one of her favourite designers to show her some good suits. Whatever else she could or could not have, Jane was determined that Bernard would be proud of his bride.

The internal phone rang as she blotted the last entry. Kay wanted to see her, with the diary.

'Happy New Year, Jane.' The editor beamed.

'Happy New Year. You look pleased with yourself. Must have been good last night.'

'What? Oh, the Chelsea Ball. Drank too much, as usual, but had the perfect antidote to a hangover just now. You'll never guess.'

'Don't suppose I will.' Jane laughed. 'So I hope you're going to tell me?'

Kay's expression was gleeful. 'I've just had a call from the BBC,' she said. 'We're going to be famous.'

'Do they want us to do another broadcast?'

'Better than that. We're going to be on television.'

'You're joking!'

'I kid you not.' Kay tapped her new straight nose. 'And it's all due to my taking the plunge.'

'A programme on plastic surgery?'

'Got it in one. The main subject is Sir Archibald McIndoe's work with the pilots, of course, going on into the realms of cosmetic surgery. That's where we come in.'

'Gosh! How exciting. But why me?'

'Because you wrote about the response from our readers after my op. And the producer heard you on Woman's Hour. Thought your voice recorded well.'

'I don't know, Kay. Sound radio is one thing, television is another. My sister pinched all the photogenic genes.'

'Rubbish! You've got a certain look about you that I think will come over well. Anyway, it's splendid publicity for *Lady Fair*.'

'True. When does it happen?'

'On the fifteenth.'

'As soon as that?'

Kay nodded. 'The programme on McIndoe's work has been planned for some time but, apparently, another programme fell by the wayside. Somebody died or something. Anyway, they needed to fill in some time so decided to expand the one on plastic surgery. Hence us.'

'Ah. So — what are the details?'

'It goes out at eight-thirty, but we have to be at the studio early for make-up and a briefing.'

Jane scribbled in her diary. 'What do we wear?'

'There's lots of points like that we need to talk about. I've asked Liz to book a table for three at Mario's tomorrow. Do you have any other appointments?'

Jane glanced at her diary. 'Kathleen suggested today or tomorrow, so that's not a problem.' She scribbled a note, then asked, 'Who's the third? Someone from the BBC?'

'Sandy, of course.'

'Sandy!'

'Well, he did assist in the operation, and the series.' Kay looked speculatively at Jane. 'There's not a problem between you, is there?'

'No. No, of course not,' Jane lied. 'I was just surprised, that's all.'

It was nearly six months since she'd seen Sandy. She thought she had succeeded in putting him out of her thoughts, but now he was going to infiltrate into her life again!

★ ★ ★

A picture postcard in the second post evoked such unpleasant memories that Jane had to wait until she had read the whole of her mail before she could shut out the image of a sleazy warehouse and look again at the splendour of the Eiffel Tower. It had been Sheila's choice to have a Christmas honeymoon in Paris. What could be more romantic? At least Jane had been a maid of honour at her brother's wedding. Jack had told his mother that enough was enough, and he and Sheila were determined that Jane would share their day. He also would dearly love his mother to be present, but the final choice was hers. She chose to stay at home.

Kathleen's finals had been even better than anticipated, so she was happily learning the legal ropes in Lincoln's Inn, not too far from Jane's office. Over lunch, they swapped their respective postcards from Paris.

'Johnny has copied ours so well,' Kathleen said. 'He really is very clever at painting. Says he wants to go to art school to learn how to be a proper artist.'

'I don't see why not. Jack was always very good and Sheila has really encouraged the boy. I thought his speech had greatly improved when I last saw him.'

'Oh, he's coming along in leaps and bounds. And the doctors are sure that he'll be able to walk properly if we could only send him to a specialist in Switzerland.'

'I know. Jack told me.' Jane didn't add that she had opened up a separate bank account for her nephew and was saving every penny she could manage. Tucking into her syrup pudding and custard, she said, 'I was surprised that Sheila decided to give up her job, but it will be good for Johnny, and it's about time Mum had a break.' Spoon poised halfway to her mouth, a thought struck Jane. 'Ironic, isn't it? The new manager already has a house so he doesn't want the little flat above the shop. It would have been ideal for me, but I don't need it now I'm getting married.'

Thoughtfully, Kathleen stirred her coffee. 'Actually, I'm thinking about renting it myself.'

Surprised, Jane looked up. 'Can you afford it?' she asked. 'You're not earning that much yet, and you'll need furniture.'

'When we talked about sharing, I thought I could just about manage it — then didn't you have to go and get engaged?' She pulled an affectionate face at Jane. 'But your uncle has offered to help me out, bless his dear heart.' Kathleen's smile faded. 'I'll admit I'm fessed at the thought of leaving your mother, just as she's losing Johnny and all. She missed him badly when Jack and Betty moved into the prefab, but we were both still at home, then.' Head on one side, she wondered, 'I suppose there's not a hope that you'll be able to come back before you're wed?'

Jane shook her head. 'I would if she'd have me, but I won't take back what I said.' She signalled for the bill. 'Don't worry too much, Kathleen. Mum has been used to you being away at university. I'm sure she'll understand you couldn't stay there for ever.'

'I hope you're right. It's just that she has been so good to me — you all have.'

Both girls put equal amounts on top of the bill and gathered up their gloves and bags. 'Talking of who's living where,' Kathleen said, 'will Eunice still live with you after you are married?'

Fervently, Jane replied, 'I hope not! But she's showing no signs of looking for a place of her own, and I can't throw her out.' It was something that had troubled Jane for some time. 'Actually, I don't really want to live there myself. I'd rather start afresh, in a new home of our own. Something that's mine, not second-hand.'

'And without the frosty sister-in-law.'

'Definitely.'

'Have you mentioned it to Bernard?'

'Not in so many words — it's a little delicate.'

'If you don't, you might be stuck with her.' Kathleen glanced at her watch. 'Must go. I'm in court with one of the junior partners this afternoon.'

'I want to hear more about your job. Why don't we have a meal after work tomorrow? Bernard is tightening up some comedy sketches he's written, so I'm not needed at rehearsals.'

'Sorry.' Kathleen hesitated, then said, 'I'm

meeting Desmond at the Corner House before we go to the theatre.'

'Desmond?'

'Yes, Desmond.' Kathleen said. 'And don't you go reading more into it than just a celebration of his demob.'

'As if I would!' Jane grinned, recalling that Desmond had dated the lovely Irish girl a couple of times when he'd been on leave. 'What are you going to see?'

'*The Mousetrap*. Agatha Christie's new play. They don't think it will run for long, so we thought we'd better get along to see it while we can.'

⋆   ⋆   ⋆

The dreaded business lunch with Kay and Sandy started off badly because the proofs were late coming up from the printers, and Jane had to check her page before she left the office. Kay had gone to the restaurant straight from another appointment. And Sandy had a face like thunder.

'If you couldn't get away before one-thirty, why didn't you say so?' he accused, as soon as she arrived. 'Some of us have important work to do.'

Jane glared at him, aborted her attempt to apologise, murmured to Kay that she would explain later and took her time reading the menu. Ignoring his impatient sighs and the frequent references to his wristwatch, she changed her mind twice before going back to her first choice. Then she sat back and smiled sweetly.

'So far as clothes are concerned, I really don't see that you were needed at all, Dr Randall,' she commented. 'You'll probably wear either a blood-spattered white coat, to create the correct image, or your one good suit.'

Kay raised an eyebrow and Sandy seemed about to retort, but suddenly stopped, staring at Jane's engagement ring. It did not take long for him to recover his ability for caustic comment.

'Well, well, well! So at last you've found someone else who's prepared to take you on. I trust it isn't anyone I know?'

'Actually, it's Bernard, and we're both very happy, in case you are interested.'

'Really?' As if defying her comment, he stared at her, with raised eyebrows. Then, with a sardonic expression, he murmured, 'I suppose I'd better congratulate the poor devil, although I feel condolences are more in order.'

Kay glanced from one to the other, as though wondering whether Sandy's tongue was really in his cheek.

Seething, Jane signalled to the wine waiter. As she poured her second glass of full bodied red, Sandy turned to Kay. 'If we have a repeat performance of the incident at the book launch, I'm afraid you're going to have to sober up your Beauty Editor by yourself. I have a very busy afternoon scheduled, and surgeons have to give priority to their patients, as I am sure you appreciate.'

Fighting back the urge to throw the contents of her glass into his face, Jane said, 'But they can be selective in their choice of priorities, can't they?'

Frowning, Sandy said, 'I really don't know what you mean.'

'Oh, but you do, Dr Randall. In fact, you wouldn't be sitting here now if you hadn't been so selective, would you?'

His eyes mirrored a wealth of feelings: perplexity; frustration; impatience; and finally — anger. Intense, cold anger. Tossing his napkin back onto the table, he reached into his briefcase and thrust a file in front of Kay. 'Here are some notes I made for this meeting. Obviously, I will be of more use back at the hospital. Good afternoon.' Standing up, he looked down at Jane, the anger only just under control. 'My one consolation is that, after the programme, we will not need to meet again. And I am sure the feeling is mutual.'

Wondering if she had gone too far, Jane watched him leave the restaurant. Kay's expression was one of extreme irritation. 'Whatever the problem is between you two, you'd better sort it out — and soon,' she said. 'I've never seen you behave so badly. As for Dr Randall . . . '

'I'm sorry,' Jane apologised. 'We shouldn't have involved you. It's something that happened a long time ago.'

'Do you want to tell me about it?'

'No, I can't. But I promise you, it will be . . . ' She paused.

'All right on the night?' Kay prompted. 'I just hope so. This is a live transmission, and I don't want to be sitting there holding you two apart.' She took some banknotes from her purse. 'Will you pay the bill for me? There is a fur jacket in the sale at Harvey Nichols that I really ought to resist — but what the hell!'

Jane sat alone, annoyed with herself for rising to the bait so easily. The waiter presented the bill and bent low over the table. 'Madame — Signor Mario — he wishes you to drink with him. Compliments of his house.'

Jane was surprised, but she had no desire to drink with anyone. 'Please give him my

321

regrets, but I have to get back. If you could just let me have the receipt, for my secretary.'

He came back with the receipt, and another message. 'Madame — Signor Mario, he say it is very important that you talk to him. In his office, please.'

Puzzled, she glanced over her shoulder to the door that led to the kitchen. A short, stocky man stood smiling and nodding at her. The restaurant had always been crowded and Jane had never particularly noticed the proprietor. Intrigued, she followed him into a tiny office, the desk littered with menus, bills and order pads. Lying on top was a copy of the *Illustrated London News*, open at a feature on Jane.

'A customer leave it on the chair, and I know I think right.' He beamed at her. 'I say to myself, this is not Helena Beaumont, famous writer. I know that face. And as soon as I read you have been to Torquay, signing your famous book, I know who you are.' He removed a pile of dirty overalls from a chair, but she remained standing. 'You look different now, but I recognise you. You are the little sister, Janey!'

The pieces began to fall into place. His face became vaguely familiar as she recalled a muddy pigsty in Devon. 'I'm sorry, I didn't recognise you at first,' she said. 'You were working on Uncle Amos's farm, during the war.'

'*Si*. You last see me with pigs. Now I cook the pigs for you to eat.' He laughed at his own joke. Jane wondered where this was leading. It didn't feel right. His gaze was slightly disrespectful.

'So, you are famous lady. Is Rose also famous lady? She said she would be famous lady on films.' Even the vague foreboding didn't prepare Jane for his next words. 'And what does she call my *bambino*?'

17

It was cold in Trafalgar Square. Cold and damp. Huddling deep into her coat, Jane was reminded of a Christmas night in Paris. The same emotions; misery and fear. If Mario carried out his threat the whole family would be destroyed. Yet if she gave in to his demands, would they ever stop?

To think he was the father of Rose's baby! But Rose had always been attracted to earthy, flashy types. She said they had more sex appeal than nice guys. But a nice guy would have looked after her when she was pregnant. She would be alive — and her child.

Jane cringed as she thought of Sandy. All these years she had believed he was the man who had abandoned her sister, just because she had seen Rose quarrelling with him the day after she had promised to contact the father. Jane had taunted and humiliated Sandy until his own feelings of friendship and affection had been trampled into the ground, too badly damaged ever to be repaired.

She couldn't even say sorry, not without revealing the truth about her sister and a nasty little Italian. A man who'd ignored pathetic phone calls from a sixteen-year-old girl, and had the nerve to declare he'd always planned to claim Rose and his *bambino* once his business was established — so sad, so sad. Silently Jane had watched him wipe a crocodile tear from his eye. She knew his conniving mind was working out how he could use this news to even greater advantage. It didn't take him long.

Now his business needed money to expand upstairs. It needed new tables and chairs, a bigger kitchen. It was too crowded, profits not so good, his prices too low. Mario sent money home to his family in Italy — his mama and papa, and many brothers and sisters. They were very poor. But the rich landlord in London, he wanted more rent. The council, they wanted more rates. The tax man — she would understand.

Oh, yes. She understood perfectly well. Particularly the suggestion that her mama and papa might be happy to meet the man who would have been their new son if Rose had not been so tragically killed — and the *bambino* with her. *Mama mia!* It might be too much for them to bear. But Mario would not bring back the pain if Jane thought it better that he stay in restaurant. His bigger, improved restaurant. Only the famous Helena Beaumont could choose what he should do.

She had soon realised that pleading with him wouldn't work, and managed to convince him that she was going away on business and couldn't do anything until she returned.

Back in the office, she tried her old trick of a piece of paper divided down the middle. Both sides made sorry reading.

If she didn't pay up, her parents would be devastated. Grandad was seventy-six. Who could say what a shock like that would do to him? Mario had said he had a customer who worked for one of the less respectable Sunday newspapers. He might be bluffing, but what if . . . ?

Even if she agreed to pay, where would the money come from? At Christmas she had bought a television set for the family, so they could watch the Coronation. The rest of her money had been invested for Johnny's operation, she couldn't touch that. So where might she borrow? Laura had ploughed all the proceeds from the sale of her house into the Coach and Horses and Uncle Len was committed to helping Kathleen, as well as his own business. It was the same with Aunt Grace, and Miss Dawson couldn't be expected to mortgage her Turner painting every time one of them was in financial need. Bernard? Out of the question. He would lend her the money if he had it, but she couldn't bring herself to ask him. Confessing her sister's shame and borrowing money to pay off a nasty little blackmailer was not the way she wanted her marriage to begin. No, she had to do this by herself.

Jane's thoughts went back eight years to the time when her twin had been desperately trying to borrow money from her parents and . . . was that why she had met Sandy in the restaurant? Rose wouldn't have told him why she needed it, but a medical student wouldn't have much money to spare. Perhaps that explained why Rose had lost her temper. She had come to the end of her tether. And after the acrimonious row with her father, she'd finally taken Gran's little nest egg and run from the house, never to return.

Closing her eyes, Jane relived that awful January morning when she'd searched for her sister. And now, after all the efforts she'd made to keep Rose's secret, it threatened to tear the family apart once again.

Her head pounding, Jane decided to go home. Home? She didn't have a home any more, just a room in Bernard's house. Even when Bernard carried her across the threshold in six months' time, she would have to share the house with his sister. Eunice, as always, would be watching every move, listening to every telephone conversation and

327

checking every letter on the mat — constantly searching for any signs of an unfaithful liaison.

Taking the powder compact from her handbag, Jane was horrified by her reflection. She looked dreadful. Bernard and Eunice would ask questions if she arrived looking like this. She couldn't face them. Reaching for the telephone, she dialled Laura's number, then Bernard's office.

★ ★ ★

The restaurant kept Laura busy and Uncle Len was working flat out behind the bar. Jane was glad to have the upstairs room to herself for a while, although her solitude was short-lived. Halfway through the evening, Jack brought her up a plate of sandwiches and a pot of coffee.

'Sorry I didn't have a chance to talk to you earlier, Sis, but it's been a bit hectic tonight.' He kissed her cheek. 'Sheila's giving Laura a hand. She'll be up later.'

'I should offer to help out myself, but I'm really too tired.' Jane poured the coffee. 'When did you get back?'

'Lunchtime. We were at Mum's when Laura phoned to say they've got three down with 'flu, and she said she'd keep Johnny overnight.' He reached for a sandwich. 'Didn't expect to see you here, though. Don't you usually rehearse on Friday nights?'

'I'm not needed tonight and I promised Laura before Christmas that I'd come over for a chat.'

Jack laughed. 'Chance will be a fine thing.'

'I know. Still, I'm staying over, so we can gossip tomorrow morning. Now, tell me about Paris.'

Jack's enthusiasm for Paris and his new bride helped revive Jane's jaded spirits a little.

'She's the most marvellous girl, Sis. I can't tell you how happy I am.'

'You don't have to. It's written all over your face.'

He looked at the door, then burst out, 'I was going to wait until it's all signed and sealed, but I really want to tell you first. We're moving to Devon.'

'What!'

His eyes were full of excitement. 'When we visited Aunt Grace in December, we went over to see Robert and Yvonne in Brixham. Their sailing school did rather well last summer and they're thinking of taking on another man.'

'You? But you don't know anything about boats.'

'I can learn, and I'm a good swimmer. It's

not as crazy as it sounds, Jane. Robert said he needed someone for inshore duties to start with. He's prepared to take the chance and train me now I'm fitter — I really don't fancy spending the rest of my life in an office.'

'How does Sheila feel about it?'

'We talked a lot in Paris.' He grinned. 'You needn't look like that, we found time for talking as well!' His expression became serious again. 'There's a good chance of her getting a photographer's franchise at one of the holiday camps. Anyway, we'd like to provide Johnny with a baby brother or sister as soon as possible.'

'Do they have a good special school down there?' Jane asked.

'To be honest, I don't think he needs a special school any more. Sheila has worked wonders with him and I think he could cope with a normal school, even though he may be in a lower stream. His teacher suggested as much last term.'

'That's good news, and it's the perfect place for him to develop his artistic talents.'

Jack nodded. 'Yvonne knows some of the artists who have a sort of colony in Brixham. She reckons he could be apprenticed to one of them when he leaves school. Learn the craft first-hand.'

'When are you planning to go?'

'We've still got a few things to discuss and decide, but I want to start navigation training as soon as possible, so we won't hang about.'

'Mum will be upset that you're all going. So will Mrs Green.'

'I know. That's why I don't want to say anything just yet.' Jack's face clouded as he looked into the fire. 'I won't ever be able to forget what happened in Burma,' he said. 'But I feel as though I've been given a second chance to live a normal life — and I'd be a fool not to take it.'

'If anybody deserves a second chance, you do.' Jane squeezed her brother's hand.

Standing up, Jack said, 'I'd better go back before they start calling 'Time'.' He looked affectionately down at Jane. It was good to see that boyish grin again. 'I just had to tell someone,' he said. 'And when it comes to keeping a secret, you're the best, Janey.'

If only he knew, she thought.

* * *

Bernard telephoned Jane the following morning. Eunice had received a letter from Miss Bluebell, asking if she would audition some dancers in the north of England. She would be away for a few weeks but it wouldn't affect the new show — the girls were well rehearsed. Would Jane be coming home on Sunday?

Thinking quickly, Jane grabbed the opportunity Bernard had given her to stay with Laura a little longer. Without Eunice living in the house as chaperone, perhaps it was not a good idea for Jane and Bernard to share the same house before the wedding. Of course Jane realised that he was not about to sneak into her bedroom because they were alone, but the neighbours would not believe their relationship could be so innocent. Wiser not to give them any ammunition which might leak out to the press, especially with her forthcoming appearance on television. Sorry — she would be working late at the office for a week or so, or taking work home, but she would keep in touch by phone, and see him at the dress rehearsal.

Jane always kept an overnight bag in the office, packed with a change of clothing and toiletries, in case she had to make an emergency trip to a cosmetic supplier, or judge a beauty competition at short notice. She decided to pick up the rest of her things on Monday morning, after Bernard had left the house. Just for now, she really couldn't face him, not until she had cleared her thoughts about Mario.

But the same thoughts rattled around her

mind like a windmill, interrupting her sleep and ever present during the daytime. Her appetite had gone and she knew her beauty article was not up to standard — Trish had raised her eyebrows more than once during dictation.

Laura accepted her explanation that it wouldn't be 'proper' to live in Bernard's house and agreed Jane could stay until Eunice returned, but she wondered why he didn't come over for a meal. Jane knew her friend was worried that there might be problems over her forthcoming wedding, and tried to sound reassuring as she made the excuse that she was nervous about the TV programme and needed time to quietly plan her notes. What Jane didn't tell Laura was that she would dearly have loved to be comforted by Bernard, to draw from his strength. But she was afraid that if he questioned her and offered to help, she would ask him for the money. The sands of time were running out and Mario was expecting to hear from her any day now.

★ ★ ★

Jane was no nearer to a decision by the time she sat with Kay in the studio, waiting for the make-up girl to finish combing and fluffing and brushing and patting. Her stomach made a rather loud rumbling noise.

'Sorry,' she apologised. 'I skipped lunch.'

The girl laughed. 'You'd better not get too close to the microphone, then, or they'll think it's thunder.'

Kay glanced sideways. 'Sure you're all right?' she asked.

'Just a bit of stage-fright, as usual. Aren't you nervous?'

'Of course. But I had some Dutch courage earlier. Did you?'

'Didn't dare. Remember what happened last time?'

'Am I ever likely to forget? Or Sandy! Have you seen him since the lunch?'

Jane shook her head. She was dreading the confrontation. When he arrived, he just nodded coolly in her direction, smiled at Kay and was obviously a little overawed by the presence of his idol, Sir Archibald McIndoe, one of the most charming men Jane had met. Two members of his famous Guinea Pig Club were introduced, and she noticed a young production assistant flinch as she entered the Hospitality Room. Jane talked to one of the airmen about Robert.

'Yes, I remember the merchant navy chap. There weren't many in East Grinstead without wings.' His smile was lopsided, but warm. 'The Boss did a ruddy good job on his nose. How's he doing?'

'Fine. He and his wife run a sailing school in Brixham.'

'That's the ticket. What most people tend to forget is that we might look different on the outside but, inside, we're still human beings.'

Looking at the stumps of his fingers holding a cigarette, Jane wondered if she could have such courage if she were suddenly unable to play the piano. As if reading her thoughts, he said, 'We have to forget the things we can't do and concentrate on the things we still can do.'

'You're absolutely right. And I would imagine that's exactly the sort of thing the viewers will want to hear.'

'You know, I was a bit nervous about going on the box, but I don't feel so bad now.' The Floor Manager beckoned the airman, who nodded. 'Tally Ho!' He grinned at Jane. 'Thanks for the chat.'

As she turned to look for a glass of water, Jane realised that Sandy was only a few feet away, a thoughtful expression on his face. Oh, what wouldn't she give to be able to tell him the truth, to apologise. Even the opportunity to speak politely for once would be something. But he turned away, and the moment was gone.

All too soon it was their turn. The interviewer mostly spoke to Kay, who showed a picture of her nose before the operation and smiled a little nervously as the cameras came in for a close up of the finished product. Sandy talked about the technical side of the operation, and the reasons plastic surgery was his chosen field. To her surprise, Jane found she was quite calm when asked for her opinion on the various forms of cosmetic surgery, and was able to discuss some of her readers' problems without reference to her notes.

It was over. With fixed smiles, they sat in their chairs while the credits rolled. After the 'Well done, everybody', they were entertained with wine and light refreshments. She skipped the wine but accepted the canapés. Sandy remained with the surgeon and his patients until it was time to leave. As he shook hands with Kay, Jane wondered if he would speak to her, but there was just another cursory nod and he left without a backward glance.

The food had calmed the hollow in her stomach, but she knew nothing would ever comfort the emptiness in her heart.

★ ★ ★

The call Jane had been dreading came the day after the television programme.

'The newspaper man. He come in for my special cannelloni today. It remind me I not hear from you.'

'I'm sorry,' Jane said. 'But five hundred pounds is a lot of money.'

'You have lot of money. Soon you will be married to rich man with big business. Only rich and famous people get married in Caxton Hall. There is no problem with money.'

'My fiancé is not a rich man. He has a very small business, smaller than yours, and he has no money to spare.' Perhaps she should appeal to the Italian affection for children. 'My money is in trust for my nephew. He needs to go abroad for an operation on his leg.'

Silence. Then, 'I remember Rose tell me about the little boy with the bad leg. But you are famous lady. I see you on television with famous people. You have more money, not for the boy.'

She had hoped he would be too busy to see the programme. 'Only a small amount I need for my wedding.'

'How small?'

'Fifty pounds.'

Again a silence. 'You give me fifty pounds.

Borrow more money. Big man in bank will not lend to small Italian businessman. But he no spit on your name. You important lady.'

It was Jane's turn to remain silent, and think. 'I will send you a cheque for fifty pounds tomorrow. The rest I cannot guarantee, but I will try.'

His voice was sharper. 'You send cheque today. And try hard for rest of money. Very hard.' His tone changed, as though he were smiling. 'Mario very busy man. Not want to visit your mama and papa. Or your bridegroom. You no want me to visit, eh?'

'No! I will try hard. But there must be one condition.'

'I listen.'

'If, and I repeat — *if* — I borrow the rest of the money, there must be no further demands, ever. Is that clear?'

'Once Mario has big new restaurant, he not need more money.'

'Promise.'

'On my mama's grave.'

'You said your mother was alive.'

'On my grandmama's grave.'

'Five hundred pounds, and no more. I need your word.'

'Mario's word is honest. Trust me.'

Jane replaced the receiver, feeling she had betrayed her integrity, and Rose. Betrayed

— the word that would haunt her for the rest of her life. She wrote out the cheque and put it into her handbag. It would be posted today, but after the last post had gone. Only a small delaying tactic, more would be needed before she could write any further cheques to Mario.

But how on earth was she going to obtain another four hundred and fifty pounds?

18

At the end of January, hurricane winds whipped the North Sea into a frenzy, and breached the dikes of Holland before venting their spleen on the east coast of England. As soon as Laura heard the early morning news item that the Thames Estuary had overflowed its banks, seriously flooding large areas of Kent and Essex, she telephoned her mother.

The storm had kept Jane awake most of the night, and she was already dressed when Laura knocked on her bedroom door.

'I'm going to pick up Bea. Her front rooms are under water.'

'Is there anything I can do?'

'Thanks a lot, but I can manage, and Desmond will be here to give Len a hand.' As the telephone rang, Laura said, 'Could you take that for me while I change?'

The call was from the WVS. They were desperate for dry clothing for survivors from Canvey Island. Could Laura contact her members, collect as much warm clothing and blankets as possible, and take it to Benfleet?

'Sorry, someone else will have to do it. I must look after Bea.'

Jane had a brainwave. 'I'll do it,' she offered.

'What about work?'

'I'll phone in. Just let me have the names and telephone numbers of your ladies.'

An hour or so later, Jane changed into her thickest trousers and duffel coat, while Desmond loaded a huge suitcase and several carrier bags into her car. 'You'd better take these as well,' he said, holding out a large pair of wellington boots. 'Mind how you drive. The roads are bad down there at the best of times, so there'll be potholes lurking under the floodwater.'

As she approached Benfleet, the puddles became larger and deeper until it was almost impossible for her to proceed. Lorries laden with digging materials splashed past and soldiers were everywhere, piling sandbags around doors in readiness for the next high tide. She wound down her window and called out, 'I've got dry clothes here for the WVS. Can you direct me?'

A bedraggled corporal blinked at her through the rain. 'Down there and round the corner, miss. But your vehicle's a bit low slung — you'll flood the engine.'

'Can I walk?'

'If you've got rubber boots. Park up that little rise. It should be safe enough there.'

Jane paddled through with the suitcase and a carrier bag. She would need to make several trips to empty the car. Just inside the door of the hall that had been commandeered as a rest centre, a middle-aged woman in WVS uniform stood at a row of trestle tables, sorting through piles of clothing. 'These are from Laura Davies's group,' Jane said. 'Where shall I put them?'

Barely glancing at Jane, the harassed-looking lady pointed. 'Down at the end, dear. Have you got any socks?'

'In the car.'

'Good. The rescue workers are desperate for them and I can't get the wet ones dried off quickly enough.'

Jane emptied the suitcase and carried it back to the car twice for refills. On her third trip, she realised what the woman meant. Her stockings were decidedly damp and uncomfortable. As she tipped out the jumpers and cardigans, a tired-looking man came into the hall. 'Christ, but it's cold down on the sea wall!' he said.

The woman handed him a mug of tea. 'Here, take this. I've only just poured it. Can I get you something to eat?'

'No, ta. We're racing against the next tide, and we've still got a lot of people to evacuate. Ah . . . ' His eyes focused on a long football scarf. 'Just what I need.'

As she handed him the scarf, Jane asked, 'Have you managed to get everybody out in time?'

'Afraid not, miss. Over two hundred bodies at the last count, but there'll be more before we've finished. The old people can't cope with the cold.' He drained his cup, then went on, 'Like the wife of that old boy in the corner. Just slid off the chest of drawers into the water. We found him hanging on to the top of the wardrobe. Poor old sod.' Wrapping the scarf around his neck, the rescue worker went out to brave the elements once more.

In the corner, a very old man with a blanket around his shoulders stared at the floor. At first, Jane wasn't sure what he was muttering. Then she realised it was a name. 'Min . . . ' He repeated it over and over.

The room was filled with dejected people trying to come to terms with the fact that their homes and treasured possessions were under several feet of water, which would turn to sludge as it receded. They were the lucky ones. Others would have to identify loved ones.

'Dreadful, isn't it?' The woman followed Jane's gaze.

'Just like the war.' Jane picked up the empty suitcase. 'This will be the last load. Is there anything I can do to help?'

The WVS member glanced at Jane's manicured hands. 'Well . . . ' she began, uncertainly.

'Don't worry,' Jane assured her. 'I'm quite capable of sorting through clothes or making tea, if it will help.'

'To tell the truth, dear, I could do with a break. I've been here since seven this morning.'

As fast as Jane sorted piles of socks, jumpers, trousers and skirts, the other ladies whisked them away into another room where the survivors were able to exchange wet garments for something that might — or might not — fit, but was dry.

'Have you any more blankets, please? I have patients suffering from hypothermia.' The voice was familiar.

Jane turned to see Mrs Randall, wearing her nursing uniform. At first she didn't recognise Jane, who grinned as she stabbed at her hair with a hairgrip. 'I know. The readers wouldn't recognise me, either. Here — I've got some knitted shawls. Will they help?'

'Anything. I'm trying to keep them alive till we can get them into hospital.'

'I suppose they've asked for all the medical staff they can get. Some of the poor souls seem to be badly shocked as well as cold.'

'And we've had quite a few injuries, where they've been trapped or fallen off furniture. Sandy's helping to make them more comfortable while we're waiting for the ambulances to shuttle them away.'

'Sandy?'

'He drove here as soon as he was off duty, to see what he could do.'

Jane was cold, dishevelled, hungry and vulnerable. The last person she wanted to face right now was Sandy. But there he was in the doorway, with his hair plastered to his head and a woman clinging to his back.

'Careful,' he warned, as his mother helped lower the woman. 'She's wrenched her shoulder rather badly, hanging on to the roof.' Then he noticed Jane. 'Good God! What are you doing here?'

Before she could answer, he was called to examine a man whose condition had deteriorated. Watching, Jane couldn't help but be impressed with the calm and efficient way he and his mother worked, assessing the priority of patients for the ambulances, writing notes for the hospital staff, then back out to meet the next lorry load of rescued people.

It was late afternoon before additional voluntary assistance arrived and Jane was thanked for her help. As she pulled up the hood of her duffel coat, preparing for the trek back to her car, the rescue worker wearing the football scarf popped his head around the door, thrust a soggy bundle into her arms and said, 'Glad you're still here, love. Find a home for this one, will you? Its owner's dead.'

She looked at the bundle. It was a dog! What breed, and what age, there was no way of telling. Its coat was covered in mud, and it seemed more dead than alive. She turned back to the ladies at the table. They all said, 'Poor little thing', but shook their heads when she asked if someone could take it home. Suddenly, it raised its head, and two dark eyes glistened amongst the mud as it looked appealingly into Jane's face. When she was a child, she had chosen a puppy in Romford market because it did just that.

Jane stroked the wet head. 'Looks as though I'll have to take you,' she murmured, 'although goodness knows what Bernard and Eunice will say.' She foraged around for a piece of old sacking, wrapped the shivering animal tightly inside her coat, and set off.

It was even more difficult keeping her footing in the dark and twice she slipped to her knees, desperately holding on to the dog. The car spluttered several times before she was able to start the engine, then stalled as it hit a stretch of water at the bottom of the hill.

Was it her imagination, or was the water rising? She turned the ignition key again, left it for a moment to avoid flooding the engine with petrol, then tried once more. The wheels spun, but the car moved forward. Thank goodness.

Suddenly, blinding headlights appeared out of the darkness! She turned the wheel hard to the left to avoid a collision, the little Morris skidded off the road, and her own headlights disappeared beneath the swirling waters. Briefly they illuminated below the surface, like a submarine, then blinked and went out. Completely out of control, the car was swept further and further away into the flood, noisily crashing into debris.

Terrified, Jane tried to remember what Uncle Nobby had once said about being trapped underwater in a car. Wait until the car filled with water, then the pressure would ease against the door, and you could swim away. But would the dog hold its breath when the water closed over its head? Of course not. She grabbed the whimpering animal from the seat and held it under the roof until the water reached her chin, then pushed her weight hard against the door. At first it wouldn't budge, but eventually she tumbled out, holding the dog high with one hand while she groped for a safe handhold on the outside of the car with the other. Her foot found the running board, but the car was settling lower into the water and she was forced to climb onto the bonnet. Soon she began to lose the sense of feeling in her limbs.

Peering through the lashing rain, she looked for a light, some sign of habitation. There was nothing — just blackness. Her cries for help were lost in the howling gale. Where was the driver who had forced her off the road? Probably in difficulties himself. Oh, God! Little Mo was sinking even further.

She would have to swim — but in what direction? Already she had drifted far from the road, and if she went the wrong way she would be swept out to sea! But there was nothing to cling to on the roof of the car. She had no choice.

Offering up a swift prayer, Jane slipped into the icy water, still trying to hold the little dog above the surface. If only she could see a little. Suddenly, she was caught in a current and spinning, as helpless as the driftwood which bounced painfully against her body. Through the darkness, a huge, vague shape loomed straight in front of her.

The thud was sickening, the light blinding and the blackness total as water covered her head.

19

Water gushed from her mouth and she felt as though her back had been pounded to a pulp. But the voice was soothing.

'Easy now. Don't open your eyes. Just relax.' Gentle hands examined her arms and legs. 'I don't think anything's broken, but don't move, just in case.' It sounded like Sandy's voice.

'Have I fallen off the haystack?' It was such an effort to speak. 'Don't worry,' she whispered. 'I'm only winded. Rose will know what to do.'

'Oh, Jane . . . ' Sandy's voice sounded funny.

She was lying face down, and she was soaked through. Why was she so wet? It had been a lovely sunny day. Everyone had said that the summer of 1939 had been glorious. No one would think a war had started. Was that a dog whimpering? Mr Green said dogs would run wild and spread rabies if war broke out, and Rover should be put down. He'd said sorry afterwards, but it was too late.

'I'm sorry, Sandy,' she croaked. 'So very sorry.' She tried to move, but the pain in her shoulder was agonising. And her head hurt.

'Shush, my love. You may have concussion. Keep very still.'

'But I want to apologise — what did you say?'

'I said you may have concussion.'

'No — before that.' The effort to talk really was too much. It was easier to mumble.

It seemed forever before he answered. 'Shush, my love, while I give you an injection.' Sandy's voice grew fainter. 'And where the ruddy hell did you get the mut that's just pooped all over the back seat of my car?'

It was very quiet and dark — except for a glimmer of light from the fanlight above the door reflecting on the white bedcover and stiff white sheets. Jane lay still, wishing her mother hadn't used quite so much starch, then looked again at the door. Her bedroom door didn't have a fanlight.

Tentatively, she moved her head. Ouch! Very carefully she raised her right hand, touched a bandage around her forehead. Toes still wriggled, no feel of plaster. Her left hand was covered with another hand. She squinted into the darkness. A sleeping man slumped in a chair at the side of the bed. It looked like Sandy. If it was Sandy sitting there, holding her hand, she must have died and gone to heaven. She'd often wondered if it was really white and hushed, like this.

Her movement disturbed his sleep. 'Hello, Jane.' There was a smile in his voice. 'How do you feel?'

'Weird.' Her voice sounded peculiar. 'If I'm in heaven, what are you doing here?'

The smile became a chuckle. 'Not heaven, I'm glad to say — just hospital.'

Wincing, she moved her head a fraction. 'Am I the only patient?'

'The main wards are full. You're in one of the isolation wards. Does your head hurt?'

'Yes.' As Jane tried to flex her left arm, an excruciating pain shot through her shoulder like a bolt of lightning. 'Oh, God! What have I done?'

'Dislocated your shoulder when a tree got in your way.' Switching on a dimmed bedside light, Sandy placed his fingers on her wrist, just as he had done when they'd been evacuated and she'd fallen off a haystack. He glanced up from his watch and shared the memory. 'I know how to do it properly now,' he said. 'You were rather waterlogged, inside as well as out, so we had to resuscitate you — that's why you're feeling a bit sore. And you've got a few stitches in your head — but you'll live. Just don't move around too much.'

'I was sure I was going to die,' she

351

murmured. 'How did you find me?'

'The guy in the lorry alerted the divers and they went straight after you in their amphibious whatsit. Even so, they wouldn't have found you if it hadn't been for the pooch.'

'I don't understand.'

'Well, my darling, you'd gone under but the dog was swimming around in a circle and they picked him up in their searchlight. He saved your life.'

Her breath escaped like a sigh, partly from grateful thanks to the little dog, mainly because of Sandy calling her 'my darling.'

'You were very lucky,' he said, 'and so am I.'

'Yes, Doctor.' Her tongue felt thick. 'Can I have a drink?'

After he poured a glass of water, gave her a pain-killing tablet, and settled her back comfortably on the pillow, Sandy kissed her lightly but lovingly upon the lips and took hold of her hand once again as she slid into a dreamless sleep.

★　★　★

Still woolly-headed, and with a throbbing shoulder and back, Jane was thankful to return to the unstarched comfort of her room above Laura's restaurant.

'A couple more days of bed rest and you'll be — well, not quite as good as new, but able to join the human race again,' Sandy diagnosed, then peered into her face as she remained silent. 'What's wrong?' he asked.

'I don't know. It's as if there's something I've forgotten. Something important.' She raised her eyes. 'Jack must have felt like this.'

'It's the concussion. Don't worry about it.'

'I can't help it. I feel as though I'm someone else, not Jane Harrison.'

'Does Helena Beaumont ring a bell?'

'Oh, yes. My stage name — no, my professional name. Oh, dear, I don't seem to know who I am or what I'm doing.'

'Well, to be honest, my sweet, I'm perfectly happy to have Jane Harrison back in my life. Helena Beaumont had turned you into a . . .' He hesitated.

'A monster?'

'You said it, not me.' He studied her hand, stroking the fingers one by one, before he went on, 'Certainly you were a stranger. But when I watched you helping out in the rest centre, with your hair all over the place, you were the old Janey — the one I've loved since I saw a little girl sitting by herself on top of a haystack, looking rather forlorn.'

'You never said a word!'

'Fourteen-year-old boys don't even realise it's love, let alone talk about it.'

'I mean later, you idiot.'

'Ah, later came exams, med school and national service. All the things young men have to deal with before they're ready to settle down. And I heard you were engaged to a Norwegian.'

'You had girlfriends.'

'One or two. None that I wanted to spend the rest of my life with. I never managed to recapture the comfortable feeling I had when I was with you.'

'Oh, Sandy,' Jane sighed. 'If only I'd known.'

'It was all in the letter I wrote after Rose was killed.'

Sadly, Jane remembered how she'd stuffed it into the fire, unopened.

'I tried to explain how I felt,' Sandy went on. 'Thought perhaps I could help you through a hard time. But you didn't answer.'

Jane felt the warm tear slide down her cheek. 'I'm sorry. It was a misunderstanding. I thought . . . '

Gently, he prompted. 'What did you think?'

Jane shook her head. She didn't want to talk about Rose. It was too painful.

At that moment, Laura put her head

around the bedroom door. 'Your parents are here, Jane.'

'Both of them? How did they . . . ?'

'Len phoned. Shall I ask them to come up?'

Mr Harrison kissed Jane and sat on the bed. Mrs Harrison put a bag of oranges on the bedside table. 'I didn't know what to get you.' Her eyes noted the bandage, but didn't linger.

'Thank you. I'm glad you came.'

'Fred said I should.'

Oh, please don't spoil it, Jane thought. We'll never get another chance to make it up.

Mr Harrison squeezed Jane's hand. 'It didn't take much persuasion,' he said.

'How are you?' Mother and daughter spoke together, then waited for an answer.

Again Fred Harrison stepped into the breach. 'Mum's had a cold since Christmas and, as for Jane, she reminds me of one of the ruins that Oliver Cromwell knocked about a bit.' He looked up at Sandy. 'But I can see she's in good hands.'

Their laughter was nervous. Sandy asked, 'Would you like me to leave you alone?'

'No, please stay,' Jane pleaded, and her father nodded.

'How's Grandad?' Jane asked her mother.

'Same as usual — just a bit older.'

For a short while the tension was relieved when Laura brought up a tray of tea and they talked about the floods, and the little dog.

'I owe him my life,' Jane explained to her parents.

'Ah — ' Laura paused. 'Correction — *he* is very much a *she*.' She smiled at the expression on Jane's face. 'We'll take one of the pups when they arrive, if you can find homes for the others. Oh, by the way, I have something for you . . . ' Laura hurried from the room and returned with her handbag. 'When I brought your clothes along this morning, the nurse gave me these.' She rummaged around the handbag and produced a small package. 'She'd put them in her locker for safety.'

One ring was a gold signet with the engraved initial *J*, a sixteenth birthday gift from Aunt Peggy. A matching ring with the initial *R* had been worn on a gold chain around Nell Harrison's neck since the day Rose was killed. The second ring in Laura's package provided the missing link in Jane's memory. It was a sapphire and diamond engagement ring. Bernard!

Laura was still speaking. 'I've been so busy this morning, I forgot to tell you that Bernard phoned from Liverpool. He was visiting his sister, and wanted to make sure we were OK

— but as soon as he heard you were injured he said he would come straight home.'

Sandy was standing by the window, his back to the room. It was impossible to know what he was feeling. Fred Harrison broke the silence.

'Your mum and I have been talking, Jane.'

Her mind full of Bernard and Sandy, Jane waited.

Nell Harrison licked her lips. 'You can't go back there before the wedding. It isn't right.'

'That's why I asked Laura if I could stay here.'

'But she's going to have her hands full, with Bea living here for a while, and Desmond out of the army, as well as the business to run.' Mrs Harrison glanced at her husband. 'Anyway, your father and I have agreed you can come back — on one condition.'

'No, Nell!' her husband protested. 'No conditions, please. I just want my daughter home.'

'And I want my daughter's name cleared.' A flash of anger crossed Mrs Harrison's face. 'All I'm asking is that Janey takes back everything she said about Rose.'

Jane closed her eyes. However desperately she wanted to go home, was she prepared to go back to the role of the wicked sister,

357

confess to a lie she had not told?

'Not now, Nell.' Mr Harrison's voice was firm. 'You can see the girl is ill. Let's just take her home and put everything else behind us.'

'How can I put it behind me, when every day I remember her accusing Rose of taking Gran's money — ' Mrs Harrison put a hand to her mouth and glanced quickly at Laura.

'For goodness' sake, Nell!' Mr Harrison sounded exasperated. 'Has it never occurred to you that Jane might be right? Rose was trying to borrow money from both of us that day. She could have been desperate enough to take Gran's money.'

'That was the last day of her life, Fred. I won't have her branded as a thief.'

'She probably intended to put it back, just wanted it urgently, that's all.'

'Don't be stupid, Fred! She was only going to the pantomime. Why on earth would she need to take the whole of Gran's savings?' Her voice was contemptuous. 'No, it's Janey who's got it all wrong — just out of spite.'

'Stop it!' Jane cried. 'Please stop it. I can't bear to keep hearing it over and over again.' She put a hand to her aching head. 'And it's not fair on the others.'

Her mother reddened. 'I'm sorry, Laura — Sandy — but I have to clear this up once and for all. It's been making my nerves bad

358

thinking about all these lies.'

Sandy's back was still to the room, his voice low. 'Jane isn't spiteful, and she isn't lying.'

Mrs Harrison appeared shocked at the interruption. 'You don't know anything about it, Sandy.'

'Actually, I probably know more than you do, Mrs Harrison.' He turned around to face Jane's mother. 'Rose phoned me that morning, and we lunched together. She was desperate for help — and for money.'

'I don't believe it!' Mrs Harrison stared back at him. 'Why should Rose go to you for money? And what sort of help?'

Sandy looked at the expectant faces. 'I wish I could spare you this. In fact . . . ' He smiled faintly at Jane. 'I suspect that Jane has been trying to spare you the truth for eight years.'

Fred Harrison gripped his wife's arm as he quietly said, 'You'd better tell us then, if it's the only way.'

Jane was not quite prepared for Sandy's answer.

'Rose came to me for an abortion.'

'No!' Nell Harrison cried out loud, then swayed a little and leaned against her husband. When she spoke, her voice was little more than a whisper. 'It's not true. It can't be true.' She looked at Jane, who nodded.

'It is true, I'm afraid.' Her voice was choked.

Mrs Harrison shook her head, still unable to believe the truth. 'I would have known if Rose had been pregnant. A mother always knows these things. And Rose wouldn't dream of having an abortion. She'd have come to me first. She'd know I would stand by her.'

'You were anxious about Jack at the time. I only guessed she was pregnant because she was sick at work — then she admitted it, Mum.'

Laura took a packet of cigarettes from her handbag. 'I confess I wondered, when she looked so unwell that Boxing Day.' She lit two and handed one to Nell Harrison. 'I'll make some more tea.'

'No — thank you — I must go home.' Mrs Harrison looked from face to face, then back at Jane. 'Why didn't she tell me? Why didn't you tell me?' The pain in her face was pitiful.

Finding her voice through the tears, Jane said, 'She had promised she would speak to you and Dad that weekend. I didn't know she had gone to the nurse until I went looking for her.'

'Oh, no! Not one of those back-street jobs?'

'I'm sorry, Mum. I thought I'd talked her out of it,' Jane sobbed. 'If I'd known, I would

360

have gone after her the night before.'

'Rose — my beautiful Rose. How she must have suffered. And I wasn't there with her . . . ' Suddenly Mrs Harrison pointed a shaking finger at Sandy. 'Was it you?' she cried. 'You were always together.'

He held up a hand. 'No. Rose and I were always friends, but never lovers. And I don't think you are the only one who put two and two together and made five.' He looked at Jane. 'Is that why you hated me so much?'

Miserably, she nodded. 'I saw you together in the restaurant, heard her accuse you of not caring, and I assumed . . . ' Jane's own tears would not allow her to continue.

'It was me?' Sandy finished her sentence, then explained. 'I tried to convince Rose that an abortion was not only illegal but dangerous, and I wouldn't lend her the money to go somewhere else.' His expression was anguished as he looked at Mrs Harrison. 'I told her you'd look after her, but she was too angry with me to listen. If I'd known she had an address, I'd have come straight to you — I swear it.'

Nell Harrison's eye twitched rapidly. She seemed too stunned to weep. 'It must have been the Canadian. He was her only lover, wasn't he?'

'I expect so. Rose didn't confide in me, but

361

Larry was her steady boyfriend.'

Jane was certain that Sandy was aware there had been other lovers, but was trying to save her mother from further humiliation.

Laura came to the rescue. 'I'll run you both home,' she said. 'You need time to accept this. Jane can stay here as long as she wants.'

At the door, Nell Harrison turned back and stared at Jane for a long moment. Her face was grey, and she seemed to have aged ten years in the last few minutes. Silently she raised her hand, palm upwards, in a helpless gesture before she followed Laura downstairs.

Mr Harrison held Jane close before he kissed her cheek. 'I'll come back for you tomorrow,' he said. 'And, Jane,' he took a handkerchief from his pocket and gently wiped away her tears, 'I'll not allow her to upset you any more. That's a promise.'

Jane grabbed the handkerchief in a vain attempt to stem the flood of tears.

Her father stood up, glancing at Sandy before he quietly said, 'I think it's about time we all stopped feeling guilty about Rose.'

After he had left, the room was silent, apart from the gentle sounds of Jane weeping, and murmurs of preparation from the restaurant below.

Eventually, Sandy asked, 'Do you know who the father really is?'

She nodded. There was no point in keeping any more secrets from Sandy — and she really needed to share the burden with someone.

He listened carefully while she told him about Mario's blackmail, then said, 'Well, it's all over now.'

Not understanding, Jane raised her head from her father's handkerchief.

'Ignore him until he threatens you again,' Sandy advised. 'Then tell the little skunk that your parents know. When he's recovered from the shock he'll creep back under his slimy little stone.'

Of course! Thank God. Her sigh of relief was cut short by Sandy's next words. 'But we have another problem which won't go away by itself.' For the first time since Laura handed over the rings, he looked directly into Jane's eyes. 'What are you — what are we going to do about Bernard?'

Through puffed eyes, Jane stared at the rings. The signet ring slipped easily onto the third finger of her right hand, but Bernard's ring remained in her palm as she listened to the sound of tyres screeching on the gravel parking area.

Sandy turned to the window, then let the curtain drop. 'Bernard has just arrived,' he said, his voice tight, as though all emotion was locked inside, like a volcano waiting to explode.

20

With an agonised expression, Sandy thumped the window frame. 'For God's sake, Jane! You can't do this. Not now we've found each other again.'

Before she could answer, there was a tap on the door and Bernard appeared, holding an enormous bouquet. 'Is it all right for me to come in, dear? Oh — hello!' He smiled at Sandy. 'I didn't know you were here.'

'Sorry — I've got to get back to the hospital.' Sandy brushed past Bernard, leaving Jane to explain his presence.

Fortunately, Bernard believed that her hesitation and tearfulness was due to her accident, and he accepted her plea that she was tired and would like to rest for a while.

'Of course, my dearest. You've had a harrowing experience and need lots of rest.' His face was full of concern as he kissed her forehead. 'I'll go down and talk to Len while you sleep.'

After he had quietly closed the door, Jane looked at the ring on her left hand. Her father had warned her; Aunt Grace had warned her; even Laura had warned her, but she had been so sure it would work out. Would it have been easier to make a different choice if Bernard had not been so caring? If he had been arrogant and demanding, perhaps she could have found the courage to tell him she loved another man. An angry row she could have tolerated, but she couldn't bear to imagine the hurt expression on his face and know she had been the cause.

Gingerly she reached for her handbag, every limb still aching, and looked into a mirror for the first time since she'd hit the tree. Her reflection was horrific, every bit as bad as the photographs in Sandy's medical album. The bruises would fade eventually, she knew, just as they had faded after Paul had attacked her. But would she be mentally strong enough to play the role of a loving fiancée — a loving wife? Why was life so bloody unfair?

She beat her fists against the eiderdown, remembering the conversation with her father at the Battersea Pleasure Gardens and knowing she had to stick by her decision and make the best of it. And after Captain Harlow had visited Jack, she had vowed that she would never hurt Bernard. She must stick to that vow, whatever the cost.

One consolation — she would not have to return to Bernard's house, although she would try to convince him that they really should look for a home of their own. Without the suspicious presence of his sister, they would have a better chance of living a normal married life.

Hoping to ease the throbbing headache, Jane took a painkiller and reflected that it would be nice to see Grandad again and to have Kathleen's cheerful company. Tomorrow, she thought, Dad will come and collect me. Tomorrow I'll be back in my own bed, surrounded by my own things. I'll have my own piano to play again — once my arm is out of the sling. Fortunately, the next show wasn't for another three weeks. Her thoughts turned to her mother, and she wondered how things would be once she returned to her home. Jane wasn't the only one who had suffered a shattering experience.

★ ★ ★

It was difficult to define the change in Nell Harrison. It was too subtle. Too many blows had taken their toll, and Jane knew her mother was finding it difficult to come to terms with the fact that her favourite daughter had toppled from her pedestal. But Mrs Harrison was at least trying to make the best of a bad job. The only reference she made to Rose was when she asked Jane not to tell Grandad about the baby.

Surprisingly, she also suggested that Jane bring the dog with her, and suggested a name. 'If she hadn't kept swimming, like Esther Williams, they might not have found you.' And when Esther climbed into her basket under the stairs one night and produced a litter of six, Nell Harrison found a home for one of the pups with the Arkwrights next door, and another with Mrs Jarvis across the road. 'Johnny is taking one to Devon, and Kathleen wants a bitch — although I think she's asking for trouble.'

'Why?'

'Can you imagine what a puppy will get up to, left alone in a tiny flat all day?'

'She said the couple next door will have it while she's at work.'

'They won't want it digging up their lovely garden, that's for sure.' Mrs Harrison had counted on her fingers. 'With Laura, that's five. Will you have the last one?'

'We're keeping Esther.' Jane looked pleadingly at her mother, who was trying to sort out the sexes of the squirming pups.

'Oh, well. I suppose I'll have to have it. Although goodness knows what your father will say. He's making plans for the garden — talking about buying a heater for the greenhouse and growing his own plants from seed.'

★ ★ ★

Jane was resting when her father knocked on the bedroom door. 'There's a phone call for you, love.'

Sleepily, she rubbed her eyes. 'Who is it?'

'He wouldn't say. His English isn't too clever, but he said it is important.'

Suddenly, she was wide awake.

Mr Harrison seemed startled by her expression. 'Shall I tell him to ring back?' he asked. 'I did say you were asleep.'

'No, I'll take it. Where's Mum?'

'Up at the shops. And Grandad's taking a nap in his room.'

Thank goodness they wouldn't be listening in and asking questions, Jane thought, as she picked up the telephone. 'How did you get this number?' she demanded.

'I ask girl in your office,' Mario sniggered. 'Say I need to speak to your papa about the booking for your wedding luncheon.'

'My secretary would never give anyone my private number, and she has made the necessary arrangements — elsewhere.'

'Not secretary. She was out. Another girl give me number.'

369

Seething, Jane made a mental note to have strong words with the new office junior. Mario was still talking. 'I know you not give me answer in office. Mario mean business. I read in paper about accident. Now you get compensation for car. Lots of money. No more bloody messing about, eh?'

Hearing her father setting out teacups in the kitchenette, Jane lowered her voice. 'Listen, you nasty piece of work. I have told my parents about Rose — and the baby. So you're not getting another penny!'

She heard him draw in his breath before he said, 'I not believe you! You not tell them I am father.'

'They know everything,' she lied. 'And if you ever call this number again, I will give your name to the police.'

The telephone clicked.

Her father put his head around the door. 'Finished, dear?' he asked. 'Shall I bring in the tea?'

'Yes, I've quite finished, thank you. And a cup of tea would be lovely.'

★ ★ ★

As soon as she returned to work, Jane immersed herself in the special issues for the Queen's coronation in June, researching,

370

arranging photo sessions, interviewing, writing. The call from the BBC was more of a shock than a surprise.

'They want me to do some of the commentary — covering fashion and make-up.' Stunned, she flopped into the chair opposite Kay's desk.

'On the radio?'

'On television.'

'That's terrific! They must have liked the bit you did last month.'

'Guess so. But to be at the Abbey — part of the Coronation. Gosh! It's a bit scary.'

'You'll be fine. Now, what are you going to wear?'

'Oh! I hadn't thought of that.'

'Your wedding outfit will be gorgeous — no — that wouldn't be fair.'

'If I was getting married two days before the Coronation, instead of two days after, I might have got away with it. I'll have to ask Mr David to do some more sketches.'

'He'll be delighted with the publicity — I'll do a piece on you for the mag.' Kay grinned. 'Bet you can't wait to tell your mum!'

★   ★   ★

It was difficult to guess whether or not her mother was pleased. She just said, 'Really?' in

371

a non-committal way, frowned thoughtfully for a moment, then untied her apron and disappeared.

Grandad looked at the empty doorway, then back to Jane, said, 'Well, I never!' and shook his head. Kathleen jumped up and down with joy. Fred Harrison was equally delighted and poured them all a glass of sherry. Jane expected Grandad to ask for a glass of brown ale instead, but he cheerfully raised his glass to 'one on our side, girl.'

Kathleen was cock-a-hoop. 'Can you imagine what the folks in the office will say when I tell them?' She shrieked with laughter. 'Even the po-faced senior partner has to be impressed that my very best friend is going to be at Westminster Abbey with all the Lords and Ladies!'

Mr Harrison smiled. 'Not just Lords and Ladies, Kathleen. Princes and Princesses as well, and a fair sprinkling of Kings and Queens — the most important being our own Queen Elizabeth, God Bless her.' Glasses were refilled and raised as the toast was echoed. Why had her mother left the house in such a hurry, Jane wondered? They hadn't had supper yet.

Jane was looking in the larder to see what was available when Mrs Harrison returned. Mr Harrison took her coat.

'Where on earth did you dash off to, Nell?' he asked.

'Oh, here and there.' A smug little smile on her face, Mrs Harrison picked up her apron. 'Mrs Ackroyd, Mrs Jarvis, the Irish family who had the party on VE Day, and the new people at number forty-four. They're all coming.'

'Coming? Coming where?'

'Here, of course — to watch the Coronation on our television set.' Mrs Harrison rattled the saucepans in the cupboard. 'They were quite amazed when I told them that Janey will be at Westminster Abbey.' She found the poacher, and went on, 'Haddock and poached egg for supper as we're a bit late. Give me a hand, Janey . . .' Mrs Harrison glanced quickly at her husband before she added, 'if you don't mind.'

* * *

Jane was working on her paste-ups the following week when the telephone rang. She waited for Trish to intercept the call, then remembered she was getting coffee and sandwiches from the canteen.

'Mario! How dare you?'

'Do not put phone down.' He sounded very arrogant. 'I read in papers you will be on

373

television again. Will see the Queen. Now very important lady will be paid big money, *si?*'

'That has nothing whatsoever to do with you. I told you, my parents know everything, so you can't . . . '

'But do your bosses know everything? Do BBC bosses know everything?'

Feeling sick, she held her breath and waited.

'Ah, I think not. And I think they might not want you near Queen of England if they read about naughty sister in papers. Not good for bridegroom just before wedding, eh? Not good for mama and papa when everyone talk about their pretty little Rose.' Mario laughed. 'You not say so much now. No, you just listen.'

'I'm listening.'

'My friend from newspaper. He come to eat tomorrow.'

She would have to pay him and be done with it. 'How much do you want?'

'Everything go up since I last talk. Newspaper will give me five hundred pounds for story. I need thousand pounds for business.'

'What! That's far too much.'

'How much you have?'

Jane thought rapidly. The insurance claim

374

had not been settled on the car, and there were some royalties due from the book, but nothing like the amount he was demanding. She would have to try to negotiate, stall him.

'I don't know. I will phone my bank manager, ask for a loan, but it will take some days even if he agrees — and it won't be all at once.'

'Five hundred to start. You have to end of week, or I sell story.'

Shaking, Jane stared at the telephone. How much more? And just as her life was becoming — bearable. She had to get rid of him, once and for all.

The bank manager would see her in half an hour, but Jane couldn't wait around in the office. To fill in the time and settle her nerves, she decided to walk to the bank instead of taking a taxi. Perhaps the air would clear her head, it was cold enough. Head down against the threatening rain, Jane walked briskly along the back streets, not noticing the man unfurling his umbrella outside the Charing Cross Hospital until they had collided.

'I'm sorry — Jane!' It was Sandy. She hadn't seen him since the day when she had slipped Bernard's ring back onto her finger. Suddenly she felt faint.

'Oh, Sandy . . . ' she murmured, as her knees gave way.

Within minutes, he'd propelled her into a cafe, ordered tea, and listened while she recounted the telephone conversation with Mario. When she had finished, he said, 'Keep your appointment with the bank manager, but don't sign anything. I'll make one or two enquiries of my own and get back to you.'

'What sort of enquiries?' Jane wondered if he was going to offer to lend her the money.

He shrugged. 'Trust me.'

Of course she trusted him. With her life, if necessary. But he must know why she had made her decision. 'Sandy — I never had a chance to explain about Bernard.'

'It was your choice, Jane, not mine.'

'But you don't know all the facts.'

Sandy sat back in his chair and looked at the ceiling. 'Bernard was in a German prison camp for five years, lost some toes through frostbite, his dancing career was finished and — when he was repatriated — his wife told him she was divorcing him and going off to America. Right?'

Jane nodded.

'On the rebound he fell in love with a younger woman, kind and caring, the sort of girl who would be good and true and — ' His eyes searched her face for an answer. 'Why did you ever agree to marry him in the first place? You don't love him.'

376

'I'm very fond of Bernard and thought I could learn to love him. He said he loved me enough to be patient.' Explaining was so complex. 'It seemed better than just being . . . '

'An old maid?'

'Yes. Does that sound dreadful?'

'Not if you're really content to settle for second best, I suppose. But I thought you loved me.'

'I do — if only you knew how much!' She reached across the table for his hand. 'But for years I thought you had behaved very badly towards Rose. In fact, I blamed you for her death. I know — I was wrong, and I'm sorry.' She entreated him to understand. 'I was afraid of falling in love with you — it was safer to marry Bernard.' She smiled, tearfully. 'In retrospect, I can see it was the most stupid thing I have ever done, but I can't go back on my word. It would be too cruel.'

'It's just as cruel for me,' Sandy said, quietly.

'I know,' she whispered. 'But you haven't suffered it all before.'

'It will be cruel for you, as well, being married to a man you don't love, and knowing there's someone else you could be happier with.'

'Please don't!' she cried. 'There's nothing I

want more than to run off with you into the sunset, like the end of a beautiful film — but I can't betray Bernard, and I promised his sister I would never put him through that again.'

'Eunice? What's she got to do with it?'

After Jane told him about her conversation with Eunice, Sandy raised his eyebrows.

'You're not going ahead with the marriage because you're afraid she's going to shave your head, are you?'

Exasperated, Jane shook her head. 'Of course not. But if I break my word, other people will be affected as well as Bernard.' She held his gaze. 'You might even lose respect for me yourself.'

Sandy didn't answer, just looked unhappy.

'So you see, my darling Sandy,' she went on, 'I have to keep my promise to another very fine man, and hope and pray that one day you will find someone who will be free to love you.' Her voice breaking, Jane picked up her handbag. 'Now I had better look for a taxi.'

★ ★ ★

The bank manager would only agree to an overdraft of three hundred pounds without collateral. All week, Jane worried about the money, and Mario, and Sandy. On Friday morning, Sandy telephoned her at the office, said it was unlikely that she'd hear again from Mario.

'What happened?'

'I went to see him, and you're right. He is a very unpleasant man. Showed me all the facts he had written down about Rose — and snapshots.'

'Oh, no!'

'However, when I mentioned that I'd been in touch with the Red Cross, and the Italian Embassy, and the Home Office, he lost some of his arrogance, and I was able to use a little blackmail of my own to recover the photographs.'

'What had you found out?'

'That our ex-prisoner of war was already married with three children when he was captured.'

Jane wondered how this affected the blackmail. 'Has his wife joined him over here?'

'She refused to leave Italy. But he hops home from time to time — now he has six kids. So I told him it wouldn't go down too well with his parish priest if it were known that he'd made a young English girl pregnant, then abandoned her. And his wife would probably castrate him if she found out.'

'Do you think he really will leave me alone now?'

'He'd better. I found out his residence visa is due for renewal, and he is very anxious to remain squeaky clean. A letter stating that he raped the niece of his employer whilst a prisoner-of-war, then tried to blackmail her sister, would definitely make his chances very slim.'

'Would you go as far as that?'

'I managed to convince him I would, if he tried to make trouble for you.'

Jane drew a deep breath. 'Is it really over?'

'Mario might be a greedy opportunist, but he knows I'm not bluffing, and he has too much to lose.'

'How can I ever thank you?'

'Oh, Jane — you know I can't answer that.'

'I'm sorry — but I am so grateful. I wish there were some way we could still be friends.'

There was a long silence, until Sandy said, 'I shall be your friend for life, Jane, if you ever need me. And I do wish you well. Goodbye, my love.'

21

In May 1953, Stanley Matthews helped Bolton Wanderers win the FA Cup Final, Edmund Hillary and Sherpa Tenzing placed their flags on the summit of Mount Everest and Chris Chattaway set the two-mile record at 8 minutes 49.6 seconds.

It was also an eventful month for the Harrisons: Sheila confirmed that she was pregnant on the day her mother exchanged her council flat for one in Paignton; Johnny won first prize in a national painting competition; and Jane, using the bank loan, was able to give Jack the money he needed for the operation on his son's leg. She also played *The Cornish Rhapsody* for her piano solo in the Coronation Celebration at the new Civic Centre and arranged some Elizabethan madrigals for Audrey, Monica and David to sing. Everyone said it was their best show ever, and Jane knew it had been good, but she wondered if they would be able to keep up the high standard without their lead performers. David and Ruth had decided to go back to Wales and were looking for a small garage to buy; Gordon was taking his double bass — and Monica — to Halewood; and Harry had accepted an offer to be drummer with a professional jazz band. They had all showered Audrey with confetti at Easter, and Jane knew the pretty soprano wanted to start a family as soon as possible. It would take some time to create another little band and find new voices of such excellence, and Jane wasn't sure her heart was really in it — or whether she would ever be able to recover her heart from Sandy. However hard she tried, she couldn't fill the hollowness inside her.

The day before the Coronation, Jane went to Westminster Abbey to check her position and last-minute details. The last person she expected to bump into again was Sandy.

'For goodness' sake, Jane! Don't you ever look where you're going?' He smiled ruefully as he helped her gather her papers from the pavement. 'My umbrella has not been the same since you tangled with it.'

'I'm sorry. I was thinking of something else.'

'Coronations and weddings, no doubt,' he said dryly. 'Not long now, is it?'

'Thursday.' She knew he wasn't referring to the Coronation. Oh, please, my darling, she thought, don't make me think about it. Let me just have this moment alone with you, even though we are surrounded by people and just making small talk.

He studied her face for a moment, then quietly said, 'How are things between you and your mother?'

'OK. We get on much better now, and she's almost back to her old self — worrying about what the neighbours think and so on.'

'The thing I remembered most about her when we were kids was how houseproud she was. Hitler might bomb her house but he wasn't allowed to make it dirty!'

'You should see her now, with a puppy to housetrain!'

'Have you found homes for all of them? Only we might . . . '

'They're all spoken for, I'm afraid. And I'm taking the mother when — ' Jane stopped abruptly.

Sandy turned away and Jane feared he might just go. But he turned back and asked, 'Has your mother come to terms with knowing the truth about Rose?'

'More or less. She'll always be Mum's favourite, and I understand that. But at least she treats me with respect.'

'Good. How's the rest of the family?'

Jane told him her brother's news. 'And Kathleen got her promotion and moved into Sheila's flat. Desmond wanted her to go over to the Coach and Horses tomorrow

— they've hired a television set for the customers — but she'd promised to help Mum make mountains of sandwiches. Half the street's been invited, and Mum's in her element making cakes and trifles.'

'Seems like everyone will be sitting behind drawn curtains tomorrow.'

'It's certainly been a boost for the television industry. Even Miss Dawson persuaded Aunt Grace that the bookings were so good, they could afford to buy one, and Robert and Yvonne are going over for the day with Jack and Sheila, so there'll be quite a party going on at the Babbacombe Bay Holiday Home! What about you?'

'Oh, I'm off duty tomorrow, but I might come here with a couple of the guys and see if this lot have finished in time!' He looked around the stands, where armies of men were making frantic last-minute preparations. Then he looked back at Jane. 'Are you nervous?' he asked.

'Terrified!'

'You'll be wonderful.' For a moment, they gazed silently at each other. Then he said, 'Would you like some good news to boost your morale?'

'Oh, yes please.'

'I've just been past Mario's restaurant, and it's closed.'

'Really? I wonder where the little rat has gone?'

'Back to Italy. I asked around and it seems he owed money everywhere, and was being hotly pursued by a pregnant waitress — oh, Jane, I'm so sorry! That was rather insensitive.'

'I'm just thankful he's gone — and I'll never forget that you were the one who got him off my back.' She smiled. 'Anyway, what are you doing here? You're a long way from the hospital.'

'Ah, well — a vacancy has come up for a Senior House Officer at East Grinstead, and Sir Archibald remembered me from our television programme. He's a consultant at the Chelsea Hospital for Women and arranged to interview me there.' Sandy ran a hand through his thatch of hair. 'I needed a walk afterwards to calm myself down, so decided to see what was going on around here.'

'When will you know if you've been successful?'

A broad grin spread across his face. 'I start in September.'

'That's wonderful news! Oh, Sandy, I'm so pleased for you.' Impulsively, Jane kissed him on the cheek. 'It's just what you wanted.'

'I know. My dream come true — well

385

— some of it.' He looked over her head and frowned. 'Isn't that . . . ?'

As Jane followed his gaze, the woman who had been watching them turned on her heel and walked quickly away. It was Eunice!

★ ★ ★

Although June 2nd was dull and showery, nothing could dampen the spirits of the stalwart crowds in London. They camped on the pavements to get a good vantage point, waved flags and cheered everyone. Even Jane warranted a ripple as she arrived at the Abbey in her deep purple grosgrain dress and matching dustcoat, with long white gloves and high-heeled shoes. She'd been tempted by a huge picture hat, but was glad she'd chosen the close fitting cap, covered with tiny aquamarine flowers. Disgustingly expensive, but just right for her task and Mr Gerard had swathed her hair into a chignon on the nape of her neck. Once the ceremony began, her nerves disappeared and she calmly took her turn at describing the gowns, the hairstyles, the jewellery and the robes. After the crown was solemnly placed upon the head of Queen Elizabeth II, and the last shout echoed from the rafters, Jane was entranced with the dignity and beauty of the slight figure who walked slowly between her curtseying and bowing loyal subjects.

It was over. Congratulations and goodbyes were said, cameras packed away, cables rewound, and Bernard was waiting by the BBC control van.

'I thought you were watching with Mum and Dad,' Jane said.

He kissed her. 'I couldn't see you, but I heard every word. You were superb!'

'Thanks — but I don't understand why you're here.'

'Can we get away from this crush?'

Curious, Jane led the way towards the Embankment. As she waited for Bernard to speak, she remembered Eunice. Oh, dear!

Eventually, Bernard spoke. 'Eunice saw you yesterday, with Sandy.'

'We bumped into each other accidentally and, before you draw the wrong conclusion, I was only congratulating him on his new job. I'm sorry if Eunice read more into it — '

'I know about his new job,' Bernard interrupted. 'But that isn't all, is it?' He took her arm and led her to the balustrade edging the river. 'As soon as Eunice telephoned me, I went to see Sandy at the hospital.'

'Why? Didn't you trust me?'

'Of course. But Eunice was convinced you were having an affair behind my back, so I thought the best way to convince her otherwise was to speak to Sandy myself.'

'What did he say?'

'That you were the most honourable person he'd ever met, and I am the luckiest man in the world. He even wished us luck for our wedding day.'

Jane waited. She could see by his face that there was more to come.

'I asked him if he loved you, and he said yes. Then I asked him if you loved him — and he told me to ask you myself.'

Closing her eyes, Jane waited for the dreaded question. It didn't come.

'I didn't need to,' Bernard went on. 'I think I have always known there was someone else, but couldn't bring myself to accept it. And when I discovered that you were prepared to make this magnificent sacrifice, I realised that I cannot let you do it.'

Jane opened her eyes — and her mouth, but no words came.

Bernard was still talking. 'I've managed to cancel the important arrangements for Thursday — I'll do the rest tomorrow. And I've spoken to your parents.' He breathed deeply. 'Now I've faced the truth, I couldn't live with you — or myself. It would be a marriage of pretence.'

Stunned, Jane could only stare. 'I don't

know what to say. I'm so sorry you found out.'

'When you've had time to think about it, you'll be pleased. But you have nothing to reproach yourself about.'

'Eunice must hate me.'

'To tell the truth, she's not particularly bothered.'

'But she . . . '

'Being Eunice, she had to make sure I knew. But she's much more concerned with her own romance at the moment.'

'What romance?'

'She met a guy in Paris when she took the girls over to Miss Bluebell. Right now she's packing her belongings ready to move over there.'

'Oh! You'll miss her.'

Bernard shook his head. 'She's a brilliant choreographer and we work well together, but we really shouldn't share a house.'

'What about the concert party?'

He shrugged. 'With so many leaving, I had been seriously thinking of winding it up and moving on once we were married.' He smiled. 'Even considered working in Paris. Would you have come?'

Jane shook her head, knowing he did not realise the real reason.

'Thought not. You wouldn't want to be too

far away from your family and friends. Anyway — I was quite impressed with the talent I saw up north, and Gordon and Monica could be founder members if I start a new group up there.' Bernard paused. 'I have a gut feeling that one day Liverpool might be big news in the entertainment world, and I'd like to be in at the beginning. If there's one thing I'm good at, it's spotting talent.' He shrugged his shoulders. 'So you needn't worry about me, my dearest Jane. I'm not going to sit at home crying into my beer.'

'Bernard.' Jane blinked as she tried to think clearly. 'How did Mum and Dad take the news?'

'Your mother seemed more concerned as to whether the shop would refund the money on her new hat, but I sensed relief from your father.'

'Dad liked you — really liked you — but I think he was bothered about the age gap.'

'At least that won't be a problem with Sandy.'

Jane fought hard to control the threatening tears. 'The last thing I wanted was for you to be hurt any more. You've been so good to me, and I really am very fond of you.'

'I know. But just being fond isn't enough — for either of us.'

She removed her glove and slipped off the

engagement ring. 'I wish it didn't have to be like this,' she murmured.

For a moment, Bernard held the ring, watching the blue and white splinters of light firing from the stones. Then he slipped it into his pocket. 'You'll be able to have your church wedding now,' he commented with a wry smile.

'Oh — I hadn't thought that far — Sandy hasn't proposed.'

'He will.'

Her head was spinning as she gazed at him. Everything was happening too quickly. She couldn't take it all in. Her knees felt as though they wouldn't support her for much longer.

Bernard led her to an empty bench. 'You've had a long tiring day. I would imagine Her Majesty feels like that just now. Listen . . . '

The cheering continued into the distance, following the route of the Royal procession.

'I don't know . . . what shall I do now?' Jane felt incapable of making any rational decision.

'Just sit here for a while.' Bernard bent his head and kissed her lips. It was a long kiss — sweet, but tinged with sadness. A kiss that said 'goodbye' more eloquently than words. Then he held her at arm's length, and softly said, 'Thank you for loving me just a little.'

Despite his slightly lopsided gait, Bernard moved quickly, and was soon lost in the crowds near the Abbey. Jane felt very strange. She closed her eyes and breathed deeply, fighting back the wave of dizziness, and wondered why Bernard had asked her to wait. Was he fetching his car? Or sending a taxi? No, only official vehicles were allowed in the area. Her mind was so confused she couldn't even remember where she had parked her own car.

She had no idea how long she waited, a million thoughts racing through her mind, before she heard her name softly called, and turned.

'Sandy — oh, Sandy!'

He held her so tightly she could scarcely breathe, and his kisses sent the most sensuous tingles down to her toes. When he raised his head, his eyes worshipped her face. 'I can't believe what he's done.' His voice was choked. 'How could anyone in their right mind let you go?'

'I told you he was a good man.'

'Yes — and I could never be that good. But I shall be eternally grateful.' Sandy kissed her again.

Her nerve ends were in fourth gear when he said, 'Can I tell Sir Archibald that I'm bringing my wife with me to East Grinstead?'

'Oh, yes, please,' she gasped, more thoughts flashing through her mind. Kathleen would make such a beautiful bridesmaid — and Mum wouldn't have to take her hat back — and — 'East Grinstead sounds like heaven.'

Ignoring the curious stares from people drifting towards the embankment, he cupped her face in his hands and kissed her cheeks, her forehead, the tip of her nose. 'It will be, I promise you.' A thoughtful expression crossed his face. 'And you will be able to commute from there.'

'Pardon?'

'To work — I know how important your career is.'

'Oh — that?' Suddenly, the publishing world did not seem at all important. 'We'll see. I've heard that being a wife and mother can be a most interesting career.'

'I love you,' he said, then suddenly laughed. 'I can't wait to see the expression on Kay's face when we tell her we are getting married!'

'She'll never believe us.' Jane was feeling a little delirious as Sandy pulled her back into his arms. Nobody, but nobody had ever kissed her quite like that.

Later — much later — Sandy gazed out across the river. 'There will be fireworks this evening. Shall we stay?'

'Mmm.' She leaned against him. 'Although I feel as if I'm floating up in the clouds already.' Her legs weakened. 'Could we have something to eat?'

The crowds were dispersing, most with the same idea. Jane thought they would never find a restaurant that didn't have a mile-long queue, but Sandy remembered a tiny cafe in a back street near Chelsea. It was resplendent with Union Jacks and pictures of the new Queen and her consort.

'Not quite Buckingham Palace, but there's one vacant table with two chairs,' Sandy said. Watching Jane tuck into her sausage, beans and chips, he threw back his head and laughed. 'I bet they don't get many in here dressed like you and putting it away like a navvy,' he said.

'That's the first food I've had since yesterday,' Jane protested, with her mouth full, then ordered apple pie and custard to follow. 'I was too nervous to touch my breakfast.'

'No wonder you were feeling — ' He stopped as a newsvendor shouted from across the road. 'The early evening papers are out. Won't be a minute.'

The front page carried a huge picture of the Queen and Prince Philip in the Coronation Coach. Attention was focused on the robes and regalia. Sandy flipped over the pages. 'Just listen to this!' He read out loud. '*Helena Beaumont not only outshone most of the ladies in the Abbey with her stunning ensemble and good looks, her illuminating commentary painted pictures of richness and colour onto our drab black and white screens.*'

'You're having me on.'

'See for yourself.'

'Gosh!' She chuckled as she handed back the paper. 'Well, you know what they say — never believe everything you read in the newspapers.'

'This time they have it exactly right.' He took her hand across the table and gazed at her, his head on one side. 'Do you remember what you said to me, on top of that haystack, all those years ago?'

Stirring a cup of tea that looked strong enough to stand the spoon in, Jane shook her head. 'Not really. I was too busy trying to keep out of the way of the boys fighting over Isabel Wallis.'

'You said you were one of the Harrison twins — the plain one.'

'Well, that's what everybody said. Rose was the one with the looks, not me.'

'That's where you're wrong, and you really must stop thinking that.' Sandy tilted her chin upwards. 'Beauty is more than a pretty face. Much more. It's all to do with the eyes.'

'Is it?'

'Oh, yes. Rose's eyes were brilliantly blue and full of fun, but she was quite incapable of giving love to anyone else.'

It was true. Rose had once confessed to Jane that she didn't know how to love.

'Whereas you, my darling — ' Sandy's voice was low. 'Once I looked deep into your eyes and saw how much love you had to give, I was lost . . . ' He paused to look deep into them again, and observed, 'They really are the colour of sherry.'

'Sherry?'

'A beautiful, tawny sherry — we once had a puppy with eyes that colour and — ' He stopped suddenly, as though a thought had just occurred to him. 'Will we have to take that pathetic little mongrel with us to East Grinstead?'

'Of course. Love me, love my dog. She saved my life — remember?'

Customers nudged each other and the waitress giggled as Sandy kissed Jane's fingertips, one by one. 'I love your dog!' he said, dramatically. 'I really — really — really love your dog.' His comic expression changed to one of concern as he softly asked, 'Are you thinking about Rose?'

'How on earth did you know?'

'You have a faraway look in your eyes — a sad little look.'

'When important things happen to me, I always feel that Rose is very close to me.' Jane sighed. 'I was just wondering how things might have worked out if she could have experienced a love like this.'

'I don't think Rose could ever have settled down with only one love.'

Jane was thoughtful for a while, then she nodded. 'Perhaps it was Rose's destiny to love unwisely — and too often. Probably because she was so beautiful.'

'No. Rose was pretty — very pretty.' Sandy gripped Jane's hands tightly. 'But you are the beautiful one.' His eyes were full of tenderness. 'And I am going to spend the rest of my life telling you just how beautiful you are.'

Suddenly, Jane realised the truth. It didn't matter whether she really was beautiful. All that mattered was that Sandy thought she was beautiful. And she was loved.

She remembered something Laura had once said. A quotation from the Bible. *A time to love and a time to hate; a time for war and a time for peace.* She and Sandy had been through the wars, had their own battlefields, hated each other — or thought they hated each other. Now it was their time to love, their time for peace.

'A penny for them?' Sandy prompted, then added, 'although, judging by your expression, your thoughts look as though they're worth a pound.'

Leaning across the table, Jane kissed him with great passion. 'I don't know what I have done to deserve such happiness, Dr Randall,' she whispered. 'But I am going to spend the rest of my life telling you just how much I adore you!'

THE END